I0659454

FATAL HONOR

SHADOW FORCE INTERNATIONAL

MISTY EVANS

Fatal Honor, Shadow Force International Book 2
Copyright © 2016 Misty Evans

ISBN: 978-0-9966470-9-0

Cover Art by Sweet & Spicy Designs
Interior Formatting by Author E.M.S.
Editing by Linda Beaulieu, Marcie Gately, Patricia Essex

Published in the United States of America.

ROMANTIC SUSPENSE AND MYSTERIES BY MISTY EVANS

The Super Agent Series
Operation Sheba
Operation Paris
Operation Proof of Life
The Blood Code
The Perfect Hostage, A Super Agent Novella

The Deadly Series
Deadly Pursuit
Deadly Deception
Deadly Force
Deadly Intent
Deadly Attraction (coming 2016)
Deadly Affair, A SCVC Taskforce novella (coming 2016)

The Justice Team Series (with Adrienne Giordano)
Stealing Justice
Cheating Justice
Holiday Justice
Exposing Justice
Undercover Justice
Protecting Justice

Shadow Force International Series
Fatal Truth
Fatal Honor
Fatal Courage

The Secret Ingredient Culinary Mystery Series
The Secret Ingredient, A Culinary Romantic Mystery with Bonus Recipes
The Secret Life of Cranberry Sauce, A Secret Ingredient Holiday Novella

ACKNOWLEDGMENTS

An author can't do without feedback. It's been an honor to bring this new series to readers and have them embrace the troubled heroes and heroines of Shadow Force International so wholeheartedly. Thank you to my fans many times over from the bottom of my heart for your love and support!

An author also needs her tribe. Adrienne, JB, Nana, Amy R, Amy A, and Steph, you made me brainstorm harder and were always around when I needed an ear to cry on or someone to bounce an idea off of. Miles and Charlotte are two very unique, out of the box characters that challenged me at every turn. Plus, my life has been complicated so far this year. I have my sanity because of all of you!

Lastly, oodles of gratitude to my new/old beta reader Tiana for offering to read for me once more. It's been awhile since *The Perfect Hostage*, but I'm so glad you're back in the crazy world of my stories, T!

From me & my Gypsy ancestors to you and yours: *Kushti bok*

To Mark,

my favorite wizard

A group of former SEALs, abandoned by the United States and
labeled as rogue operatives, who now work as a black ops team
performing private intelligence, security, and paramilitary
missions for those who have nowhere else to turn.

Cine seamana vant culege furtuna.
Who sows wind will harvest storm.

How shall I hold on to my soul,
so that it does not touch yours?
~ Rainer Maria Rilke

CHAPTER ONE

The one thing Navy SEAL Miles Duncan would never do was betray his SEAL team brothers.

On a cold January night in a castle on the right bank of the Danube River in eastern Serbia, he did just that.

"You are one ugly terrorist, mate," MI6 operative Andrew Hardy joked as he and Miles crawled across the cold parapet, working their way toward the corner tower of the castle where the object of their mission was located.

The British Intelligence officer looked like Henry Cavill and sounded a little like Alan Rickman, drawing out some of his words here and there like Snape in the Harry Potter movies. Miles wondered if he practiced in the mirror back home in London. He probably tried different hairstyles there too, aiming for the latest Bieber look.

Even with the face paint Miles had layered on Hardy, along with the dark camo suit, the operative looked like a movie star. A movie star taking on a role in an action film that would make him look like a badass while in real life he got manicures and ate caviar while men like Miles and his SEAL teammates gutted it out with MREs. "I didn't realize being beautiful was a requirement for being an AK-47-toting terrorist. In that case, you should take the lead on this mission, pretty boy."

That garnered a chuckle from the terrorist team listening in on their comms. Miles' teammates and several of Hardy's were the good guys this round, while Miles and Hardy and a handful of SIS pretended to be the tangos. The good guys had stores of

1

weapons, ammunition, and food. The bad had none of that. Miles and Hardy were in charge of setting off a bomb to distract the guards so their teammates could confiscate the resources they needed.

Hardy, good natured as well as slightly egotistical, laughed along with their tango buddies. "I'm good, chief. Lead the way."

The night was cold, the bite of the fast-approaching winter in the air. A partial moon hung over the castle's east turret, a half-lidded eye watching them as they attempted to breach the tower where they would set off the bomb.

The bomb wasn't real, but the training lesson was serious. It was quite possibly their last tactical engagement together and Miles had every intention of making it a success.

The joint team training operation with the CIA and SIS had come about on short notice. MI6 agents had been in the area working with CIA agents to track down a British operative who'd gone undercover with the Romanian crime lord and was now believed to have gone rogue. The operative was identified only by a code name, Butter. Apparently the Queen didn't take kindly to her agents going off the reservation and wasn't about to share the details.

So the British guys were waiting on orders to come from Vauxhall Cross on the double agent's whereabouts and bring in the crime lord, a guy named Bourean, with her. Both SIS and the CIA wanted Bourean. Problem was, no one could pinpoint exactly where the MI6 gal was hiding out. Every lead from Vauxhall, every expedition into the nearby towns and countryside, had turned up zilch.

Miles and his team had also been on standby along the border, waiting on orders to carry out a complicated extraction of an Islamist Syrian terrorist who'd once been with Al Qaeda and was now traveling Europe to set up splinter groups. He'd formed his latest group with former Guantanamo Bay detainees and the U.S.—along with a dozen other countries—wanted him bad. Latest intel suggested he was working with Bourean to get his hands on weapons and had holed up in the mountains to ride out the winter months.

Not ones to sit on their hands and do nothing, they'd been training relentlessly day in and day out. The big wigs at the SIS and CIA had decided a joint training op would benefit all parties involved. The SEAL team had gone on a couple of scouting missions with the spies to see if they could scare up Agent

Butter. With no luck, the MI6 guys had wanted to play terrorist for a while. Win-win.

Hardy wanted his double agent. Miles wanted his terrorist. Looked like neither of them was going to complete their mission, however, because now, a nasty storm system was moving into the area within the next twelve hours. Planting their fake bomb might be their one and only success this round.

Which sucked, but Miles had learned that sometimes you had to take whatever success you could eke out and be happy with it.

Before he and Hardy could breach the tower, however, even their plan to plant the bomb eluded him in the end when Senior Chief Hunnan called a halt to the exercise.

The senior chief was big, burly, and gruff, barely giving his men time to file into a circle around him inside the flanking tower where he'd set up their HQ before he started barking out a change in their mission. "A plane has gone down in the Southern Carpathian Mountain range. It was carrying a high-value asset. A nuclear physicist named Alexander." He marked a spot on a map and then tapped a large tablet to blow up the same map with a more detailed topography. "DIA believes he was kidnapped by several Syrian sympathizers through a deal with Romanian crime lord Nicolae Bourean. He was being transported to Turkey where the kidnappers planned to meet up with a Syrian intelligence operative and turn him over. Syria wants to develop nuclear weapons. The plane was shot down and an intercept from the crash suggests our scientist is still alive."

The exfiltration mission they had been waiting for was finally here. Only now, it was a search and rescue of a completely different target.

Hardy danced on the balls of his feet as he eyed the map. "Bloody hell, that's the area our girl was last spotted."

The Carpathians, a rugged arc of mountains that stretched nearly a thousand miles from one end to the other, were nothing to fool with, especially with a blizzard approaching. The second longest mountain range in Europe, they'd been divided into three sections: Eastern, Western, and Southern. They were separated from the Alps by the mighty Danube. Getting in and out of the rugged area was challenging for their kind of missions.

Hardy's boss put a hand on his shoulder. "Sorry, mate. We're pulling out. With no new leads and the storm coming in, we have to go. Butter got the best of us."

A few minutes later, as Miles' team suited up for the helicopter ride to take them deep into the Romanian mountain range, Hardy pulled Miles aside.

"Agent Butter," he said, handing Miles a snapshot of the woman. The profile view showed pale blond hair, a perky nose and lovely skin. Her hair, no doubt the reason for her codename, was pulled back behind her ear and a lightening bolt earring nestled in the lobe. "Keep your eyes out for her. She's dangerous. If you do come across her, do not engage. Notify us."

Miles took one last look at the photo and nodded. She hardly looked like the woman all the MI6 agents talked about as though she were a ghost, but perhaps that's why they had such a lousy photo of her. She was a ghost in the wind.

"You think I'll find her in the plane debris?" he joked.

Hardy didn't smile. "If Bourean is in on this, she is too. SIS wants Bourean, but I want her more. No MI6 operative sells out my country and lives to talk about it, you feel me?"

"Yeah, pretty boy." Miles clapped him on the back. He didn't run off to remote areas of the world and put his life on the line for grins and giggles. He lived and breathed being a SEAL. Would do anything to protect his country. "If I see Agent Butter, you'll be the first to know."

<hr/>

Southern Carpathians
Five hours later

Miles floated in a hazy cloud of pain and bliss. How the two sensations could exist at the same moment, he wasn't sure. He blinked his eyes open but the scene before him didn't compute. Open beams on a ceiling, dried flowers and plants tied with strings hanging down. Shadows dancing over rough-hewn log walls, the comforting smell of a fire.

A woman hummed as she rocked in a rocking chair near a fireplace, a book open in her lap. She was beautiful, with long, dark blond hair flowing over one shoulder, thick eyelashes hiding her eyes as she stared down at the book. Graceful fingers twirled the end of one section of her hair as she hummed. Her left leg was drawn up under her, toes of the right foot pushing off the floor, keeping up the chair's cadence.

Where am I? What is this place?

His memory was thick as pudding. He closed his eyes for a second, trying to swim through it, grasping at the fleeting images.

It was no use. The last thing he remembered was Andy's face, the seriousness in his eyes.

Scientist. Plane.

Butter.

The helicopter explosion. It all came back to him in flashes, nothing concrete, just out of his brain's reach.

The rocking chair creaked and he opened his eyes once more. The woman was no longer reading; she was watching him.

Dark eyes locked on his, her expression steady and serene.

His tongue was thick, his mouth dry. Pain shot through his lower leg, his ribcage, when he tried to move. "Hello?" he said, but it came out a croak.

She stood from the chair, putting her book down on the side table. The hem of her long white gown fell to floor and she hugged a sweater around her body as she walked softly over to peer down at him.

"You're finally awake. I was worried you might have a concussion, but there wasn't anything I could do but wait and see. We're kind of stuck here in the middle of nowhere, I'm afraid." She motioned to a window across the room. "How do you feel?"

He could barely see through the frosted pane but it appeared a blizzard raged outside. "Like I fell out of a helicopter."

"I didn't see it, but that sounds possible."

"Where am I?" This time his voice was stronger.

"A cabin in the mountains. You're lucky to be alive."

How *was* he alive? A flash of memory jarred his mind—the helo shifting too suddenly; panicked voices; losing his balance as he hung in the open door.

"I found you in the snow. I thought you were dead."

"And the others?"

She looked to the fire, shook her head. "There was an explosion. The helicopter crashed."

The pain radiating throughout his body took on a sharper edge. He closed his eyes and sensed her moving away. "How?" he whispered to himself. *Explosion. Crash.* It didn't make sense. "How did that happen?"

As he replayed the memories he could dredge out of his brain over and over, the bed moved with her weight as she sat on the edge and handed him a cup of water. "Drink this. You need fluids."

He was gutted.

Let me die.

He turned his head away, stared at the opposite wall where a desk and bookshelf sat.

"I know what it's like to lose someone," she said, quietly. "The pain, the survivor's guilt. The need to understand why it happened, who was responsible. Blaming yourself doesn't help. Getting answers sometimes doesn't either. Nothing can bring them back."

For long moments, Miles wished her away. She didn't say anything else, didn't touch him. Just sat with him as if sharing his grief.

His ragged breathing slowed. His parched throat yearned for the water she held. A thousand daggers stabbed at his heart but eventually, the desire to know what had happened made him look at her once more. "I'll take that drink, now."

She gave him a sad smile. With her help, he propped himself up on his elbow, enjoying the soft touch of her hands, her patience with him. He grasped the cup, his fingers lacing with hers. His skin tingled where their fingers met, his hand trembling with weakness. She held onto the cup, guiding it to his mouth.

Their eyes met over the edge of the cup. The water was cool and tinged with a flavor he couldn't place. The raw burn in his throat vanished. "What's in it?" he asked.

"A tonic my mother used to use on me when I was feeling ill. All natural, nothing harmful, I promise."

She smiled again and his mind went blank. She was strikingly beautiful, her voice soft and soothing. Her touch...

While the realization that his SEAL brothers were gone was a nightmare, he, himself, had apparently fallen into a dream. He was alive and stuck in a cabin in a snowstorm with the most beautiful woman he'd ever laid eyes on.

Maybe I died, too, and went to heaven.

While that seemed unlikely, he hoped that was the case. Living without his team wasn't an option. If they were dead, he wanted to be dead with them.

Taking the cup from his hand, she glanced down at it.

Shadows from the fire danced across her tanned skin, but he swore he saw her cheeks blush. "My name is Sarah," she said.

"Miles."

Those dark chocolate eyes of hers came up to meet his. Her smile made his pulse jump. "Nice to meet you, Miles."

She turned and leaned over to put the cup on the nightstand and his little slice of heaven went straight to hell as he saw her in profile. The blond hair and the pert nose. The tiny lightening bolt earring in her right earlobe.

She turned back and adjusted his blankets. "Your left ankle is busted up pretty bad, but I do have some medical training, so hopefully the set job I did on it works. You've got a couple of bruised ribs and some other minor injuries." She gave him that knockout smile. "You'll live but it could be a while before you can walk on that leg. Since we're probably going to be snowed in for a few weeks—this is Romania, after all—we'll have plenty of time for rehab."

He tried not to stutter, his pulse now double-timing it as he looked into her beautiful face and knew he was hip deep in shit. "I guess I don't have a choice."

It was no lie.

She chuckled and put a hand on his shoulder as she pushed him back down into the bed. The lightening bolt flashed. "Well, don't you worry. I'm going to take good care of you. I assume from the gear you were wearing and the look of your..."—another blush as her eyes scanned his chest. "You appear to be military. U.S., yes? Doesn't matter, I don't need to know. But your physical appearance suggests you're quite healthy. I'm sure you won't have any trouble recovering from your injuries."

He smiled back, hoping she didn't see the worry in his eyes.

The beautiful, charming woman he was stranded in the Romanian mountains with—the women his very life depended on at this moment—was Butter, the dangerous MI6 traitor Andy had warned him about.

THREE WEEKS LATER

Charlotte could tell Miles was feeling better. The worst of

the pain from his broken ankle was over. She'd reset it, splinted it, wrapped it. A medicine cabinet full of Gypsy remedies kept his wounds disinfected and they were all on the mend. The bruises dotting his body had disappeared.

Initially, he'd been fighting the pain. Once that abated to tolerable levels, he'd fought depression. She'd done everything in her power to keep his spirits up. A tough job when the snows came every night, burying them deeper in the cabin, and the wind whistled through the cracks in the logs and the uneven windowpanes.

There was nowhere for them to go, no other human beings to interact with. Communication towers in these mountains were unheard of. She'd taught him Tile Rummy and a card game called Macau. He'd shared stories about his childhood and discussed politics. He'd taught her how to whittle small dogs from their stash of firewood. She'd explained the local Gypsy culture and demonstrated one of the clan's favorite rituals to clear the body of toxins, hexes, and demons. While she danced the required steps of the banishing dance, he laughed.

But there was something more in his eyes now. A hunger she recognized and felt inside her own body.

The nights were long, the cabin chilly. There was only one bed. Now that he was better, he insisted she take the bed while he dozed in the nearby chair or slept on the floor. He brewed coffee every morning and brought her a cup while she was still in bed.

Her body ached for him. Not because he was the sexiest man she'd ever been around, or the most honorable. Certainly not because she was alone and on the run from a monster. She was used to being alone, independent. But even in another time, another place, she would have fallen for him. He was an impeccable specimen. Beautiful. Strong. A man worthy of a woman so much more than she could ever be.

And yet, she saw it in his eyes. He wanted her too.

She hadn't told him who she really was—he knew her only by her middle name, Sarah. He hadn't told her much about his job as a SEAL and hadn't demanded to know about hers. Early on, she'd seen the suspicion in his eyes. He knew she was more than a single woman living in the woods on the side of a mountain, but he never probed too deeply about her present situation.

Night was upon them once more, Miles standing at the

single window staring out at the snow. A full moon hung low in the sky, its light playing over his rugged features.

"It's time to change your bandage," Charlotte said.

Every day it was their ritual. He sat on the edge of the bed, she unwrapped the old bandage, rubbed cream on the healing skin, and rewrapped it. She'd discovered he was ticklish and enjoyed teasing him about it.

Tonight, he shook his head. "I'll do it myself."

His tone was brusque, he wouldn't look at her. Had she done something to annoy him? "All right. I'll get you the supplies."

When she returned from the bathroom he was in the chair, head in his hands as he leaned his elbows on his knees. She set the basket of fresh cotton strips and salve next to his foot. Without looking at her, he removed the thick, wool sock and began to unwrap the bandage.

Charlotte made busy work of stoking the fire, getting a glass of water. From the corner of her eye, she watched him toss the used bandage down and slap the salve on, all with a pissed look on his face.

"I'm sorry if I've done something to upset you," she said softly.

His hands stilled. He leveled her with a look so intense, she nearly took a step back. "It's not your fault."

The words lacked conviction. "Isolation is challenging for most people."

A long silence. Then, "True, but we're not most people, are we?"

For half a second, she thought he knew she was an intelligence agent. That maybe he knew everything. "I'm sure, as a SEAL, you're trained to withstand isolation."

"And you seem quite adept at living alone out here in the mountains."

It wasn't her first choice, but it beat being chained up in Nico Bourean's belowground torture chamber.

"I don't know who you're hiding from," Miles went on, as if reading her mind, "but I want you to know, your secret is safe with me. I won't tell anyone you're here."

He thought she was hiding from a partner perhaps. An abusive relationship.

If only he knew. "I appreciate your discretion."

"I need to leave, Sarah. For your sake as well as mine."

Leave? The thought made the pulse at the base of her throat

fire like a tiny, trapped bird. "You can't travel until the snows melt."

"If I stay…"

He shook his head, let go of a ragged sigh.

Her nerves bounced around in her stomach. "If you stay, *what?*"

Again, that intense gaze hit her. It did a slow perusal down her body, back up to her eyes, lighting every point it touched on fire. "If I stay, I can't promise not to touch you."

Her breath caught. Her knees felt loose in her joints. She grabbed onto the fireplace mantel.

The air between them shimmered and shifted. The hunger in his stormy gray eyes was back, everything he was feeling shining in them like the flames from the fireplace.

She wanted him to touch her. Longed for the feel of his hands and lips on her body. Day and night, she'd found herself fantasizing about him.

"You've been touching me everyday," he said. "Torturing me with your fingers, your laughter, your simple presence. I want you so badly, I can hardly stop myself from throwing you on that bed and stripping you naked."

Her nipples peaked under her thin nightgown. "Perhaps, I'd like that too."

His brows crashed down over those beguiling eyes. His voice came out raspy. He searched her face as if looking for deception. "You shouldn't. Being with me, even if I don't share your bed, is dangerous."

"I'm used to dangerous men. I know how to handle myself."

"What kind of dangerous men?"

She came to stand in front of him, looking down into his handsome face. "My past is checkered with them, but I'm leaving that life behind as soon as I can. I have an incredible radar system that lets me know who's dangerous and who's not. You're not, Miles. I know that. You've been sleeping in my bed for weeks. I'd like to truly share it with you."

"Are you sure?"

Grasping the gauzy material of her gown, she bunched it up, raising the hem higher and higher. It grazed her thighs, her hips. Using both hands, she lifted it over her stomach and breasts. At last, drawing it out, she freed it from her head.

Closing the last bit of distance between them, she dropped it at his feet. "I've never wanted anything more."

He gazed at her body with a look of wonder. "God, you're beautiful."

Letting him draw her into his lap, she sucked in a breath as his lips closed around one of her nipples.

Knowing this was all a dream—that it could never last—Charlotte tipped her head back and let herself be carried away.

CHAPTER TWO

SAN DIEGO
NINE AND HALF MONTHS LATER

He was being followed.

Two days ago, Miles noticed a black hybrid following him to the Hit & Run where he grabbed a bottle of caffeine and a protein bar to overcome the previous night's whiskey-induced hangover.

Fresh off of his last job for Shadow Force International, he'd been lying low and kicking back, enjoying the mild Southern California weather and the fact he had running water again, unlike the Bosnian hellhole he'd been in just days before. Even the last job he'd had in the States, helping keep news journalist Savanna Bunkett from dying at the hands of the president, had been a cakewalk compared to Bosnia.

But Bosnia was a stone's throw from Romania. Romania held answers. Answers he needed to know what had happened nearly a year ago when someone destroyed the helo his SEAL team had been traveling in. In those mountains with a beautiful brown-eyed blonde who haunted his dreams. He was going back to find her, or at the very least, the person responsible for the death of five good men, as soon as Emit Petit let him.

Which wouldn't be anytime soon. He was finally due some R&R from SFI, and what did Emit say to him? *Do me a favor. Run the West Coast Division of Rock Star Security until a replacement can be found.*

The Rock Stars were the cover business for SFI, and in this day and age of rich, famous, and reality TV wannabes, the security service was booming. Every man on the team was a former SEAL with a shady past. Each of them went by a codename in order to protect their real identities. Their skill sets were perfect for the bodyguard and security service work needed.

Although Miles had dabbled in the RSS side of things, he didn't know much about running a group of bodyguards. But he couldn't let Emit down, no how, no way. The man depended on him and Petit was a stand-up guy. An honorable one. He'd rescued Miles from Romania and gave him a job and a place to stay upon his return.

Miles had never wanted to be a leader—he preferred being in the field. At least the men working for him understood the job and the chain of command. They all shared a similar sense of duty, loyalty, and honor.

So, thanks to the debt he owed Emit, he was here in San Diego, recovering from his last paramilitary stint and wondering who his stalker was. The bodyguards now suddenly in his care were doing a decent job of handling themselves without him and for that, he was grateful.

Today, he'd seen the black hybrid behind him in the late afternoon rush hour traffic. Tonight, it was sitting a block south of his apartment.

He'd been declared MIA after his team had been destroyed in those mountains. His ankle had healed, but it wasn't strong enough for him to return to the Teams once he was back home. He'd found he didn't have the stomach for it anyway. He didn't deserve to wear the emblem of the United States Navy anymore.

With his fellow SEALs all dead and him missing, the U.S. had presumed he was dead too. If it hadn't been for that mysterious guardian angel who'd found him and patched him back up, he would have been.

Her luscious curves and beautiful face invaded his mind day and night even all these months later. Every time he thought of her—her tender, healing touch, the hours she spent tending to his wounds, the way she'd used her own body to help him regain his strength—he missed her. They'd shared food, shelter, and physical comfort in each other for six weeks, and yet he didn't even know her real name. Sarah, she'd told him, but she looked close enough like the picture of Agent Butter that Andrew Hardy had shown him, Miles knew it had to be her.

During their time together, he'd played it careful, trying to draw out her story without being obvious. Outside of a few throwaway childhood stories, she'd never talked about herself, always switching the conversation back to him or distracting him with sex.

He hadn't seen her since the night she'd disappeared from the cabin and Emit Petit had shown up in those godforsaken Carpathian Mountains to rescue him. Truth was, at that point, he hadn't wanted to be rescued.

He missed her fiercely. Her wildness, her kindness, her laughter. Some days, he wanted to escape his current life and go back to that time. To her.

The solid gold cross lying under his shirt warmed the skin next to his heart. The only thing he had from their time together. That and the memories.

He'd drawn a sketch of her face, ran it through the SFI facial recognition software. The closest ID he'd come upon was a British Intelligence agent named Charlotte Carstons. There were no decent photos of Carstons anywhere in the system. No social media or public photos either. Which only made him more convinced she was an undercover operative.

While the Brits wouldn't give him any info on her, Miles had done research, asking contacts and putting out feelers. Being part of SFI helped. Beatrice Reese, Petit's second-in-command, was former NSA and knew everyone and everything. She'd put out a few feelers too, before getting her hands slapped by the Queen of all people. If their intel was correct, Charlotte Carstons had been MIA since that very time period Miles had spent healing and making love to a woman who still haunted his dreams. If she were indeed Butter, it was rumored she had been feeding Nicolae Bourean classified information and helping him sell it to the highest bidder.

Just my luck, I fell for a traitor.

Miles' cell rang and he answered it without taking his eyes from his night vision goggles. "Whatcha got for me, Rory?"

"Not much, Poison." Rory, the SFI tech specialist, referred to Miles by his Rock Star bodyguard name. Rory stayed behind the scenes keeping them all on track. A former SEAL as well, he'd done wet work for the CIA for a bunch of years before ending up with SFI.

The man had a voice only a mother could love. He sounded like he'd smoked too many cigars and enjoyed too many shots of tequila that evening. Probably had. "Car's rented from a smalltime dealership in La Jolla. Name on the rental agreement is Veronica Whitman. Ring any bells?"

The name meant nothing to Miles, and yet, he felt a quickening of his pulse. A strange woman following him. Was it…?

No. It had been just over nine fucking months since he'd been in the States. Why would his guardian angel come looking for him now?

Nine months. *Shit.* Was he a father?

The thought rocked him. He had to take a couple of deep breaths. Finally, his brain engaged again and he discarded the idea. If the woman he'd known as Sarah had given birth to his baby, why wouldn't she simply knock on his door and drop the bomb?

Because she's the No. 1 on the MI6 Most Wanted list?

They'd fucked like rabbits but used condoms every time. They'd been careful.

And maybe she *had* been looking for him all along. He wasn't exactly on Twitter and Instagram, telling everyone where he ate, slept, or worked out. "That name doesn't even ring a distant bell."

"Not a high school sweetheart," Rory offered, "or former babysitter?"

"Nope. You got a picture?"

"The dealership does a lot of backdoor stuff, so no copy of her driver's license is on file. I ran her name through the DMV and there are a dozen Veronica Whitmans in the United States. Four of them live in California alone. I have Facebook pages, YouTube videos, LinkedIn profiles, but no idea which one could be keeping tabs on you or why. Yet," he added.

"I can help if you send me the links."

"I'm cross-referencing each of them with your name to see if anything comes up. If that doesn't give us a lead, I'll start with the California girls and do more in-depth background checks."

"Probably a false ID."

Computer keys clicked on Rory's end. "Then it'll be a long night, but I *will* figure it out."

That was the great thing about working with the former SEALs who formed Shadow Force International. They were all good men. Men who'd been screwed one way or another by the government they'd served, and who still kept the same determination to see justice done and to help the innocent. They helped each other too. Every one of them had the other's back.

Miles leaned against the window frame. All was quiet on the street out front. He'd left the lights off in his living room and kitchen to make sure he couldn't be spotted in this window. His bedroom light and TV were on at the back of the apartment. If the person in the car was casing his place, they'd think he was watching TV in bed.

"Did you check the airlines for her?" he asked. "If she's renting a car, she might have flown in from somewhere."

More clicking of keys. A long pause. "No Veronica Whitmans have landed at San Diego International in the past week. I can check LAX, but she probably would have rented a car up there, so that's a long shot. Did you get a tracker on her?"

"Stuck a Shadow Tracker on the bumper as soon as the sun set."

He'd crawled under the cars behind the black hybrid until he'd gotten close enough to tag the underside of the back bumper with the tiny GPS device. The size of a quarter and charged by the sun, the tiny tracker was specifically designed for asset and vehicle retrieval. "Do that cross-reference thing and I'll follow her when she leaves, see where she goes." Miles said. "Call me back when you've got something."

"Copy that. If you send me the tracker's ID number, I'll keep a watch on her, too, via my software."

"Done." They disconnected.

Miles went into the bedroom and suited up. A nine-millimeter went into his shoulder holster, a couple of listening devices went into his Kevlar vest pocket. He pulled on a dark knit cap, a black jacket over the vest, and his motorcycle boots. Snagging his car keys and a power bar from his stash, he turned off all the lights and let himself down the fire escape in the back. He found the perfect surveillance spot not far from his car and sat in the dark with his binoculars and waited.

As suspected, Veronica and her Ford pulled away from the curb a few minutes later.

Miles got in his car and followed.

Tracking a former Navy SEAL who now worked for a private

protection agency wasn't easy. Tracking Miles Duncan, a *paranoid* former SEAL who once held the esteemed, if unofficial, nickname of Evasion God among his team brothers, was one of the most challenging missions of Charlotte Carstons' career.

But she'd found him. Finally.

The bathroom was thoroughly steamy after her long, hot shower. After the sun had gone down, the car had gotten cold. She hated cold.

Being held in a Romanian crime lord's torture chamber six feet under ground for months had done that to her. Like a person who'd had heat stroke and could no longer stand direct sun, she couldn't stand the slightest chill. It took her right back to the living grave she'd endured and those horrible months at the hands of Nicolae Bourean.

She wiped the mirror off with her towel. The shower had done her good, warming her and relaxing her muscles. The scanner built into her phone had alerted her that Miles had somehow put a tracking device on her car. She had top of the line night vision goggles that had detected him standing in the shadows of his living room watching her. She'd waited until he'd left the window before she snuck out and removed the device.

Winding around the city's hills and down to the wharves, she'd tried to pick up his truck following her. She'd never seen him. Not once. Still, she'd tossed the tracker into another car at the gas station before she'd gone back to the motel.

She wanted to talk to him, she did. So much better for both of them if she didn't. She needed to make sure Nicolae's men hadn't followed her and that no one was already watching Miles. As far as she knew, Nico didn't know anything about Miles, but the Romanian clan leader had a knack for figuring out and exploiting weaknesses. Miles Duncan was Charlotte's one and only weakness.

He was also her only hope.

Nine months. Eighteen days. What were the odds he still had the cross necklace she'd put around his neck before Emit Petit had arrived to whisk him away?

The cross was her lifeline. The only way she could retrieve proof she wasn't a traitor to her country. Inside the cross was a key that opened a secret safe. A safe that held the intel to clear her name and put Nicolae Bourean away for good. Without it, she would have to stay on the run forever.

The scar over her collarbone, the last one Nico had given

her, was still pink but fading. She had some color in her cheeks again, not just from the heat of the shower, but because she was stronger, healthier than she'd been in a long time. Her hair was no longer falling out from malnutrition although her ribs and hip bones still jutted a bit. The hunger never left her, much like the cold that had seeped into her bones.

Somehow Nico had found out she was MI6. Going undercover inside his organization had taken months of planning and manipulating her way into his trust. She'd been careful, feeding him legitimate intel her handler passed onto her that helped Nico get what he wanted. He'd graduated from crime lord to international arms dealer and Charlotte's job had been to find out how and why.

Sometime during her time in the cabin with Miles, her true identity had been revealed to Nico. After she'd left Miles to try to uncover the truth about the plane crash and the follow-up terrorist act that had brought down Miles' helicoptor, she'd walked right into a trap.

Nico had beaten her, drugged and starved her, trying to get her to admit she was a spy, trying to get her to give up the identities of her fellow MI6 operatives in the area. Under his abuse, she lost her sense of time and direction. Her very humanness. Delusions and hallucinations invaded her brain. She would see Miles, sure he had come to save her, only to have him fade away when she reached for him.

That had been the worst...the desolation. Knowing he would never come for her. No one would. If she were going to defeat Nicolae Bourean, she had to do it herself.

She never told him the truth about who she was, never endangered any other MI6 operative. Instead, she convinced Nico she didn't have any idea about the accusations he continued to bring against her. A dangerous game, since he could decide at any time she was useless and kill her, so she'd fed him less crucial information that was accurate and gained him something. A name of a gray market contact, a location, anything that led him on a treasure hunt where he scored money, drugs, weapons, revenge on his enemies.

After a few weeks, he came to rely more and more on her. Became convinced that she was, indeed, true to him and his syndicate. The beatings continued, and she was little more than his slave, but she was alive. Bit by bit, she regained her sanity and began forming a plan of escape.

Escaping had come at a high price. Charlotte had been forced to leave behind a young girl Nicolae used for sex. Madeena. She'd sworn she'd go back for her, but would it be in time? Would Maddy ever want to see her again after she hadn't been able to secure the girl's escape to begin with?

Time was of the essence but Charlotte couldn't rush things. Once she'd learned that MI6 thought she'd gone to the dark side, she'd had no choice but to go it alone. The journey to America had been tough enough. Securing papers, a passport, a driver's license. Then having to track down the most evasive man in the world, all while staying completely under the radar.

Nico was after her. MI6 was after her. The Queen wanted her head on a platter. With her luck, even Miles would be less than happy to see her after she'd abandoned him.

Wrapping her hair in the towel and securing her gun inside it, she snagged a second towel from the rack and tucked it around her body. Tomorrow, she would wait for him to leave his apartment and then she would search his place for the necklace. He didn't appear to wear jewelry of any kind; she'd scanned his neck for the gold chain the cross had been on, but hadn't seen it. She hoped it was still in his possession, in his apartment. His security system was decent, but not too tough for her to crack.

Opening the bathroom door, Charlotte stopped halfway across the threshold. The bedroom was dark.

She'd left the light next to the bed on, hadn't she?

Normal people would wonder if the bulb had burned out. Charlotte knew better.

Her fingers instinctively went to the light switch on the bathroom wall, shutting it off so she wasn't backlit. She whirled her body behind the door, crouching and undoing the towel around her hair to arm herself. Her pulse thrummed against her temples, blood pumping in her ears.

Outside in the bedroom, silence reigned. Nicolae wouldn't sit in the dark. He would have all the lights on and be waiting for her with a smile and a sickle knife. If it were one of his men, they would have taken her out in the shower.

Who then?

Miles?

MI6?

She waited, slowing her breathing, commanding her pulse to slow with it. Biding her time and listening for any telltale noise.

One of her best skills was patience. A hunter after prey would only sit still for so long, but she had learned to remain still and silent for hours.

Being held prisoner for nine months did that to you.

Her Beretta had a fresh clip and a round in the chamber. Her makeup case held hairspray, a lipstick case with an injectable poison pen, a perfume bottle that when broken would act like a flashbang grenade. Not exactly an arsenal, but she'd made do with less.

Please let it be Miles. At least he didn't want to torture, imprison, or kill her. At least, she didn't think so. As careful as she'd been to keep her presence a secret, it would be no surprise if he'd spotted her, figured out she was watching him.

There was no other exit from the bathroom unless she would squeeze herself down to the size of monkey to fit through the window at the top of the wall. She sat on the floor, the tile cool and sweaty, leaning her head against the wall. *Definitely not Nicolae.* He had the patience of a squirrel.

The fear thrumming under her skin eased slightly. Nico's minions were ruthless but lacked imagination. If there were only one, she could take him.

MI6 wouldn't kill her. They'd haul her back to Vauxhall and interrogate her. After escaping Nicolae, she'd had to lay low, but had tried contacting her old handler. He'd told her she'd been branded a traitor and MI6 had her on an internal wanted list. She had no proof she wasn't a double agent or that she'd been held against her will by Nico, except for the scars on her body. Those wouldn't be enough for them to grant her a pardon. She had to retrieve the video intel she'd shot back on that mountain when the scientist's plane—and then Miles' helo—had been shot down.

She'd lied when she'd told him she hadn't seen what happened with the helo. Not only had she witnessed the horrible explosion, she had most of it on video. The terrorist responsible was on that footage as well. Worse, Madeena knew the man. Knew where he hid out.

Charlotte had no doubt Miles would kill for that information.

The air around her shifted, causing her to stop breathing, to strain her ears. She'd heard nothing, saw no movement in the shadows, yet she felt a very distinctive presence. Close.

Too close.

"You going to come out of the bathroom on your own, darlin'," a lightly accented Southern voice said from the doorway, "or am I going to have to come in there and carry y'all out?"

That voice. A tiny thrill went through her, every cell in her body rejoicing at the sound of that deep, husky voice.

Charlotte remembered the first time she'd heard him speak. He'd been unconscious for days, barely clinging to life, in and out of consciousness. Exhausted from caring for him and keeping her location a secret, she'd fallen asleep next to him in bed, her head lying near his. He'd touched her face with the tips of his fingers, waking her, and said, "You must be my guardian angel."

He'd fallen right back to sleep, but it had made her giddy that he'd woken up and spoken to her. Twenty-four hours later, he was fully awake and wanting to know what had happened.

She was no guardian angel. Angel of death was more like it. It was her fault the scientist's plane had been shot down in those mountains. Her fault he'd needed rescuing by the Navy SEALs.

If Miles had found out she was the cause of all of that—the trouble that killed his teammates—no wonder he hadn't knocked on her motel room door and kissed her silly when she opened it.

Maybe he *did* want to kill her. She wouldn't blame him.

Tucking herself closer to the wall, she tried to see through the slit in the doorframe. Her eyes had adjusted to the darkness but she couldn't make out his whereabouts.

She could feel him, though. Every place that he had touched, every spot he had kissed in her cabin in the mountains, was suddenly alive again. Not scarred and bruised and broken, but tingling with anticipation.

Laying her brow against the cold metal of the gun barrel, she closed her eyes for a second. She'd been waiting for this moment, looking forward to a reunion with him. Never in all those fantasies had she envisioned herself sitting on a dirty bathroom floor, wrapped in nothing but a towel with no way out.

In her version of the reunion, she'd planned on retrieving the video from her hidden safe first, putting Nicolae behind bars where he could never hurt anyone again, and *then* showing up on Miles' door with a clean slate and the tiniest hope for the future.

Best laid plans...

Without warning, the door banged fully open, smacking her body and nearly knocking the gun from her hands. A shadow moved, hands grabbing her and smacking the wrist of her gun hand into the edge of the sink. She grunted, trying to hold onto the Beretta as she kicked out at the same time with her right foot.

She landed a solid hit to her attacker's shin. He grunted and knocked her wrist against the sink once more, the impact sending a shockwave up her arm and forcing her to let go.

No stranger to pain, she suppressed the cry that exploded in her throat, kicking out again with both legs and nailing him in the knees this round. The towel covering her backside slid on the tile floor from the effort, causing her to go down on her back as he released his grip on her wrist.

But now he had her gun.

A large hand wrapped around her ankle. One jerk and she was flipped over onto her belly, the towel coming completely undone, her chin bouncing on the floor.

Ow.

The tiles chafed against her naked skin. She fought, reaching for anything that would give her purchase, anything that could be used as a weapon.

Her fingernails scratched against something hard. The tiny garbage can under the sink. It was only plastic, but it would work if...she could...reach...it...

Miles plopped down on her butt, his heavy weight pining her to the floor. She heard him eject the Beretta's magazine, clear the chamber of the round. He reached down and knocked her outstretched hand away from the direction of the garbage can; one of his did the job of restraining both of hers above her head.

"Don't fight me, *Veronica,*" he said, his lips close to her ear as he held her immobile. His breath was warm, sending a fresh wave of goose bumps over her skin. "Or should I call you Charlotte? Or my favorite, Sarah?"

Grinding her teeth, she ignored the pain in her wrist, the chafing of the tile against her breasts and hips bones, the weight of him. "Get off of me, you lughead."

He chuckled. "That's not what you said the last time I was on top of you."

Even with the cold tiles under her, a hot flush wormed its

way under her skin. The memory of him on top of her, of his body working its magic on her, was enough to make her stop fighting.

He's not the enemy, she reminded herself.

If only she could breathe. "My first name is Charlotte. My friends call me Charlie."

"Ah, but we're not friends, are we? Fuck buddies, lovers, maybe. Not friends. Friends call one another, they don't leave in the middle of the night with no goodbye and disappear for nine months." He still pinned her down, his nose brushing against her head as he spoke in her hear. "What are you doing here?"

He'd kept track of their time apart. Charlotte took hope in that. "Let me up and I'll explain."

The light drawl evaporated. "You must think I'm naive or incredibly stupid."

"I don't believe either. Why?"

"You slipped away me from once before, Agent Charlotte Carstons. I'm not turning you loose so easily again. Start talking."

So he *did* know her true identity. She closed her eyes for a moment, breathing in his familiar Miles scent of citrus and warm male skin, wishing she could tell him the one simple truth burning in her throat. *I love you.*

He wouldn't believe her after all the lies she'd told, and saying the words out loud wouldn't change the fact she would have to lie to him again. Leave him again. For his safety and for hers.

Struggling to breathe under his weight, she shoved thoughts of confessing her love aside and opened her eyes. "Nicolae Bourean, head of the Corsicani clan in Romania. I'm on the run from him. The reason I left you was to save your life. You and I survived that brutal winter in the mountains, and it's one of my fondest memories, but when spring came, I had to ensure no one knew you and I had been together. It was too dangerous for you. I made contact with Emit Petit, told him where to find you and I left. I had work to do on my case, information I still needed before I could close it out, and I had to go to Nico to get it. Unbeknownst to me, he'd figured out I was MI6. He took me prisoner. I escaped a few weeks ago, but he's after me. He wants me back. Badly."

She forced herself not to shiver at the thought of what Nico would do to her if he ever did get hold of her again. Death would be a blessing. "You, Miles Duncan, literally hold the key to my survival."

After a long, quiet pause, Miles slid off of her, took her gun and stood a few feet away. She couldn't see him without turning over and any sudden move could cause him to straddle her again. But she felt that solid, unwavering presence of his behind her. A second later, he flipped the wall switch and the bathroom flooded with light.

Charlotte blinked, tried to right the towel as she kept her gaze on the tiles. The rough, dull cotton was askew, barely covering anything but a stripe across her buttocks. Her back and legs were completely bare.

A growl tore from Miles' lips, raising the hair on the back of her neck.

The scars. He was seeing the scars that crisscrossed her back and thighs. Nico liked his leather belt, liked his sickle. The welts had left their marks. The tip of his knife as well. Her once flawless skin was now a mess of damaged and disfigured scars.

"Jesus, darlin'." Miles voice was low, controlled. "What the hell did he do to you?"

Carefully sitting up, she drew the towel around her, hugging her knees and keeping her gaze pinned to the floor. "The cross I put around your neck before I left you," she said. "Please tell me you still have it."

He was immobile for a moment, then moved as swift as he always did, bending down and clasping her chin with his big, warm hand.

He lifted her chin, forcing her to look at him.

Their eyes locked and he scanned her face, her wet hair falling in a tangle around her head. His gray eyes were sad, angry, as they searched hers for answers. He gingerly pushed a lock of hair away from her eyes.

His free hand unzipped his jacket, dug under the vest and shirt covering the base of his neck. Her breath caught when she saw him drag out the very thing she was looking for.

Still searching her eyes, he held up the ornate golden cross and let it rock in the air. "I have it," he said. "It was the only thing of you I did have."

Light from overhead bounced off the inlaid gemstones, her future sparkling between them.

CHAPTER THREE

Miles' guts crawled at the scars on Sarah's—*Charlotte's*—body. She clutched the towel to her chest, trying to cover them, but he could see a fairly fresh mark on her collarbone.

Her face was devoid of any, and even without makeup, she was quite simply beautiful.

He saw her throat work as she swallowed, staring at the cross. She held out a hand, her gaze meeting his. "I need it back."

His phone vibrated inside his pants pocket. He'd shut off the ringer, but he recognized the three short pulses of the personalized tone he had for Emit Petit.

Slipping the cross back under his shirt collar, he watched as Charlotte followed his every move. She licked her pale lips and his mind blanked out for a moment.

The things she'd done to him with those lips, that mouth. It was enough to make him hard.

Yet, after what she'd just told him, he had the sick, uncanny feeling she'd only been using him in some personal undercover operation to double-cross her own country.

The phone buzzed again, insistent in his pocket. "I want to hear the whole story," Miles said, rising and offering her a hand up. He dug the phone from his pocket with his other hand. "Put some clothes on and we'll talk."

Snatching Charlotte's gun from the vanity counter and moving a few steps back to give her room to grab her clothes, he answered the phone. "Yeah."

His boss's voice sounded annoyed. "Yolanda Fernandez needs your services asap."

Yolanda was a West Coast security service client. A thirty-something dynamo who ran her own import company and had been going through a nasty divorce a few months back. Miles had played a hybrid security services specialist and bodyguard to her. "I'm kinda busy."

"Her ex is at the house threatening her."

Miles stuck Charlotte's empty gun into his belt at the small of his back. "Then she should call the police. She has a restraining order."

"This is the third incident in the past two months. She called the local badges, but no one's responded yet. You're only half a mile from her place."

More like three miles since he was at this rundown motel on the north end of the city.

Charlotte had moved to the vanity where she was playing around with a makeup bag on the counter. She'd secured the towel around her ample breasts, having made no move to get dressed.

A warning bell went off in Miles' head, and he moved behind her in record time, grabbing her hand out from inside the bag. She clutched a travel size lotion and raised an eyebrow at him in the mirror.

"Come on, man," he said to Petit, steering Charlotte away from the vanity and toward the other room. "I'm on vacation."

"You're on a bender, and I totally get it after what went down in Syria, but I need to know I can rely on you to keep the West Coast Rock Star office running while I work on setting up the Chicago satellite. You said you needed a few months off from Shadow Force and could handle the personal security division out there, so what's it going to be? Can you keep the West Coast division at top speed or not?"

He had the skills, he had the talent. All he needed was the motivation.

Charlotte had gone over to a suitcase lying open on the bed. Her bra and underwear were laid out on top of the comforter.

She rummaged around inside the suitcase. A telltale zip of energy ran up Miles' arms. She was looking for something besides clothes.

In two strides, he was next to her, nudging her out of the way with his hip. He ran his hands inside the suitcase, searching, searching…

Nada. No weapons.

With swift movements, he yanked out a pair of jeans and a purple blouse, tossing them on the bed next to her undergarments and pointing from her to the clothes.

"Poison?" Emit's voice was strained. "You there?"

Petit had rescued him from the foot of those damn mountains in Romania. Had given him a solid job and helped him keep his demons at bay. He owed the man a hell of a lot. Besides, he couldn't in good conscious strand Yolanda. Her ex was a blowhard, full of self-importance and bluster, but the guy had a mean streak that made him dangerous. "I can handle it, boss."

"Good, I'm counting on you. Now get your ass over to Yolanda's and make sure our client is safe from her ex-husband."

"I'll take care of it. Tell Rory I found Veronica. He can quit digging around about her."

Emit didn't ask who Veronica was, thank God, and they disconnected. Charlotte was staring at him, making no moves to put on the clothes he'd laid out for her. "Please," she said. "All I need is that cross and I'll be out of your hair. You never have to see me again."

That was the problem. He *wanted* to see her again. Traitor or not, he wasn't letting her leave him again.

"So Romania. That was all a lie, then? You and me. You needed someone to get this cross"—he tapped his chest where the cross lay under his shirt and the flak vest—"out of the country. To keep it safe until you could retrieve it."

Her eyes went soft. "Nothing that happened between you and I was a lie."

If it hadn't been for her, he would have died on that mountainside. She hadn't known he was going to be there, so surely she hadn't planned to save him for her own purposes.

Or had she?

Did it matter now? Somewhere along the line, she'd seen a way to get the cross out of Romania. What was so important about it?

He had to get to Yolanda but he wasn't done with Charlotte. Not by a long shot. "We need to go."

"I do need to go, but not with you. It's too dangerous for you to be around me. Just give me the cross and I'll get out of your life again."

"You're coming with me, like it or not. So put on those

clothes or I will drag your half naked ass out of here. Your choice."

Her nostrils flared as she sucked in an irritated breath. "If Nicolae—"

"If Bourean comes anywhere near you,"—Miles moved into her personal space and stared down at her—"I will tear him apart, limb by limb. Let him come. I look forward to it."

He thought he saw her shiver. "You don't know who you're dealing with."

Snatching the shirt off the bed, he handed it to her. "Get dressed. We're leaving."

She let the towel fall, donning the bra and slipping the blouse over her head. "Where are we going?"

"To help someone." He moved away to give her some privacy, but there was no way he was taking his eyes off her. He leaned against the doorjamb and cocked his chin at her suitcase. "And quit going after weapons. I know who you really are now and how you think. You're not getting this cross off of me until I'm good and ready to give it back."

"But you *are* going to give it back, right?"

He let his eyes drift over her hipbones, her thighs. He couldn't help himself. She was underweight and there was a haunted look that never seemed to leave her face, but nothing slacked his desire for her. She was a goddamn traitor—the thing he hated most in the world—and even that didn't turn him off.

Fucked. He was totally, one-hundred-percent fucked. From the moment he'd first laid eyes on her, he'd been a goner.

She donned the jeans and slid her feet into a pair of shoes next to the bed, raking her wet hair back as she waited for his answer.

Scars and betrayal be damned, he still wanted her. He glanced out the window, checking the area for Bourean or anyone else who might be watching.

"We'll see," he said, as he tossed her her jacket and hustled her out the door.

"Where are we going?" Charlotte said, jerking her elbow out of Miles' grasp.

His hair was short now, his body as lean and muscled as she remembered. There was a hardness in his eyes that hadn't been there before. A hardness that took her breath away when he looked at her.

Unlocking the truck, he hustled her into the passenger seat. "To help someone."

She needed her passport, her wallet, her gun. "Bringing me along will not help them. I'm—"

He shut the door before she could finish her sentence. Skirting the front of the truck to his side, he scanned the parking lot and then hopped in to the cab.

Fluid movements, focused concentration. Just like in the bathroom when he'd studied her naked body from head to toe.

"Nicolae Bourean is after me," she reminded him. Why didn't he understand how vicious and tricky Nico was? "MI6 thinks I'm a traitor. Anyone I'm around is in danger. *I'm* in danger. Especially since you've left me unarmed."

He started the truck and put it in reverse. "You don't need a weapon. I'll protect you."

The night was dark and still. He pulled out of the parking lot and followed the access road to the main highway, seemingly unconcerned about her current situation.

Miles was one man. Nico had hundreds of men—ruthless mercenaries—at his beck and call.

They waited at a stop light, silence filling the cab. "What happened after the cabin?" Miles asked. "Where did you go?"

Maybe if she answered his questions, that hardness would leave his eyes. He'd be satisfied and would give her the necklace. "After I contacted Emit Petit to come pick you up, I went to see my handler."

"How do you know Emit?"

"I crossed paths with him a few years ago in Moscow when an American businessman was accused of spying activities and needed help getting his family out of the country. His wife is a British citizen and so are the children. I was in the area and had been called in to try diplomatic avenues. Those were failing and Mr. Petit arrived with a less diplomatic, but more efficient, solution. I lent a hand in the exfiltration; made sure the wife and kids made it back to London."

Lights from a car behind them illuminated the cab. Miles' face was devoid of emotion. "What did you go see your handler about? To tell him you pumped the American sailor for intel?"

"I set your broken ankle and nursed you back to health. I never pumped you for intel."

A muscle popped in his jaw. He kept his focus on the highway as the truck topped eighty.

Could this reunion be going any better? "I went to see my handler because I hadn't checked in with him for six weeks." She turned toward the window and stared at the all-night gas stations and restaurants dotting the landscape. *The best six weeks of my life.*

If only she could reach out and touch him, tell him how sorry she was.

Charlotte stared at his shadowed profile, the pulse at the base of her throat beating like the wings of a trapped bird. It took all her willpower not to touch his hand on the shifter, run her fingers across his tight jaw. He wouldn't accept her touch any more than her apology, and she didn't have time for this...whatever *this* was. "How about you answer one of my questions? Like, who are you so fired up about going to help?"

They passed a slower moving car. He unclenched his jaw. "A woman whose ex is threatening her."

A woman. Charlotte's heart tweaked a little. Of course he'd found someone new. He probably had dozens of women he spent time with. *Good for him.* It wasn't like they could resume their past relationship, anyway.

But, God, the thought of him with someone else made her heart feel too small inside her chest. As if all the blood were drying up, her heart cracking.

She forced casualness into her voice. "You really think it's a good idea to bring me to meet your girlfriend?"

"Girlfriend?" He sent her a confused look. "She's a client and he's a lousy SOB who needs to be taught a lesson."

Client, right. Rock Star Security—the front for Shadow Force International. She'd figured Miles wouldn't go back to the SEAL teams, figured Emit Petit might have use for him. While SFI kept the identities and whereabouts of the employees strictly confidential, it hadn't taken long for her to figure out Miles wasn't in D.C. when she arrived in America. He was working out of the West Coast branch.

Without signaling, Miles took an off ramp and interrupted her thoughts. "How did you end up kidnapped by Bourean?"

She debated whether to answer. Decided it didn't make a lot of difference. He wasn't going to answer more of her questions and she needed him to understand the severity of what he was doing. "In recent years, Britain has been hit by a Romanian crime wave, including rapes and murders all led by Nico. MI6 sent me to infiltrate his organization. It took time, but I got in deep enough to start gathering intel on several of his criminal activities and overheard a disturbing conversation. He'd hooked up with a terrorist and formed a collaboration to export certain members of his clan to the UK in order to set up sleeper cells."

They drove past a fancy, gated community, and took a left onto a long drive that rose to a house on a hill.

"Sleeper cells for what purpose?" Miles said, slowing the truck and scanning the dark expanse of yard.

All the lights were on in the two-story mansion. Outside lights revealed a Mercedes in the circular drive, parked at an odd angle, and a man standing on the steps with his hands raised into the air, shaking his fists and yelling.

"He was going into the terrorist business. I just needed to prove it."

Miles cocked his chin at the man on the front steps. "This guy is trouble. If I don't shut him down, he will eventually hurt the woman inside. He's probably drunk and needs to know, right here tonight, that he can't keep doing this. Help me out a minute, would ya?"

He was out of the truck and striding toward the man before Charlotte could ask how.

She checked over her shoulder, saw no one had followed them. She debated, then exited the truck.

"Ted." Miles stopped at the bottom of the stairs. "I told you to stay away from her."

The man whipped around and snarled. "And I told you to butt out. She's my wife!"

Miles took the stairs two at a time, putting himself face-to-face with the guy. "Not anymore. She divorced your sorry ass for this very reason. You're a violent drunk. Let her go. Get some help. Move on."

Ted growled and took a roundhouse swing. Miles easily dodged it, grabbed the man's arm and tossed him down the steps.

A couple of flips, arse over teakettle, and he landed at Charlotte's feet, moaning.

He wasn't all that big, but probably a good thirty pounds overweight. He lifted his head and looked up at her, his eyes bloodshot. The smell of beer wafted up from him. Something changed in his demeanor, and a second later, he reached out and snagged hold of her ankle.

She stomped on his wrist with her free foot. The man howled and let go. Miles, having followed the man down, grasped his flailing arm and hauled it behind his back. Then he forced Ted to his feet, rolling his eyes at the man's string of curses.

Spittle formed on Ted's lips and the alcohol fumes made Charlotte take another step back.

"The police are on their way to arrest you," Miles told him. "This is your third violation of the restraining order. We can't have this, Teddy, ol' boy. Not on my watch."

Ted spit at the ground. "Fucking cops won't do anything to me."

"No, but I will," Charlotte said, moving closer.

Miles looked at her over Ted's shoulder. "Yeah, my friend here doesn't like men who abuse their wives. You know, if it was just me, I'd kill you and make your body disappear, but Charlotte here, she likes to make domestic abusers suffer."

Ted stopped struggling.

Charlotte gave him her best psychotic smile and ramped up her British accent a notch. "Do I get to take him apart limb by limb? I so love all that blood."

Miles spoke close to Ted's ear. "She has a spot out in the desert, keeps you alive for days while she tortures you."

"Fuck you," Ted said, blustering again. "I don't believe that."

Charlotte licked her lips. "Want me to show you what I can do?" She ran a finger over the side of his face, eyeing him like he was a piece of meat. "I learned from the best, you know. Serbian war criminals. Russian mobsters. Romanian Gypsies. They all know how to inflict tremendous pain without killing you."

"Gypsies?" Ted reared back from her finger. "Who the hell are you?"

Funny that the term Gypsy carried more fear for him than war criminals and mobsters.

She could work with that. She tapped the end of his nose. "We're going to have lots of fun, you and I. And while you're dying, I'll curse your bones so your ghost walks the desert from now until eternity."

She began chanting a Gypsy song her mother had taught her.

The man reared back again but went nowhere since Miles

was holding him. "You're sick." He tried to twist away from Miles' grip. "Let me go. I want out of here."

Lights from an approaching car spotlighted them. Charlotte startled and turned. A black and white cruiser. Police.

A violent relief flooded her and she backed away, out of the spotlight. As Miles handed Ted over to them, she slipped quietly into the truck, keeping her face in shadows.

A woman erupted from the house, flying down the stairs and hugging Miles as the cops shoved a handcuffed Ted into the backseat of the cruiser. He was yelling and cursing and Charlotte could hear him through the windows.

She caught his eye. He stopped mid-curse and stared at her, almost daring her.

She gave him a little wave and licked her lips. Then she gave him what she hoped was a full-on serial killer smile.

He drew away, sliding across to the other side of the seat.

Miles finally detached himself from Yolanda and guided her to an officer who began taking her statement. Miles climbed into the truck a moment later and put it in gear.

"She seems quite happy," Charlotte said.

"Thanks for your help." They drove down the long driveway and stopped at the gates. "He'll think twice about threatening her again. Meantime, I suggested she start keeping these gates closed and locked. I taught her self-defense while I was working for her, but she needs to quit making it easy for him to get to her."

Miles used a Bluetooth to call his boss and report in as they hit the highway headed back toward the city. Once the two men had disconnected, he glanced at her. "You did good back there. I appreciate it."

"Sure," she said, keeping her gaze on the passing night scenery. While this whole side trip was keeping her from her mission, she'd told the guy the truth. She'd learned torture from the best.

They drove for a few minutes in silence. She could feel Miles' questions hovering in the air around them. His citrusy scent tickled her nose.

They were a few blocks from her motel when he finally spoke. "So why all the sneaking around, Charlotte? Why didn't you come straight to me and ask for the necklace back?"

"It was safer to stay out of your life. To get in, get the necklace, and disappear again. No one could track me to your doorstep."

"Seems more like you were chickenshit to say hello."

That too. "I was protecting you."

"Being chickenshit doesn't seem like you. Not the woman I remember. You weren't scared of anything back in those mountains."

He was wrong, but she never let anyone see the underlying fear she lived with. She'd been brought up by a military father who expected her to be fearless, courageous, to value honor and loyalty. And then he'd betrayed her.

That was all in the past. *No dwelling*, she reminded herself. "We're all scared of something. I just don't let my fears get in the way of what I want."

"Which makes you a good spy, I imagine."

A siren sounded behind them. "I'm not a double agent, like they say. I love my country. I would never betray her."

Red lights flashed through the rear window. The siren blared louder, a long mournful sound that made the hair on Charlotte's forearms stand up.

Miles slowed and pulled to the side. Charlotte checked over her shoulder, fearing the police were chasing them.

But it wasn't the police. It was a large red fire truck that whooshed by them, another one on its heels.

Once they were gone, Miles pulled back onto the road. "How did you end up on that mountainside and find me?"

No point in playing dumb. "I had followed Nico. He was meeting a man I believed to be the terrorist he was going into partnership with. I was trying to get the man's identity and record any interaction they had. They were testing new weaponry Nico had secured from the black market through me. My handler had set it up. Weapons so advanced and new, the U.S. and Britain hadn't even given them to their soldiers yet."

"What happened?"

"I hooked Nico up with the weapons as instructed by my handler. It was part of my cover in a sting to set up Nico and the terrorist. I was inside Nico's organization, but just barely. I had to get him to trust me, believe I could help him, in order for him to bring me deeper into the clan and find out who the terrorist was he was working with."

"Dr. Alexander, a nuclear physicist, died because of your sting. My men died because of it."

She fisted her hands. The frustration that ate at her night and day burned in her stomach. "No one was supposed to die.

My instructions were to do whatever it took to hook Nico up with the terrorist. There wasn't supposed to be a plane in the area. No plane crash, no SEAL team sent to rescue anyone."

They made a right turn, swung a corner. "So it was simple coincidence that the plane, and then our helo, was used as target practice?"

Charlotte sat up straighter as a line of gray smoke intersected the distant night sky. Memories of the plane crash, a similar trail of smoke rising into frigid night air, assaulted her. Her throat tightened.

"Charlotte?" Miles stopped at a red light, glanced at her, then followed her line of sight. "What is that?"

"How far are we from my motel?" She estimated less than a mile. "Tell me that smoke isn't coming from there."

More sirens split the air, another fire truck and a police vehicle racing through the intersection. Miles wheeled the vehicle through the red light and accelerated.

A minute later, they navigated past the gathered crowds, parking as close as they could get. Jumping out of the truck, she didn't wait for Miles to catch up with her before she ran toward the scene.

The entire east end of the motel where her room had been was ablaze. Firefighters blasted it with water from long hoses. At the opposite end of the L-shaped building, a body, covered by a white sheet, was being rolled out to an ambulance.

Miles, suddenly by her side, touched her arm. "Stay here. I'll find out what happened."

But Charlotte already knew. Nicolae.

Putting up the hood on her sweatshirt, she faded backward into the crowd, searching for his goons, anyone who seemed more interested in watching the people rather than the fire.

Miles spoke to a police officer, showing him an ID. Charlotte watched as the cop replied, motioning at the flames, the front desk. Miles glanced back to the spot where he'd left her. His face went hard—harder than before—and he nodded at the officer before he began fighting his way through the crowd toward her.

She should run, disappear again. He was in too much danger if she stayed.

But she had nothing, just like when she'd escaped Nico.

Her eyes danced over the flames that were at that moment engulfing her clothes, her shoes, her money, her passport, everything. Where would she go without the necklace? Who else would help her?

So stupid, Charlie. She never should have left her belongings—as meager as they were—behind.

"Going somewhere without me?" Miles voice, low in her ear, made her jump.

He took her hand and drew her deeper into the shadows. "The desk clerk was shot in the head. Double tap, execution style. Nothing is missing but it looks like they messed with the office computer, might have been checking security camera footage and names of those registered."

Another man had died because of her. A creeping numbness spread through Charlotte's body. "I need to get out of here."

He started to lead her back to his truck. "Let's go."

She tugged her hand out of his. "Not with you."

Her took her by the elbow and forced her feet to move along with him. "You're on my turf, my country, and I'm not giving up the cross until I have answers, Charlotte."

They stopped next to his truck a block down. As he dug his keys out and hit the fob to unlock the doors, she tried to whirl away from him.

He was too fast for her, grabbing her wrist and drawing her back. She lost her balance and stumbled into his chest. He pinned her against the truck door and held her immobile.

Even in the shadows, she saw his jaw dance with irritation. "We're not done here."

She stared up into the brooding eyes and wanted to kiss him. Kiss away his irritation with her. Kiss away this awful night.

"Don't you see?" she said, fighting against the rising tide of hopelessness inside her. "Everywhere I go, people die. He won't stop until he brings me back to Romania. If he doesn't get me first, MI6 will."

The hold on her wrist loosened. He rubbed his thumb across the sensitive pulse there. "Bourean is never touching you again."

For that alone she really *did* want to kiss him. His protective stance. His determination and loyalty after what she'd done to him.

Instead of kissing him, you should knee him in the balls and rip the necklace from his neck. Make him hate her and get the hell out of his life. It was the only way to save him.

She was about to raise her knee and hate herself even more than she already did, when he leaned down and kissed her.

Chapter Four

He'd wanted to kiss her from the moment she walked out of the bathroom. He had to know if it would be the same. If it would *feel* the same.

It didn't.

Oh, no. It didn't feel the same at all.

It was a hundred times better.

So fucked.

Her lips were as soft as he remembered, still as full and responsive. He ran the tip of his tongue along her bottom lip, tasting her, then deepening the kiss when she moaned into his mouth.

Once upon a time, she'd tasted like comfort and salvation. Now, she tasted like danger.

Deception.

Risk.

God help him, if that didn't make her kiss better. Sexier.

He wanted her even more.

Not here. Too vulnerable.

He broke the kiss. Released her wrist. Stepped back. "We need to move."

Her eyes were half-lidded. She licked her bottom lip. "*I* need to move. You need to go back to your life and forget you ever saw me."

"Enough with the 'I'm a danger to you' shit." He opened the truck door and boosted her into the seat against her protests. "Every job I've had, outside of dog sitting in middle school, has involved danger. Danger is my middle name."

He belted her in, shut the door and hit the lock button on his key fob. She grabbed the door handle and tried to get back out, but the child safety locks were on. She went nowhere.

Keeping a close eye on the surrounding area, he took off his flak vest, adjusted his weapons.

"You can't hold me against my will," she said once he'd climbed in the truck and started the engine.

He did a U-turn in the street and took off north. "Watch me."

She bit her lip and stared out the window. Thinking about the kiss? At least she hadn't hauled off and smacked him, which he totally deserved.

The scars on her body were testimony to the fact someone else had held her against her will, and after a minute of her silence, a twinge of guilt gnawed at him. "I simply want to keep you safe, Charlotte."

"You can't. The only way for me to ever be safe again is to put Nico away for good and clear my name."

"That's exactly what we're going to do."

Nothing about her body language changed, but he sensed a change in her mental outlook. *That's right, sweetheart. Resistance is futile.*

When they'd been stuck in that cabin in the mountains, he'd become so in tune with her mentally, emotionally, and physically, he could often tell what she was thinking without even looking at her.

Had that all been conjecture on his part? Had he simply wanted her so bad, he'd imagined he knew her? He never suspected she was an operative, and he had plenty of experience working with undercover agents from the CIA to Special Ops. He should have known.

He took the highway out of San Diego, heading for a private residence up the coast. A place with top-notch security where he could catch his breath a minute and think.

Charlotte continued her silence for a long while, not even asking where they were headed.

The night closed in around them. Miles kept an eye on his rearview, traffic thinning in the hour after midnight.

When she finally did speak, her voice was low and quiet, like the night. "Thank you for pulling me out of that motel room. Otherwise, I might be dead at this moment."

"How do you think Bourean tracked you?"

"Wondering the same thing and I'm quite clueless. I escaped three weeks ago and I've stayed off the grid, used false identities, moved around constantly. Tonight was the first night I checked into a motel. I've been sleeping in cars, varying my appearance. It makes no sense." She glanced over at him. "How did *you* find me?"

"Slipped a tracker on your rental."

"I tossed that tracker into another car."

"I saw you do that." He grinned and shrugged one shoulder. "You didn't really believe that was enough to stop me, did you?"

"So you're a ghost now? Or is it a chameleon, blending in with your surroundings?"

He looked a heartbeat away from amusement. "I'd tell you my secrets, but what fun would that be?"

"Hmm." She gnawed on her lip and clasped her hands tightly in her lap. "You're good, but I lost my edge while I was inside."

Inside Bourean's mafia. The thought made him want to punch the dash. "Hard not to under those circumstances. How long were you under?"

"Four months before I got snowed in with you at the cabin."

She fell silent again. A stiff, hard silence that filled the cab of the truck and made his jaws clamp together and his fingers grip the steering wheel.

Once more, the urge to kiss her overcame him. He wanted to make her forget the cruelty she'd suffered. Make her remember the passion they'd shared. He'd never experienced anything like those weeks in the cabin with her. Never wanted a woman as much as he wanted her.

Even now, when he knew she was only with him at the moment in order to get her necklace back.

"It's a key, right?" He tapped his shirt where it covered the cross. "Where's the safe? The one it unlocks."

"I can't tell you."

He slowed and took an off-ramp. "Well, sweetheart, you're going to have to since I'm going with you to recover the contents."

Frustration rang in her voice. "The less you know, the better. If you come with me—and that's still a *big* if in my book—you'll have to trust that I'll lead you there."

"Why can't you simply tell me?"

She looked down at her hands, still clasped in her lap. "If Nico catches you, he'll torture the information out of you."

Offended at her lack of confidence in his skills—first that he would get caught, and, second, that he would give up information—Miles had to give her credit for protecting her own backside. She seemed damned good at that. "And you can't risk anyone giving up that intel to him."

"I know it sounds callous, but yes. If you choose to come with me, so be it, but I can't risk the location of the safe falling into Nicolae's hands before I secure the video that will expose the terrorist he's working with and prove I'm not a traitor. It's not personal. Anyone stupid enough to go with me would receive the same treatment."

There was a hint of teasing in her last statement. Teasing she'd used regularly on him back when he was recovering from his injuries and was desperate to escape the painful therapy sessions she put him through.

The safe house was just ahead on the left, part of a group of large, expensive homes with views of the Pacific. As he crawled through a couple of adjacent neighborhoods, he continued to watch for anyone following him. Satisfied they were in the clear, he circled back to the community he wanted. Nearing the gated entrance, he pointed at the glove compartment. "Small, blue box, looks like a garage door opener. Hit the button, would you?"

She opened the glovie, the tiny light illumination allowing her to see as she rummaged through the napkins, old parking tickets, and miscellaneous hand tools. She produced his backup weapon, a small pistol he usually strapped to his ankle, and laid it in her lap. Finding the box in question, she pulled it out and hit the button as Miles drove up to the gate.

The light next to the unmanned guardhouse went from red to green and slowly, the gates retracted. With one last glance in his rearview, Miles goosed the gas pedal and crossed into a place where he could breathe again.

"Now I need the black box," he said.

She dug some more and handed a small, plastic remote to him.

This one was a garage door opener for Emit Petit's vacation home. To his wife's dismay, the place had been converted into a safe house since Emit didn't take vacations anymore. Like everything Emit owned, it was tricked out with the latest technology and security system. The man was paranoid, but in this business, you had to be in order to be successful.

"Wow," Charlotte said. "What is this place?"

Outside lighting spotlighted the walkway and landscaped areas around the front of the modern multi-story beach house. An American flag was on the south side, also spotlighted, the red, white, and blue fluttering gently in the breeze. A large wraparound porch extended to the back, where a lap pool, an infinity pool, and a wide beach with sand dunes led to the ocean. A dock and a boat in a boat slip were waiting for them if they needed to escape land.

The garage door glided up and Miles drove in, waiting until the garage door shut again before turning off the key and popping the locks. Charlotte carried his pistol as he exited the truck, her eyes scanning the three-car interior where two other vehicles—a Land Rover and a Mercedes SUV—silently waited.

Miles punched in the security code and opened the interior door that led to the expensive, modern house.

"Welcome to the West Coast Division of Rock Star Security," he said to Charlotte as she walked by him, her eyes going wide as she took in the commercial kitchen and open living room filled with vintage art and antiques that cost more than a year's worth of Miles' salary.

She gravitated to the glass doors at the other side of the living room. Come morning, there would be a beautiful ocean view.

"A safe house?" she said, tapping the gun in the palm of her hand as she sauntered back to him.

"Well, I couldn't exactly take you home to meet Momma."

"Funny."

He checked the house alarm and held out his hand for his pistol. "Lose the clothes."

"Excuse me?"

"I need to burn them in case there's a tracker on you. You'll find a closet of clothes with a variety of sizes and styles in the master bedroom on the top floor."

"I only bought these clothes two days ago. They're all I have left."

"Can't take chances."

With a testy sigh, she relinquished his pistol. "When do I get my gun back?"

Removing it from his waistband where it had dug into his back on the ride, he set it on the kitchen island. "All yours."

She held out a hand. "Bullets?"

He grinned, then rooted them out of his front pocket and handed them to her.

"Privy?" she asked.

"Guest bath is around the corner, under the stairs." He opened the fridge, surveyed the contents. "Master bath is upstairs where you'll find the clothes. Wanna a drink?"

"I'd love whiskey, but I'd better stay sober."

Because of Bourean or because of him? "Water, soda, sports drink?"

"How about coffee?" She headed for the guest bath. "It's going to be a long night."

Was it? Was she going to tell him all her secrets? Entertain him with a new round of fake stories?

Fuck his brains out?

He could only hope.

The coffee in the walk-in pantry was imported and came in a fancy bag with a picture of rainforest birds. It was labeled fair trade, organic, and bird friendly, whatever the hell that meant.

The coffee maker was a fancy Italian espresso machine that he never used. He wasn't much of a coffee drinker, but Charlotte was and she liked hers strong. He poured in water. dumped in a few scoops of the ground beans, then hit the button.

The machine made noise, chugging as it started brewing. Charlotte returned, wrapped in a robe with her clothes in hand. "Here you go."

"Coffee's on." He sorted through the pile of clothes and found no trackers, but he left her at the breakfast bar and headed outside. A few yards from the house lay a large fire ring and a pile of charred wood. He burned her clothes.

Once he was back inside, he found her sitting on the couch, coffee cup in hand, staring blankly at the cold, lifeless fireplace. Her gun was on the cushion next to her leg.

The coffee smelled good and he needed a shot of caffeine, so he got himself a cup as well and came back, hitting the gas switch on the fireplace. The fake log sprang to life.

Taking a seat beside Charlotte, he switched on the nearby table lamp. He both hated to be the bearer of bad news, and liked the idea of getting her out of the robe for any viable reason. "I need to check you now."

"Check me? For what?"

"Bugs, tracers, GPS."

"Where exactly do you think I'd have any of that hidden?"

He sipped his coffee—gad, the stuff was strong enough to wake the dead. The flavor was decent though. "Under your skin."

She stiffened, thought about it a minute. "You think Nico injected me with a tracker?"

Miles shrugged. "Are you sure it's him chasing you?"

"MI6 wouldn't kill innocents and burn down my room."

"Then how do you think he's following you if you're not bugged? Your clothes were clean like you said."

"I already checked myself over. If I had a chip or tracer under my skin, I would have found it."

"Not if he hid it in your blind spot."

"Shit." She sat forward and put her cup down on the glass coffee table. "I've definitely lost my edge."

Untying the robe, she slipped the thick collar down over her shoulders and swept her long, blond hair off her neck, baring her back to him. "Go ahead. Do your worst."

He started high, kneading his fingers into the back of her head. Her shoulders dropped an inch. He massaged his way along her cranium, down the back of her neck, feeling the tight muscles there.

A soft, sexy sigh escaped her lips and Miles' fingers stalled.

Charlotte shivered and glanced at him over her shoulder from under half-lidded eyes. "Did you find something?"

"Uh, no." He stood and moved away before he ended up sliding the robe the rest of the way off of her and touched her in places that would make her moan. "I need my scanner."

The thickness between his legs made taking the stairs to the second floor uncomfortable, but he did it anyway. *Fuck.* Seeing her porcelain skin—skin he had kissed, licked, and sucked on—and hearing her sigh had nearly done him in. He had to keep his head.

Both of them.

Inside the master bedroom's closet, he opened a hidden panel, flipped a switch, and entered a room of security equipment. Tracker chips inserted under the skin were often embedded too deep to be seen or felt. Examining Charlotte's entire body by touch would be more of a challenge than he could handle. If she was carrying a tracker, they didn't have much time before Bourean's goons showed up.

Grabbing the handheld wand from a peg on the wall, Miles started out of the hidden room, only to be brought up short by Charlotte filling the doorway.

Her gaze scanned the room's contents. "Sweet equipment. MI6 would be jealous. I don't even know what half of this stuff is."

He closed the space between them and flipped the switch on the wand. "Hold still."

The wand was soundless as he scanned the front of her body. When he turned her around, however, the first swipe down her backside set off a beeping alert. He hovered the wand over her neck and three bars on the display lit up. Moving lower, the fourth and final bar pegged the readout between her shoulder blades and the beeping sped up.

"Found it," Miles said. "In a spot that's difficult to see or reach on your own."

"That wanker." Her British roots broke through. "He drugged me when I went back to him, believing I was an undercover agent. I eventually convinced him I wasn't, but he must have inserted the tracker when I was unconscious."

"We need to get it out. Pronto."

"Can you do that? Extract it?"

"I can."

She nodded, resigned compliance. "I'll need that whiskey after all."

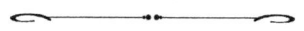

The man stole through the backyards of the neighborhood, assessing each as he went. Although it was dark, plenty of folks in the gated community had their curtains open, lights on. Modern day families putting the kids to bed, cleaning up the kitchen from dinner, the murmur of news shows and late-night television filling their zombified heads.

A few of the homes were dark, security lights and cameras here and there giving their absent owners peace of mind.

He hadn't been able to follow the pickup past the gate, but didn't need to. By process of elimination, it wasn't difficult to figure out which house Agent Charlotte Carstons was now hiding in.

In the years before 9/11, CB Norris had been obsessed with hunting down Osama bin Laden. Stationed in Khartoum, he'd spent months trying to locate the man living in exile in Sudan and gaining a reputation as a brash, egocentric operative inside the walls of the CIA.

His boss had been dull, unimaginative. Plodding along and refusing to chase the one man guaranteed to bring America to its knees.

Look what his ignorance had got them.

After the towers fell, CB had revived his career inside the CIA, moving up the ranks with his intimate knowledge of bin Laden using some well-placed informants in London and the Middle East. The president and his cabinet weren't ready for the real world of terrorism, though. While he'd laid out a very specific plan on how to take down the terrorist leader everyone suddenly wanted, his plan was watered down by his boss, the Pentagon, and eventually the president. They all thought they knew how to find and annihilate bin Laden without his insight.

Ten years later, they'd finally succeeded.

Ten years. What a fucking waste of time and resources. If they'd listened to him, let him run the op, he could have had bin Laden inside of a few months.

Norris' specialty was hunting people. Once his plan to find bin Laden had been stripped apart and diluted to the point there was no saving it, he'd told the CIA to fuck off and ventured across the pond to London, planning on living on his pension in seclusion.

The Queen had other ideas.

Soon, he was seduced back into espionage. Effective intelligence work depended on a mix of things. Some soft, such as recruiting assets. Others hard, such as hunting down and eliminating terrorists. He'd sucked at the soft stuff; excelled at the hard. When they'd given him Charlotte Carstons to handle, he'd done a bit of both.

She'd been the ideal operative, the fastest at learning what he'd had to teach. She'd soaked up his wisdom and begged for more. Her brain was lightening quick, her hunches on the money every time.

She'd reminded him of himself back in the day when he'd had righteous fire shooting out of his ass, and was determined to save America. Determined to prove to the CIA that they could stick him in any hellhole they wanted and he would still be the greatest operative who ever lived.

But Charlotte Carstons had been more than his operative. He'd fallen for her wit and her beauty. For that mind of hers that could, at times, outthink his. She kept him on his toes, made him hungry for the hunt again.

The irony was that he'd handled her mother back in the day. No one knew that, outside of a certain assassin, but that man couldn't talk. His tongue had been split and partially removed by a Romanian crime lord who made Nicolae Bourean look like a puppy. Even if Orlo could talk, he wouldn't share his secrets. He didn't care about pain or torture, unless he was inflicting it. The bastard was a freak, but a useful tool.

CB's mission for MI6 had been to eliminate Nicolae Bourean, but when Agent Carstons slipped into Bourean's mafia and began funneling intel back, he'd realized he was sitting on a gold mine. Romania had remained unaffected by terrorism for years. Bourean, in all his scavenging, criminal glory, had seen to change that.

Somehow, some way, Bourean had made contact with one of the last of bin Laden's lieutenants, an Afghan known only as Blackwater that the U.S. had never caught. A terrorist now recruiting throughout Europe and doing a fine job of spreading Islamic bile.

Just when he was ready to hunt down Blackwater and take Bourean out with him, Carstons had unknowingly interfered. She wasn't supposed to follow Bourean's men into those mountains. Wasn't supposed to be near that exchange of weapons, video taping it.

And she most certainly wasn't supposed to save that damn Navy SEAL.

A dog two blocks over barked, sensing his presence, or perhaps smelling him on the salty night air. He found the house he was looking for, one that met the criteria for a safe house.

The house kitty-corner of the two-story was empty. CB jacked the security alarm and made his way upstairs. A lovely view from the master bedroom gave him unfettered access to the safe house. He unpacked his backpack and laid out his tools.

His scope picked up two heat signatures, adults.

Between his night-vision binoculars and the scope on his rifle, he picked up cameras and infrared trip wires all around the property. The back led to a beach, a long boardwalk, and a docked boat that rocked on the waves.

Once Carstons had escaped Bourean, she'd headed to America. He assumed, rightly so, that she was going after the SEAL. Duncan no longer worked for the Navy, but wasn't far from the same type of duties with his current job. Officially, he worked for Rock Star Security. Unofficially, he was out of the country a lot, messing with black arms dealers, kidnappers, and hackers of all varieties.

Bourean's minions had gotten close to Carstons a couple of times and he'd had to step in and throw them off her track. He needed to know what she'd given Duncan, how much she'd told him.

What damage they could do now that they were back together.

No one was going to stop him from taking Blackwater. Not like they had with bin Laden.

All he had to do was watch and wait.

CHAPTER FIVE

Charlotte's ancestors included a rowdy bunch of Irish fishermen as well as the bastard son of a French king mixed in with her British roots, and that was just on her father's side. She knew how to put away good liquor and could hold her own with the best of them.

While she would have loved to drown the pain from Miles' scalpel with the bottle of gold colored whiskey he gave her, it was neither her preferred brand nor worth dulling her senses over since Nico's goons could show up at any moment.

Passing on the whiskey, she placed a clean dishrag in her mouth, lay on her belly on the kitchen breakfast bar, and nodded at Miles to go to work.

She told herself she wouldn't scream. By the third slice of the tiny knife, her eyes started to burn. Not from the fresh pain; from the horrible memories that cascaded through her mind. Her body held too much suffering in its tissues, yet she refused to give into it. A ragged moan escaped her throat, muffled by the dishrag.

"I see it," Miles said, his finger jabbing into the superficial cut he'd opened. "I just can't get hold of it."

The tears broke free, sliding down her cheeks. "Just do it," she yelled into the dishrag, the muffling making the words sound like *uss doo id.*

"Hold still," he commanded and she nearly turned over and clocked him.

The sting of the scalpel bit a bit deeper and Charlotte sucked in her breath, grinding her teeth into the dishrag.

"Got it," Miles said, holding out bloodied fingers in front of her.

Her vision swam as if she were indeed drunk and she closed her eyes, sweat slicking her forehead. She spit out the rag and cracked one eye to act interested in what he was showing her.

"Tiny bugger," she murmured.

"T16ZR." Miles lifted it to the light and rolled it around in his fingers. "I haven't seen one of these in eons. This is old technology, years out of date."

The bar was cool against Charlotte's cheek. She could feel blood running down her back, along her ribs. The horrible memories tugged at her brain, trying to take her back to the torture chamber.

Get up. Don't let the demons take you back there.

Doing a modified pushup on the bar, she pushed the memories away. "Nico gets top dollar for the modern tech equipment. Deals in everything from iPhones to surveillance cameras, but his clients don't want old stuff. Any equipment he can't get enough money for, he uses on his own people."

Miles gently touched her shoulder. "I'm sorry I hurt you."

She waved his apology off. "Had to be done. Now destroy that thing."

"This model only sends out a pulse once every fifteen to thirty minutes, and it's easily disrupted by cell towers and magnets. That's why no one uses these anymore. Not even to chip dogs. This safe house's security blocks everything from EMF waves to digital scans. Tech this old could never hold up against it."

Wooziness made her arms tremble. "But that explains how his goons have been one step behind me all this time." She pushed herself up the rest of the way and closed the robe over her chilly skin. A dull ache now pervaded her upper back. "The pulse is sporadic and getting interrupted frequently."

"If you were sleeping in cars with On-Star or any type of internal computer, really, it probably messed with the tracker. Hell, a microwave could throw it off."

"He never expected I would actually escape. He probably just shoved it in there for grins and giggles."

"Stay put." Miles wiped off the tiny device and stuck it in his pocket. Then washed his hands. "Let me clean and close that cut."

"Slap a bandage on it. I'll be fine."

"You're bleeding and I know for a fact you're in pain. Drop the robe and let me clean you up. It'll only take a minute."

Without her permission, he nudged her knees sideways so her back was facing him again. Then he gently loosened the robe from her grasp and lowered it to get to the incision once more.

His fingers were more gentle this time, washing off the blood and coating the wound with a cool cream. She shivered under his touch, not from the cream, but from a new onslaught of memories assaulting her. Memories of his fingers trailing down her spine, his lips following.

"You need a few stitches, darlin'."

The words snapped her out of her revelry. "We don't have time for that."

"Yes, we do. I put a numbing cream on the area. It'll take thirty seconds to kick in and another minute for me to stitch you up."

She felt the cream already going to work. Lowering her chin to her chest, she breathed through her nose and let her mind wander to the past again. "Stitch carefully. I don't need another scar."

It was meant to be a joke. Miles didn't seem to think it was funny. "I never should have left you."

"You didn't. I left *you.*"

"I could have found you. Kept you out of Bourean's clutches."

"Don't be ridiculous." The past was in the past. Charlotte didn't see a reason to rehash what might have been. "You had no idea who I was or what mission I was working. You couldn't have stopped what happened."

He stilled. "Charlotte…"

She waited. He didn't continue. "What?"

She heard a terse sigh.

"Look, it's all right. You can help me now, so let's get to it, shall we?"

Miles went to work sealing up the incision, the numbing cream doing its job. Charlotte only wished that cream could numb the hum under her skin everywhere Miles touched.

"The men following you will have lost the signal from the transmitter—if they were receiving anything—the moment we hit the gate outside," he said.

"We still need to move. And warn the others in the neighborhood. They'll go door to door killing people and burning places to find me."

"I called in reinforcements while I was burning your clothes. They'll handle neighborhood security, and I'll send the tracker off on a new course to distract Bourean's men."

The tracking device now lay on the counter. "Are you sure that's the only one?"

He patted the wand on the bar next to her. "This baby could find a tracking device six feet underground. You're clear."

She slid off the breakfast bar as he headed for the double doors that led out to the boardwalk and the ocean.

"Where are you going?"

"I'm putting the device in a little plastic buoy that will take it out to sea. That will give us time to get you ready to travel."

His phone went off and he checked the screen. "It's Shinedown. He'll be coming through the side door."

"Shinedown?"

"He's going to fix you up with a new passport."

"Codenames, huh? I knew Emit Petit ran a tight ship."

"It's a safety precaution. Most of us who work for him prefer our true identities stay as private as possible." He headed for the door once more. "There are wigs, glasses, colored contacts, and other accessories upstairs in the bathroom to change your appearance. Help yourself."

Change her appearance. How many times had she done that already in her lifetime? Would she ever get to be herself again?

Did she even know who that was anymore?

Tightening the sash on the robe, she headed for the stairs.

Charlotte stopped under the lovely blown-glass chandelier at the top of the curved staircase. Was she really going through with this? Letting Miles come with her?

Age-old fear crawled under her skin. It never seemed to leave her these days. She remembered when she was a young operative, excited at the prospect of the next mission, the next covert op, the next interaction with a criminal, a traitor, another spy turned double agent. The lure of the dark side had always intrigued her more than the bright, shiny heroic side of life. Yet, she had too many morals, too many scruples, to be anything but loyal, honorable, and out to see justice done.

After five years in the field, those morals and scruples had been tested beyond her limits. She'd been forced to make choices—choices that looked like the opposite of what she stood for. Now, *she* was the criminal, the traitor, the double agent.

At least that's what her employer believed.

Fear sucked, but she couldn't let it cripple her. Couldn't let her fear stop her from doing what needed to be done.

Her mission hadn't changed. *Stop Nico. Prove my innocence. Rescue Madeena.*

Straight forward, easy.

Except, of course, for Miles. He complicated everything.

Giving him the necklace had seemed like the perfect solution at the time. If only she hadn't. If only she'd gone back to her hiding place, grabbed the video she had and escaped without going back to Nico's compound.

But without the proof of who the real traitor inside MI6 was, she faced a trial and certain imprisonment since the evidence pointed to her. She'd believed if she went back to Nico, she could figure it out. Someone working with him had betrayed her, but who?

In hindsight, she wondered if being convicted of high treason and life imprisonment by Her Majesty's Prison Service would have been preferable to the torture and brutality of Nicolae Bourean.

Didn't matter now. Regrets about what might have been different if she'd left Romania with Miles were pointless. She didn't have time for fantasies about how her life might have been better.

Time was running out. She had to consider her options.

She could disable Miles—it wouldn't be easy, but she could do it—and take the necklace by force, leaving him behind so he wouldn't be in danger. She'd have a rough time getting a new passport and securing transportation, but she'd done it before. With the tracker gone, she'd have an easier time staying ahead of Bourean's goons.

Or she could change her appearance, get the fake passport from Shinedown, and let Miles go with her. A much easier solution, but more dangerous for the only man she'd ever truly loved.

Was it love? Or another fantasy? Six weeks wasn't really enough time to know someone before deciding that, was it?

A memory from their last night in the cabin flashed through her mind. Miles was back to normal, except for a slight limp.

He'd been working out, hundreds of push-ups, sit-ups, jumping jacks. He'd stuffed an old jute bag full of straw, weighted the bottom with stones, and used it as a punching bag. In the small cabin, there was little room to get out of each other's ways, so Charlotte had sat in the rocking chair near the fire, watching him go through his workout while pretending to read her favorite Harry Potter book. Her eyes wouldn't stay on the page, and kept traveling to look at his naked back and chest, glistening with sweat as he attacked the bag with a series of kicks and punches.

"How's the book?" he'd asked her, never breaking his rhythm.

She'd been so focused on the movement of his taut abs and muscled thighs as he bounced on the balls of his feet, she startled. "What?"

"The book." He half glanced at her with a grin. "What's it about?"

"Oh, it's an old copy of Russian erotica stories," she lied.

His rhythm slowed by a fraction. "Seriously?"

He couldn't see the cover and she'd removed the dust jacket months ago. She was probably safe lying. "Yes, would you like me to read one out loud to you?"

The footwork stopped. His fists lowered. He was already breathing heavy, his beautiful gray eyes picking up the dancing flames in the fireplace.

Those eyes skimmed over her face, down her neck and lower. Everywhere his gaze touched her through the sheer nightgown—her cleavage, her breasts, her thighs—felt a tingle of anticipation. "I have a better idea," he'd said.

He was healed. The winter snows were melting. *Time to say goodbye.* Her heart had clenched at the thought. But it was the right thing to do. "And what is that?"

He moved forward, drawing her out of the chair and bringing her close. Deft fingers untied the bow at her cleavage, slipped one strap off of her shoulder. "How about I clean up and you act one of them out for me?"

He smelled of sweat and male. *Hungry* male.

She let the other strap fall off her shoulder, the loose gown sliding down over the swell of her breasts. Miles ran his fingers over the hem, helping it down, down, down, slowly, ravaging her with his eyes. Charlotte shimmied and the gown fell to the floor, baring everything to him. "How about we act out one of them in the tub together?"

He'd swept her up in his arms, crushing his lips to hers. At the time, she'd known she would never feel the same way about any man. He was all wrong for her—her job required secrets and deception and he would never tolerate that. He consumed her, inside and out, and still wanted more. Wanted to explore every inch of her mind as well as her body. During their time at the cabin, he'd asked her thoughts on everything from Chinese politics to whether nuts belonged in chocolate chip cookies.

She longed to give in to him now as much as she had then.

But she couldn't.

A noise downstairs signified the arrival of Shinedown. Brushing aside the memories, Charlotte went into the bathroom and inventoried her choices for a new look.

The closet inside the master bath held a collection of hair dyes. Red? She'd loved being a redhead in her early twenties. Her brown eyes and pale skin looked good with that color.

Red hair stood out, garnered a lot of attention. Not what she wanted on this mission.

Sadly, she moved that box of hair color aside.

The names of the colors gave her pause. Toasted Walnut, Sun-Kissed Brown, Chocolate Copper. All pretty shades, but most were too dark or would clash with her skin and make her look like she belonged in a zombie movie.

She couldn't help it, even undercover, her hair color needed to be something she could live with.

Next.

Warm Butterscotch. Hmm.

It would darken her blond hair without completely washing her out, and from the guide on the back, it would give her a very subtle hint of red with the yellow tones.

Warm Butterscotch it is.

She worked the color into her hair, wrapped it in plastic and found the colored contact selection.

Brown eyes were the most common, so she decided to go with blue.

Downstairs, she heard voices. Miles and Shinedown talking in low murmurs. She ventured into the giant, walk-in master closet. A chest of drawers was labeled with her size and inside she found brand new foundation garments. She slipped them on under the robe and surveyed the selection of clothes.

She went with jeans a half size too big, a long-sleeved purple T-shirt and a sweatshirt with the Southern California

University emblem on it. She eyed a pair of boots she liked, but chose a pair of blue and white trainers instead. Better for running.

At the last minute, she went back for the boots. They would be heading into rough terrain and possibly bad weather. It was the beginning of winter season in Romania. She needed to be prepared.

An assortment of luggage lined one end of the closet. She found a duffel and filled it with a couple days' worth of clothing changes, including some long underwear.

Back in the bathroom, she rinsed the dye from her hair, combed it out and used the blow dryer on it.

The color came out darker than she'd anticipated, but the guides on the side of the box were rarely accurate. With the new blue of her eyes, the light brown with red highlights worked well.

Her face devoid of makeup, and the So. Cal sweatshirt providing context, she appeared younger than her twenty-nine years. She could easily pass for an undergrad. She grabbed a pair of fake designer glasses with heavy frames and added them for good measure.

A knock sounded from the bedroom door. "Charlotte?" Miles said.

"Yes?"

"You ready? We need to get your picture for the passport."

Smoothing down the sweatshirt, she took a deep breath, giving herself one more glance in the mirror. Ridiculous as it was, she hoped Miles still found her attractive in her disguise.

Stop acting like a schoolgirl and get on with it.

Slowly, she walked out of the bathroom and saw Miles standing in the doorway of the suite. His eyes did a double take but she couldn't tell if it was because her appearance was so different or because he liked it.

"That'll do," was all he said, before turning on his heel and walking out.

Irritation burned in her stomach. Passing his inspection should have made her happy. Instead his casual remark made her feel as if something was lacking.

So he prefers blondes. Get over it. This is a deadly mission, not a lovers' reunion.

Snatching up the overnight bag, she followed him, reconsidering leaving him behind out of spite.

CHAPTER SIX

Charlotte was as striking as a blue-eyed brunette as she was a brown-eyed blonde. Miles couldn't take his eyes off of her.

You're horny. That's all.

He hadn't wanted a single other woman since he'd left Romania. Not even a twitch when he saw a sexy woman on the street or when one handed him her phone number in a restaurant or bar. Not one fantasy that didn't have Charlotte and only Charlotte starring in it.

All the lonely nights, missing her and wondering if she were even real. Like a starving man in need of comfort food, he couldn't stop flicking his gaze over to her where she sat for her passport picture in front of a generic, off-white background.

Shinedown, a former SEAL who's real name was Colton Bells, adjusted the lighting, then touched her chin. "A little more to the right." He lowered his face close to hers, scooted her fake glasses a bit higher on her nose. "Perfect."

She smiled up at him and he smiled back and Miles' blood pressure went up twenty points.

His phone rang, the readout telling him it was the last person on Earth he wanted to talk to.

"Take the damn picture," he growled at Colt, and then barked, "What?" into the phone.

"Rory tells me we have a new client," Beatrice Reese, out in Washington D.C., said without preamble. "Tell me why I have no paperwork for her in my inbox."

Word traveled fast. Colt still leaned over Charlotte, saying something too soft for Miles to hear and making her chuckle.

Her eyes met his across the room but then skittered away.

Gripping the phone, Miles gave it a squeeze, knowing he needed to get control of his sudden jealousy as well as his ongoing obsession with the woman in the chair. He wanted to run his fingers through her newly dyed hair and make her blue eyes go hazy with lust. "I'm working on it."

"Who are you assigning her to?"

Colt finished primping Charlotte and moved behind the camera. Miles could finally take a decent breath. "I'm handling this one on my own."

"You're now head of the West Coast division of Rock Star Security. You no longer work assignments, you assess clients and assign other team members to their cases."

"This one is...different. Special."

Charlotte must have realized he was talking about her. Her eyes met his, an intensity in them that nearly sucked Miles' breath away again. At that same moment, Colt snapped her picture.

Beatrice's voice cut through the white noise in his head. "Is this the woman Rory said was stalking you?"

Breaking eye contact, Miles had to step away. Carrying on a coherent conversation with Beatrice while Charlotte stared at him like she wanted to hug him was impossible.

Colt moved to the office computer-printer setup and fiddled with both.

Miles cleared his throat and lowered his voice. "She needs help. I'm going to give it to her."

"Not until she signs our contract and I've cleared her."

Beatrice was no stranger to traitors and spies. Not only had she worked for NSA, she'd been handpicked for a secret intelligence group called Command & Control and knew her way around the political landscape as well as anyone. Betrayal and honor were two sides of the same coin she understood well. She'd been labeled a rogue agent at one point and escaped execution by an assassin who now worked for her.

Second chances. That's what Shadow Force International was all about.

But there was a fine line between helping those in need who deserved it, and helping those who'd betrayed their country for real and didn't.

Miles still wasn't sure which category Charlotte fell into.

"She's filling out the paperwork right now," he lied, motioning

Charlotte to a chair next to the desk. He dug a computer tablet out of the drawer, brought up the client contract and handed it to her. "You'll have the contract in a few minutes."

"Good. I'll run the background check once I receive the papers."

"You already have. She's the agent you helped me look into."

There was the squeak of a chair in the background. In his mind, Miles saw Beatrice rocking in her leather office chair, thinking, calculating.

Beatrice was labeled a genius. Her intellect and cunning were off the map; hence, her past career with the NSA and now running Emit Petit's dual organizations. "I assumed as much. Should I be expecting a call from the Queen, then?"

"Not if I can keep this on the down low."

"How is our new client paying for services rendered?"

Miles shifted his weight from one leg to the other. "I'll cover it."

"How?"

Sarcasm wasn't part of Beatrice's repertoire. Neither was incredulousness. She was logical to a fault and knew she had him on this one. The men in SFI were paid handsomely, but fees for Rock Star Security were astronomical. Which was why only the very rich and very famous hired them. "I'll work pro bono, and you can dock my future pay until the bill is paid in full."

Charlotte was staring at him, a frown knitting her forehead. Miles turned away.

"What I'm wondering," Beatrice said, "is why you would put your life and career on the line for her?"

"Been wondering the same thing," he muttered.

"If MI6 catches up to her and you're with her..."

"I know. Aiding and abetting. Prison. I've got the picture."

"Do you?" Another squeak of her chair. "Because if you get caught with her, I may not be able to get you out of jail. MI6 and the Queen may bury you so deep, I can't even find you. You'll be rotting in some South African prison or working the coal mines in Wales."

Miles turned back, watched as Colt stamped the passport with some foreign country's stamp and blew on it. Charlotte used the stylus on the tablet to sign her name. She looked up at Miles and gave him a hesitant smile.

She'd never been hesitant about anything during their time in the mountains. She'd been wanton and direct, doing what she felt like when she felt like it. Bourean had done more than leave scars on her back. He'd beaten some of the spirit out of her as well.

"She's worth it," Miles found himself saying into the phone.

A beat of silence went by. "I'll find someone else to take charge of the West Coast Rock Stars while you're gone. Now, get me that paperwork."

Beatrice was tough, but she had his back. Every one of the men working for SFI, whether they did security details for the rich and famous, or ran covert ops in foreign countries, took their cues from her. They were all a team. "Thank you."

"I assume you're heading back to Romania. I have contacts there. Let me know what you need and I'll find someone to help."

He sent up a second, mental thank you to her. "I need a plane."

"I'll make sure one is fueled and ready at Greenbow."

Greenbow was a small, private wing of the Van Nuys airport that Rock Stars and SFI used for clients. "Shinedown can handle things until I get back."

"Hmm." Her pause suggested she had serious doubts about that. Colt, however, looked thrilled. "Have him call me."

She disconnected.

Colt held up the passport and showed it to Miles. "All done."

"You're sure it will pass inspection?"

A hurt look passed over the former SEAL's face. "Homeland taught me well. I'm the best at this and you know it."

Colton had unique skills and had worked for a brief time for DHS before the SEALs, tracking the often fake passports of terrorists. "Thanks, man."

Miles took the tablet from Charlotte, closed out the form, and emailed it to Beatrice. Colt locked a Rock Star bracelet on Charlotte's arm, giving her the rundown about the high-tech piece of jewelry. "GPS, the tiniest wire saw in the world, a pick for locks."

"All in this?" Charlotte held up her wrist and examined the gold bracelet. "Handy."

"Ready?" Miles said.

She stood and pocketed the passport. "Lead the way."

"Call Beatrice," Miles told Colt. "Everything you need is here in this house to run things. Schedules, assignments, etc. Anything you can't find, ask Rory."

They shook and clapped each other on the back. "God's speed," Colt said.

In the living room, Miles handed Charlotte her coat. He grabbed her go bag and his—he kept one ready to go in his truck—and headed for the doors on the ocean side of the home.

"Security cameras show no activity," Colt said. "Clutch and Chevelle are outside keeping an eye on things. You're clear."

As Miles walked ahead of Charlotte, heading for the wooden boardwalk that would take them to the dock, she snagged his coat sleeve. "Where are we going?"

"To the boat."

"I thought we were going to the airport."

The crashing waves of the Pacific echoed in the night air. The normal fog was already rolling in. "We are, but it's safer if we take the boat up to Greenbow. Trust me."

Her face, already in shadows, tilted down. "Miles, you really don't have to do this."

He took her chin between his finger and thumb and lifted her head. "Yeah, that's just it," he said. "I really do."

What was this now? The SEAL and Carstons had snuck out the back of the house. They were headed for the boat.

He hadn't been able to eavesdrop on them, the safe house protected by electronic interference. The neighborhood had grown quiet, the late nighters finally giving up and going to bed. Another man had arrived at the safe house and the three of them had been tucked inside one room for the past hour. Two more had set up guard around the perimeter of the house outside.

Carstons followed the SEAL down the boardwalk to the boat. Where were they headed? He'd lose them if they got on that boat.

Back in the day, drone technology had been in use by the military but mostly used to spy on America's enemies. He'd been all in favor of arming the things and using them to take out those enemies. It was the first thing he'd proposed after 9/11 when he'd been asked to present his plan to find bin Laden to the president. The president had liked the idea; Norris' boss hadn't.

Eventually Predator drones were armed, and these days, every Tom, Dick, and Harry had some camera-only version they'd bought at the local big box store.

He had one too. Smaller than the ones on the consumer market, with a high-powered camera equipped with night vision lenses. Firing it up, he smiled at the low hum from the engine. Tapping a couple of buttons on his smart phone, he watched as the app linked with the drone's onboard computer and gave him the all clear.

Another check on the two people moving to the dock, and he pocketed his binoculars. He patted the drone and took it downstairs and outside.

Flying was freedom. He envied the drone as it lifted off and hovered, waiting for his command. The engine purred, the camera engaged its night vision. MI6 had plenty of toys. Using the digital joystick on his phone's app, he guided the drone toward the boat.

As the boat left the dock and sped north, Norris locked the drone onto his target. Then he went back inside to make himself some coffee and watch the images the camera fed back to his phone.

There wasn't much to see, the boat's profile occasionally breaking through the fog. He pulled up a map on his phone and scanned potential destinations the boat might be heading to.

If Carstons had convinced the SEAL to help her, they'd head for an airport. She'd lost her papers in the motel fire, but had probably gotten more. The organization the SEAL now worked for used private planes.

A quick inventory of the closest airports revealed what he was looking for. Rock Star Security had their own private wing at the Van Nuys airstrip.

He had Carstons. He had the SEAL she'd given the cross necklace to. If the two of them left the U.S., he'd lose them, even though he knew their ultimate destination.

All he needed was that necklace and for her to tell him where she'd hidden the intel on Bourean. He could give a shit about the crime lord, he was after bigger fish. The big fish that Carstons had on video.

For all he knew, she and the SEAL might be running for good. They might not be heading back to Romania at all, and then, where did that leave him?

Holding shit.

He couldn't take that chance.

Loading his equipment into the backpack, he continued to keep an eye on the drone. The fresh coffee smell filled the house. He didn't bother turning off the machine.

Back in his car, he set the phone in its cradle and headed north, debating whether to make a very specific phone call.

The boat was actually a small yacht. Spacious, well-appointed, fast. No surprise, Miles drove it like an expert through the dark, foggy night.

He was focused on coordinates, wind speed, knots. Charlotte wandered off and found the galley.

She hadn't eaten in nearly twelve hours. The cabinets held a nice assortment of food. Within minutes, she'd pulled together a peanut butter and marmalade sandwich. She washed it down with an orange soda.

The man called Shinedown had forged a birth certificate and social security card for her along with the passport. As of two o'clock that morning, she was now Charlene Smith, an official American citizen born in Topeka, Kansas. She'd have to work on her mainstream American English accent.

The bench she sat on was padded and comfortable, the engine noise a soft lullaby dulling her senses. Her eyelids grew heavy, the caffeine in the soda not enough to keep her awake.

Her chin dipped, her eyes giving up the fight. She dozed intermittently, flashes of memories and odd dreams mixing together and keeping her from full sleep.

Her exhausted body needed rest. As the boat rocked on the waves, her body relaxed more fully. The images flowing in and out of her mind turned to Miles and cold winter nights. She floated for a time in a pretty dream where the two of them lived in a real house. He was carving wooden animals for a little boy by the fire. She was knitting.

She'd never knitted in her life, but in the dream, she was damn good at it.

Outside the window, flowers overflowed window boxes. A dog lay on the porch in the sun.

The little boy turned to look at her, holding up his latest animal. His face was a much younger version of Miles'.

The boat lurched and suddenly Nicolae's face, the blade of a knife, flashed behind her closed eyelids. Gone was the gentle, happy dream of life with Miles and their son. In its place, a monster came for her, slashing at her, laughing at the damage he wrought on her skin.

She jerked awake, heart pounding, breath rushing in and out of her chest. Panic raced down her limbs and she was off the bench and moving before she realized where she was.

The papers on the table brought her back to reality. *Charlene Smith.*

She was safe for the moment. She'd avoided Nico's goons. Miles was helping her.

Miles. Her touchstone.

A cold, hard shiver wracked her body. She needed to see him. Touch him. Make sure this was all real.

Pocketing her papers, she focused on regulating her breathing. Then she grabbed two energy drinks from the refrigerator and headed to the bridge to find Miles.

He had the radio on and was humming along to some angsty rock ballad as he stood at the helm, his gaze going between his controls and the night view out the wide, wrap around windows.

She stood, mesmerized for a moment, taking him in. The short hair, the square jaw, the broad shoulders. He *was* real.

He glanced at her as she entered and stopped humming.

"Brought you a drink," she said, handing him the cold can. By her calculations, he hadn't slept in nearly twenty-four hours.

"Thanks." He popped the lid and took a swig.

"Are you hungry? I could make you a sandwich."

"I'm fine." His lips twitched ever so slightly.

"What?"

He glanced her way again. "Huh?"

"Your lips. You smirked."

"No, I didn't."

"Yes, you did. Is there something funny about me wanting to bring you a sandwich?"

His gaze focused on a gauge in front of him. "No."

"Then what?"

"Nothing."

She moved so she was mostly in front of him, plopping her bottom against the control panel and blocking half the gauges as she sipped the drink. She couldn't understand why people liked these energy drinks. They tasted like balls to her. "Tell me what's humorous about my offer."

He half rolled his eyes. "You're still, after all this time, trying to take care of me."

"It was a simple offer of a sandwich. You're risking your life for me, and I offered you a kindness in return."

His stare intensified. "You sure that's all it is?"

Her throat tightened. They had only spent six weeks together, under somewhat false pretenses, but he knew her better than most people ever would. *No, I love you, you big dummy.*

He'd made it quite clear that, while he still found her attractive, he wasn't interested. Fair enough. She was trouble, right down to her toes. No man would willingly get involved with her knowing even half of what she'd done.

His eyes flicked away, out to the fog teasing the pointed bow of the yacht. "How did Bourean catch you after you left me?"

"I went back to him on my own."

Confusion clouded his face. A muscle in his jaw jumped. "Why would you do that?"

"I needed to find out who Nico was working with to get those weapons—the ones he used to shoot down that plane and your helicopter." She pushed off the control panel and turned to face the bow. "It didn't make sense. The only reason I told him about the plane and the scientist on board was because I knew he had no interest in a nuclear physicist. My handler gave me the information. I'd been cleared by Vauxhall to pass it on to him. It gave me credibility since he could verify Dr. Alexander was indeed on that plane, but it shouldn't have endangered anyone."

"Yet it did."

"Nico was just getting into weapons when I infiltrated his organization. He had a couple of locations in the mountains where he would meet sellers and buyers and test the products. I overheard two of his men talking about the place and a seller who had missiles. They were meeting him there. I hadn't yet figured out where the location was, so I followed them, hoping to glean some intel. The road into the mountains was rough terrain and I lost them a couple of times. By the time I caught up, I realized they had set up a surface-to-air missile."

She set her drink on a nearby surface, her stomach roiling like the waves outside the boat. "As you know, cell phones and other communication devices are pretty worthless in those mountains. A storm was brewing just over the horizon. There was nothing I could do to warn the people onboard the plane. Plus, by the time I got there, it was only minutes until they fired that missile and the plane came down."

The details of that afternoon were etched in her mind, as fresh as if it had all happened yesterday. "I recorded the whole thing, then followed them to the crash site. The only way to stay out of sight was to use the tunnels in the mountains, so I hid and watched and continued recording. That winter, while you and I were stranded, I kept turning it over in my mind. Why shoot down that plane? I could see Nicolae wanting to capture the scientist and sell him on the black market, but there was little possibility shooting down the plane would leave the doctor alive."

"He *was* alive. After the plane crashed, we were activated and they told us the doctor had communicated with them. Alexander made it to what was left of the cockpit and sent out a transmission."

"I saw him. He was alive, but badly injured. He was calling for help. At first, I thought Nico's men would take him. That Nico was, indeed, kidnapping the scientist. But one of the men used a piece of the metal wreckage to club the doctor in the head. I should have..." She swallowed hard. "I should have stopped them, but I didn't realize they were going to kill him."

She felt Miles' touch on her arm. "You can't blame yourself. If you'd tried to save Alexander, they would have killed you."

"It all happened so fast. The bodies...the carnage." She shuddered. "I got it all recorded. What happened with your team, as well."

Miles' features clouded. "We were just over the border."

"You surprised them. They weren't expecting a search and rescue team to show up so quickly. I was hiding in the caves, and right before your team showed up, Nico arrived and another truck with two men met him there. I couldn't get a good look at them, but they seemed satisfied by the wreckage. They were shouting and laughing. I believed one of the men was a terrorist the UK and the US have been searching for for a long time."

"What happened when we showed up?"

"Nico told them to shoot you down too. He was trying to impress his new friend."

What happened next, they both already knew.

"What did you do with that recording?" Miles asked.

She rubbed her eyes, her arms. The energy drink's caffeine made her nerves buzz. "Hid it. In the caves."

"Did you ever retrieve it?"

His reflection in the glass windshield was faint, like a ghost. She glanced at his chest reflected there, the spot where she knew the cross lay against his bare skin. "That's what we're going back for."

"Wait, the necklace opens a safe hidden in the caves?"

"Those tunnels and caves inside the mountain have been used for thousands of years by the local peoples as far back as the Romans to avoid invading armies, crisscross the mountains during winter months, meet up with secret lovers, escape slavery. There are trap doors, hidden rooms, treasure troves everywhere. But the caves are said to be haunted, cursed. Not many locals will venture into them anymore. A few Gypsies still use them, and people like me who don't believe in curses or ghosts. A friend of mine helped me hide the video in a special safe located in one of the offshoot caves. That cross belongs to my friend." She pointed at his collarbone. "When inserted in the slot, it becomes a key to open the safe."

"Did you ever find out why Bourean shot down the plane?"

She nodded. "There were three men on that flight with ties to Syrian criminal syndicates. Men the Romanians—both the criminals and the politicians—wanted."

"Crashing the plane killed them. Didn't they want them alive?"

"It was a hit. No one cared about Dr. Alexander. They wanted those three Syrian mobsters dead. Nico got a new buyer for his weapons and a young girl in the trade, and he received a large reward from the government, if you can believe it, for taking out those Syrian mobsters. And I...I have to live with Alexander's death on my conscious. With what happened to your men."

Miles touched her arm, pulling her to him. "It's not your fault. You were following orders from your handler."

He was so sincere, so sure of her innocence. "If I'd done a better job of infiltrating Nicolae's organization, I would have known what he was up to."

"He'd never been in the assassination business until then, had he?"

"Not that kind, no."

"Then you had no reason to suspect he'd suddenly blow up a plane to make some quick cash."

Dr. Alexander's death would always weigh on her. All the deaths that day. "It's the terrorist. He's the key to all of this."

His face was close to hers. Too close. The night, the rocking boat, the danger…it all gave her tingles up and down her limbs.

Or maybe it was too much energy drink.

He released her, and she automatically took a step back, feeling a touch dizzy. She reached for a nearby chair and sat.

"You okay?" he asked.

"It's been a long twenty-four hours." *A long nine and a half months.*

A cluster of lights to the east came into view, hazy in the fog. The eastern horizon was starting to lighten. Miles downshifted the boat. "Grab your stuff," he said. "We're here."

Chapter Seven

The Gulfstream jet sat on the runway facing north, sunrise brightening the eastern sky.

The air in Van Nuys was a cool 67 degrees, raising goose flesh on Charlotte's arms even under the shirt and sweatshirt.

Miles hustled her up the steps where a man in fatigues greeted them with Styrofoam cups of steaming coffee. "She's all ready," he said to Miles.

"Good." Miles handed him their bags and sipped his coffee. "Megadeth, this is Charlotte Carstons. Charlotte, Megadeth."

Charlotte exchanged nods and "nice to meet yous" with the man. "Thank you for the coffee."

"No problem," he said, ushering them into the plane.

The inside of the cabin was done in rich leather with dark blue carpet and matching curtains over the windows. The seats were white, the table tops as well.

Megadeth loaded their duffels in a compartment and shut the door. "Flight plan?"

Miles directed Charlotte to a pair of generously sized seats by an east-facing window. "New York first. Then London. Once we get to London, you're free. I'll take us on to Bucharest."

Megadeth gave Miles a quirky smile. "No can do. Beatrice told me to stick with you for the entire ride. Said you needed someone to cover your backside."

Miles set his cup on the table facing the chairs, seeming to ignore the last statement. "Go ahead and file the flight manifest. I want to look things over."

"Don't trust my evaluation of the plane's readiness?"

"If I'm flying the plane, I'm doing an inspection."

Megadeth raised a thick eyebrow and scratched his bearded chin. "Who said you were piloting this trip?"

Miles flipped him off and Megadeth headed for the front cabin, chuckling.

"*You're* flying the plane?" Charlotte said.

"Consider me a full-service provider."

"You have a pilot's license?"

"Don't you?" His voice was teasing. "Let's see. You can't drive a boat or fly a plane. MI6 failed you, Agent Carstons."

Charlotte sighed and looked out at the peach and pink stripes on the horizon. "In more ways than one."

The sun was fully up by the time Miles completed his inspection. While she was waiting, Megadeth returned, a laptop, magazines and a couple of paperback books in hand. "The plane is equipped with Wi-Fi, and there's a printer and other office supplies in the back," he said. "If you need more coffee or some food, the galley's stocked. Help yourself."

"Does Miles fly a lot? Is he a good pilot?"

That quirky smile moved the man's lips. "Don't trust him?"

"Flying isn't my favorite thing in the world."

Megadeth produced a couple of airsick bags. "Keep these handy."

So she was in for a rough ride. Great. "Thanks."

"Don't worry. As co-pilot, I'll make sure the flight is as smooth as possible."

Miles suddenly appeared. "We got company. Let's move."

Megadeth tore off toward the front of the cabin.

Charlotte looked out her window. "Who is it?"

"Don't know," Miles said, "but two black SUVs rolled up fast to the main office. Could be Feds, could be Bourean's men. I didn't stick around to find out. Buckle up. We're out of here."

He disappeared into the front. Craning her neck, Charlotte saw part of the main office behind them. Sure enough, the SUVs Miles had mentioned were parked at a weird angle to the private airport's main building. As the Gulfstream's engines roared to life under her, she saw the men emerge, looking in their direction.

The four men had short, slick-backed hair, expensive shoes, and the air of superiority. *Not Nicolae's.*

Charlotte braced herself as the plane began to move in a slow arc heading toward the runway. The men picked up their pace.

Oh, God. They weren't going to make it. The men in the suits would catch them, stop them.

She'd be screwed but good. Miles, too, for helping a fugitive.

What could she do? Give herself up to save him?

She couldn't get off the plane even if she wanted to. They were already picking up speed, the runway only twenty yards away. The men were yelling now, running.

Charlotte's heart jackhammered inside her chest. *Hurry, hurry, hurry.*

The plane pulled up to the long, straight runway.

...And stopped.

Her heart sank, blood running hot beneath her skin. He was giving her up.

Any sane man would.

She started to unbuckle herself, mentally preparing for the coming hours of interrogation, the real possibility she'd be in some dank, awful prison before nightfall.

Could she run? Outwit them somehow?

She was contemplating the idea when the engines kicked up, roaring loud. The plane began a quick acceleration. Charlotte was thrown back in her seat, sudden G-forces pinning her into the soft leather.

The men outside waved at the plane, their mouths moving. Sunlight glinted off weapons.

Would they fire at the jet?

Charlotte held her breath and prayed, the nose of the plane tipping skyward. A moment later, they were airborne.

Finally able to sit forward again, she stared down at the black blobs of the men growing smaller. How had they found her?

Her stomach heaved like a tsunami that had nothing to do with flying. She eased back and closed her eyes. There were no other trackers on her, no way for MI6 to have followed her.

Which meant someone had told them where she was going to be.

There were only four people who'd known.

Shinedown, Megadeth, the woman Miles had spoken to on the phone, Beatrice...

And Miles.

As an operative, Charlotte knew there were no friendly intelligence services. CIA officers learned the same thing. "Friendly" foreign intelligence services might be useful for joint operations, but they weren't to be fully trusted. The more you relied on someone else during an operation, the more likely the operation would get blown.

Trust no one had long been her mantra. Still was.

So which one of them betrayed me?

SIX HOURS LATER

Miles exited the onboard bathroom to find Charlotte waiting for him.

"Who told them?" she asked. Her eyes were wide, her fingers shaking as she played with her hair. "Who told MI6 I would be at the airport this morning? Shinedown? Megadeth? The woman on the phone?"

They'd avoided Miles' original route, heading into Canada and refueling in Newfoundland. Over the North Atlantic, on their way to Ireland, he'd finally broken down for a pee break. "How do you know those men back in California were MI6?"

"They were." She chewed on a nail. Her hair glimmered under the cabin lights. She must have fallen asleep in her chair; one side of her hair was matted down. "Trust me."

"I thought one of them looked familiar. I was too busy getting us out of there to care."

"One of them looked familiar?"

"Andy Hardy."

"Hardy? You know him?"

"Do you?"

"Yeah." She ran a hand over her face. "He's the best tracker MI6 has."

"Trust me, Charlotte, no one in my organization would sell you out."

"How else did MI6 know I was going to be there?"

He'd been wondering the same.

No one had been waiting for them at the private airstrip in Newfoundland, but then, if the snitch was Jax—Megadeth—he hadn't had a chance to call anyone since Miles had been seated two feet from him during the entire trip so far.

But he knew it wasn't Jax or Colt.

The one person who had political as well as personal contacts all over the world and might know who to call at MI6 was...

No. Couldn't be. Beatrice would never betray him.

Would she?

He didn't want to believe it—that she could undermine him and put Charlotte at risk—but she hadn't wanted him to take this job. She'd been adamant that it could destroy his career and he'd end up in a foreign prison. In looking out for him, had she betrayed Charlotte?

No matter what, if someone inside Shadow Force gave Charlotte up to MI6, they'd betrayed him too. "I don't know how MI6 found you, but I'll figure it out."

"Will they be waiting for me when we land?"

Her tone was accusing. As if she might actually suspect he was in on it. It pissed him off. "Well, if they are, it won't be because I told them. I jammed the plane's GPS transmitter so we can't be tracked and we aren't sharing our change of flight plans with anyone. My boss has called multiple times trying to contact us and I've ignored her. For you," he added.

He brushed by her, felt her hand grip his bicep, stopping him.

"What?" he said without looking at her.

"I wasn't accusing you of anything." She released her grip. "I was simply asking a question because my life depends on it. You would do the same in my situation."

Her voice was low, tense. Turning, he met her eyes. Her face was pale, scared. She rubbed her arms, took a step back.

Modern day warfare was fought in the dark corners of the world. Caves, back rooms, tunnels. Right now, Miles saw Charlotte fighting her own war, the war zone in her mind as harsh and desolate as the battlefield she'd survived inside Bourean's compound. She trusted no one.

"You're right," he said, keeping his voice even. "I would do the same in your situation. Question everyone's motives and everything that seems out of place. You have every right to be paranoid and skeptical of my team, but at some point, Charlotte, you're going to have to trust someone. I'm hoping that someone is me."

If possible, her face paled even more. "I'm just...I'm gonna..."

She jerked around and ran for the bathroom.

"Charlotte?"

He followed and found her leaning over the sink, hyperventilating. Sweat trickled from under her hair, running down the side of her neck.

"I hate planes, hate flying," she said, splashing water on her face.

She also hated trusting anyone but herself. He understood where she was coming from. While he'd been trained to rely on a team, she'd been trained to be a lone wolf. To infiltrate criminal and terrorist organizations all on her own.

Working as a SEAL and as an operative for Shadow Force, Miles valued loyalty, honesty, bravery. Charlotte, on the other hand, had been taught to betray and expect betrayal in return.

He found a washcloth in the cabinet and wedged in between her and the sink. "I love to fly. Up here, you're away from it all. Disconnected in so many ways."

She propped herself against the wall as he wet the washcloth. "More like trapped. I'm flying over an ocean and have no control over where I'm going. I don't know what will be waiting for me when we land."

He wiped her face with the cool washcloth. Her eyes fluttered closed and she sighed, reminding him of those nights in her bed again. "So it's the lack of control that you hate," he said, encouraging her to talk.

"That's part of it. The other part is where my stomach is upside down, doing the hula."

"Why didn't you say something?" He tossed the washcloth into the sink, then went to the galley kitchen and pulled out a bottle of motion sickness pills from a cabinet, a water from the small fridge.

Returning to the bathroom, he handed both to her. "What is this?" she asked holding up the pill bottle. "I don't like drugs."

The control issue again. "They're all natural. Won't make you sleepy, but they will help the queasiness. They're the only kind I take."

"You get motion sickness?"

"On occasion."

Her dubious stare lasted a moment before she broke down and helped herself to one of the white tablets.

"Make sure you drink plenty of water with it," he said.

She did, her delicate throat working as she swallowed down half the bottle. When was the last time she'd had a proper meal? Something besides an energy drink or bottled water.

He headed to the galley, putting a cup of water in the microwave.

"I never lied," she said from behind him. "At the cabin. I didn't tell you everything, but I never lied. My middle name is Sarah."

A box of teabags was stashed behind a box of coffee packs. In the mountains, the only tea she'd had was a loose leaf kind that had tasted like flowers and dirt to him. "Well, Charlotte Sarah Carstons, do you prefer mint or vanilla chai tea?"

"You have mint?"

The earnestness in her voice made him look over his shoulder. She stood near the narrow doorframe, clutching the bottled water with one hand, the other clutching the frame itself.

He raised a green bag from the box and held it up for her to see. "Southern Plantation. Claims to be smooth and refreshing."

The microwave dinger went off. "Sounds lovely," she said, nodding.

Once he had the bag steeping, he searched for some food. The plane was owned by Petit, used to fly rock stars and film moguls around the world while providing security services for them. But no one had been scheduled to use the plane, so the selection of food was limited to expensive crackers, unopened jars of fancy olives, and crap Miles would never let pass his lips. Caviar. Gross. Hummus. Double gross.

Wait. There were cans of soup.

Soup? Seriously?

Yep, there were two cans of good old chicken noodle tucked into a drawer with some other cans to keep them from flying around if the plane hit turbulence. Who knew? Even the rich and famous liked comfort food on occasion.

"Hungry?" He held up one of the cans.

Walking gingerly, she set down the bottle and removed the teabag from the cup of hot water. Her nostrils flared as she brought the cup to her face and drew a deep breath. "I'll start with the tea, thank you."

Food would do her good. She was too skinny, too pale.

Those scars...

Fury, sadness, rage, it all warred in his stomach. He handed her a sleeve of crackers. "Try a couple of these with your tea."

She seemed reluctant to put down the tea, but did so she could keep a hand on the counter and accept the crackers.

He went to work warming up the soup, such a stupid, normal thing when they were in the middle of a clusterfuck.

"You were correct at the motel." She munched on a cracker, her eyes unable to meet his. They jumped around, past him to the wall, back to his hands as he poured the soup into a bowl, up to his face, and away again. "We were lovers, but not friends. I...I don't have friends. I've been on my own, alone, for a long time. It's comfortable, familiar. I can't tell anyone who I really am—an agent for MI6—or share details about my job. So I never let anyone in. I can't. That rubbish about my friends calling me Charlie is just that. Rubbish. No one has called me Charlie since primary school."

Being an undercover operative was hell on relationships, and if anyone understood being alone, he did. "What we shared in the cabin..."

Was he really going to tell her it had been more than a six-week fling for him? That he'd fallen for her? He truly didn't even know her, this beautiful creature standing before him. The woman he'd fallen in love with was an illusion.

But he wanted more than anything to figure out who the real woman behind the illusion was. "...it wasn't just about the sex."

She made a big deal about sipping her tea. "For me, either." Her gaze finally made it to his and stayed there. "Unfortunately, being with me carries a great risk. As I've mentioned, it could cost you your life."

The microwave dinged again, letting him know the soup was hot. "I'm willing to take that risk."

A sad smirk passed over her lips. "I can see that. You could have stopped this plane back in Van Nuys and handed me over to my counterparts. Instead, you probably caused an international incident."

He shrugged, retrieving his dinner from the microwave. "I always say, go big or go home."

She looked like she wanted to laugh. "I'd say you went big on this one."

The soup was the perfect temperature and smelled like rainy afternoons at his house growing up. On weekends, his mother would make soup and they would cuddle together on their old couch and she would read to him.

Comfort. Security. He wanted to give those things to Charlotte.

She'd been tortured, beaten, chased by men who wanted to do her harm, and was still determined to finish her mission. She trusted no one for good reason.

He wanted to change that. He held the bowl under Charlotte's nose, letting the delicious aroma drift up. "Sure you don't want some of this?"

Her gaze softened as she inhaled. "It does smell rather good."

Smiling, he took her hand and dragged her back to the cabin where he guided her into a seat and put the soup in front of her. "Eat," he commanded.

Before he went back to get her tea, she was already digging in.

They had a long, dangerous road ahead of them, but for the first time in nine months, Miles felt truly alive.

And now he had her where he wanted her. *Well, sort of.* He wanted her underneath him, naked, but this would do for now.

He had a lot of questions that only she could answer, and this time, she wasn't getting away.

CHAPTER EIGHT

Miles was good at taking care of her. She didn't know how to handle that.

Once she'd started on the soup, she couldn't stop. She was famished. The tea was quite excellent too. Her stomach had settled, thank God, and her nerves relaxed somewhat.

His words about being away from everything, virtually out of reach of the real world, rang in her ears. The hum of the engines lulled her like the boat's had. The pretty blue sky, filled with whispers of clouds, calmed her mind.

With him sitting next to her, she could enjoy the soup and tea and the silence.

He was trying not to watch her, sipping at his own cup of tea, but she felt his gaze flit over her and away each time he thought she wasn't paying attention. She owed him big for this. Not just the cost of using Rock Star services, but for risking his life for her.

"Why exactly does MI6 think you're a traitor?" he asked.

Her cheeks heated. Why, indeed? She'd been a model agent, commendations galore in her file. "I don't know, really. My handler told me that when I went off grid last winter when you and I were stuck in the cabin, my superiors assumed I had gone in with Nico and that he and I were working with the terrorist. Even my handler believed I'd thrown my lot in with Nico. It's maddening. I've never given any of them a reason to believe I wasn't one-hundred-percent loyal. It pains me that they never thought that perhaps something bad had happened to me? I explained everything to CB and he went to the higher ups, but he said they didn't believe him. That they had proof I was a traitor. What proof? Apparently when he asked, they wouldn't share what that was. I have no idea what it could be."

"Why not give yourself up and explain it all?"

"Talk is cheap. I need that video, and I have detailed accounts of Nico's criminal pursuits on that USB. Pursuits involving the terrorist. I don't know who I can trust inside MI6 and I want that USB in hand when I do talk to them."

"You have the scars on your back. Seems like proof enough to me that you weren't in cahoots with that bastard."

The sky was so lovely. So serene. *Focus on that. Sip your tea. Don't slip back into that dark hole of memories.*

"Yes, it does, doesn't it?" A cold slice of fear still managed to snake down her spine. "But I fear it may not be. My gut says there's more going on with the situation than it appears. A simple explanation and a few scars won't convince them. I need to figure out the rest of the story and look at the video again before I can snap the pieces together to form the whole picture. I can't let Nicolae get away with what he's done. The terrorist either."

"I'm onboard with that. I want both of their heads on a platter for what they did to my brothers."

He was still grieving. She heard it in his tone. "I know I've said it before, but I'm so sorry."

A muscle jumped in his jaw. He stared at his hands, seemingly unable to respond.

She'd thought he'd moved on. Now, she saw he'd only been in a holding pattern.

Give him some space.

She didn't want to. She wanted to throw her arms around him and help him through the grief like she'd tried to do in the cabin. The distraction of physical comfort took the mind off the past and, she'd believed, it helped heal a broken heart. Now, she wasn't so sure.

Her attention on the scene outside the window, she wasn't prepared for Miles' touch. His hand glided over her arm, gently, lightly. "I'm sorry. I shouldn't have brought up the scars."

He was worried about her reaction to the scars comment when she was worried about him hating her for inadvertently killing his men. What a pair they made.

Change the subject. "I have my suspicions about who the terrorist is, but I was so rushed that day, I couldn't place him. I need to look at the video, follow the trail back to him and his followers. Until I do, I can't trust anyone inside MI6."

"Why give me the key?"

A knot had formed in the spot between her neck and shoulder. She'd removed the sweatshirt earlier and now slid her fingers under her collar so she could work her fingers into the kink.

As the engines hummed, vibrating the table, tiny ripples formed in her tea, rolling out from the epicenter of the liquid, one after another.

Ripples. Like the ripples in her life from her decisions. "When I realized I had to go back to Nico to try to figure out who the terrorist was, I needed a safe place to hide that key. I planned to give it to my handler, but he was never around. I'd only seen him a few times after arriving in Romania; we used dead drops if we needed to physically exchange information. The day I called Emit Petit to come get you, I thought I'd have a few days before he arrived. Turned out he had someone who could pick you up immediately. My timeline moved from a few days to hours. I had to make a call. No way could I leave the key in the cabin. Nico might have his men toss the place, and I couldn't get in touch with my handler."

His fingers brushed hers away as he took over massaging her shoulder and neck. "Smart move."

She raised her gaze to his, the feel of his fingers kneading her tight muscles making her want to moan. "Was it?"

He worked on her shoulder, ran his fingers along the sensitive spot where her neck met her collarbone. "I probably would have done the same thing."

His voice had grown huskier. He drew the edge of her shirt down over her shoulder, baring her skin to his expert manipulations.

"You were the only person I trusted," she said. The kink was slowly loosening. Other parts of her were doing the opposite, growing taut, begging for his attention. A deep longing for his touch infused her very bones.

"How did you contact Petit when communications were so limited?"

"Once the snow melted, I could get up to the top of the hill. I hauled the portable satellite tower and antenna up there one afternoon while you were in the forest gathering fire wood."

He leaned closer, his hand going to the back of her neck and holding her in place as he spoke in her ear. "Thank you."

His warm breath brushed over her skin. Memories of his lips on her, his tongue teasing her, made her close her eyes. She never expected to hear those words. *Thank you.* Two simple words she hadn't heard a lot of in her life.

But it wasn't the words causing goose flesh to run up and down her arms. If she turned her head, their lips would be close enough to meet. She wanted a repeat of the kiss at his truck. Did he want that too?

She hated unanswered questions. They led to sleepless nights and regret. Turning her head slowly, she looked directly into his eyes. A hunger she remembered from the cabin haunted them. "You're...welcome."

They stared at each other, silence descending. His thumb drew tiny circles on her shoulder, his intense stare sending vibrations through her body like the waves in her teacup. He brushed a strand of hair that had broken free from her ponytail off her neck, sending a fresh wave of goosebumps over her skin.

He lowered his lips, eyes still locked with hers, to the vulnerable skin on her shoulder. His kiss was gentle, his lips lingering. A question...

Did she want more?

Charlotte's breath stuck in her throat. A shock of electricity went straight to the spot between her legs. The need to have his hands on her, his mouth kissing every inch of her, became a singular, driving force that nearly blinded her.

She touched him then, letting her hand land on his thigh. The muscles bunched at the contact and she did a slow, smooth stroke, trailing her fingers from his knee up to parts higher.

"You really shouldn't get involved with me again," she said.

His hand moved into her hair, kneading the back of her skull, gently tugging at her pony as he kissed the sensitive spot under her ear. "I agree. You're trouble, but I'll take my chances."

His tongue flicked out and caught the bottom of her earlobe, sending a fresh shock of electricity coursing through her nerves. She moaned and tilted her head, giving him full access to her neck.

He didn't need any further invitation, his lips kissing her skin, teeth nibbling at her ear, her jawline. Strong fingers worked through her hair, pulling the ponytail loose, his nose sinking into her hair and as he drew a deep breath.

Through half-lidded eyes, she saw movement, heard a voice say, "Don't mind me."

Jolting like she'd been pinched, Charlotte flew to the far side of the seat. Miles' jaw jumped and he glared at Megadeth.

"Plane's on autopilot." The man wasn't looking at them, hands up blocking his view of them as he passed by. "Gotta take a whiz, man."

A second later, he disappeared behind them into the back area. Miles stood, returning her shirt to cover her shoulder and leaning over to plant a chaste kiss on her forehead. "I'm going to divert the plane to a new location while he's in the head and call Beatrice. I want to know if she's the one who gave us up."

As he pulled away, Charlotte grabbed his shirt, dizzy with a whirl of emotions. "I want to be in on that conversation."

He touched her elbow, slipped his hand down to entwine his fingers with hers. "It's better if I talk to her alone first." His intense gaze bore into hers, that charged silence falling between them again. He squeezed her fingers. "I'll be back in a bit."

He didn't say it, but there was a promise there. In his eyes, in his voice. He was coming back for more. He still had questions, doubts. He still wanted to get her naked. The two desires warred with each other, but he wasn't afraid of waging that war. He was going into battle with her.

Charlotte just hoped she didn't let him down.

* * *

Beatrice had called his cell phone eight times. She'd stopped leaving messages after the third call.

Miles punched in a new destination for the flight log, put on his headset, then called her back on the SFI secure communication line.

Her greeting was less than genial. "What the hell are you doing?"

"I was about to ask you the same thing."

There was a pause. "Where are you? Why is the plane's GPS disabled?"

He checked his dials and readouts. "I'm twelve clicks south of Newfoundland over the Atlantic, no thanks to you. I disabled the GPS because I don't want you to know where we're going."

Another slight pause. He could see her shifting back in her seat, her pregnant belly jutting out in front of her. She was married to Cal Reese, who led Shadow Force Alpha Team, and they were expecting their first child in a month. "Explain."

"What's to explain? You betrayed us at the airport. I'm not letting that happen again."

"I betrayed you? How?"

"MI6 showed up. I'm sure that was no coincidence."

"The manager of the hangar called and told me. He and everyone else who deals with us were questioned quite extensively after your daring getaway. You think *I* called SSI?"

"Who else knew Charlotte's real identity and that we would be at the Van Nuys airport at that time?"

"The safety of SFI employees is always my number one priority, so while I'll admit to having serious misgivings about this assignment because it's clear you have feelings for this woman, and I guarantee, that will be an issue down the line— she is certainly not the first hot client we've had, nor would I ever betray one of my own men."

A "hot" client for the security service was anyone too hot to handle for law enforcement. Those with special security needs or unique situations, such as Savanna Bunkett who'd had the president of the United States stalking her a few months prior.

"Sorry, Beatrice. I'm not buying it. While Colt and the others knew I was hustling Charlotte out of the country, none of them know who she is or that MI6 is after her. You and I are the only ones with that tidbit of info."

"She must have a tracking device on her person."

"Nice try. Already removed one at the house. Nicolae Bourean inserted that puppy, not MI6."

Interference crackled over the comm line. "You're confident that was the only one?"

"Positive."

"So unless MI6 has advanced technology we don't know about, she's clean."

"Yes, and if they had an advanced tracking device on her, they'd have caught up to her long before the safe house."

"I haven't been able to verify the identities of the men at the airport. You're positive they're MI6?"

"Yep. One of them is an operative named Andy Hardy. He was in the Carpathians with me last winter."

"I don't get it." No one ever heard those words from Beatrice's mouth. "I'm at a loss."

Jax appeared in the cockpit, nodded at him and took the

co-pilot's seat. "You and me, both," Miles said to Beatrice, "but you can understand why I suspected your involvement."

Beatrice's superior intellect made her good at her job. She never let emotions guide her thinking; facts and logic defined her decisions and directives.

So what came out of her mouth next surprised Miles. "I don't know your client, nor do I give a monkey's backside about her, in all honesty," she said. "You, however, I do care about. You're one of my team. I would not, under any circumstances, jeopardize your future."

He hated to admit it, but he believed her. In the time he'd been with Shadow Force and the Rock Stars, he'd seen Beatrice go to bat for every one of the men, under many different and challenging circumstances. They didn't always play by the rules. Hell, they rarely followed rules period.

Except hers. They all respected and trusted her. For some of the men, after their past experience with the government, she was the *only* person they trusted. She'd earned it, time and time again.

"Why, boss, I do believe that pregnancy is making you soft."

Another rarity—she chuckled. "We don't have all the facts surrounding your client's past missions or her work with Vauxhall. I suspect she isn't telling us everything. Someone knew she was in the States and making contact with you. They may have been tracking you as much as they were her."

Miles didn't doubt that was true. "I'm working on intel gathering. Getting her to open up after what she's been through will take time, though."

"I'm glad your feelings for her haven't completely short-circuited your common sense and training. I'm sending you a file, some information I dug up from some very deep sources about her. There are holes, and some of it's not pretty, but it may help you steer this...mission...and not end up dead or in prison."

Beatrice might not be happy with him, but she did, indeed, have his back. "Send me whatever you can on Bourean too. His business partners, his personality, the chinks in his armor. He was working with a terrorist. I have no intel on the man, but see if you can find any connections."

"Rory is working on it. There's a lot of intel out there on Bourean. He even has an Instagram account. Rory will comb through it all and we'll be in touch with anything pertinent."

He wasn't used to saying thank you, but it seemed like those words had tumbled from his mouth an inordinate amount of times in the past few hours. "Appreciate it, but here's the thing, I'm not turning the GPS back on. No one, with the exception of me right now, knows where this plane is headed and that's the way I'm going to keep it. I'm going dark until we land. I'll make contact once I'm sure it's safe to do so."

"I understand."

He knew she did. That she wasn't taking his actions personally.

"Be safe," she added and the connection went dead.

Jax didn't say anything for a long time, but he fidgeted with the controls, with his seat. Finally, he offered up an apology. "I didn't mean to interrupt. You know,"—he cocked a thumb over his shoulder—"back there."

If he didn't need a co-pilot, he would dump Jax's ass at the first available spot. "You didn't interrupt anything."

"That so? I suppose that's your 'intel gathering' technique."

Miles shot him a stony look. "You got an issue with my interrogation methods?"

"Not at all." Jax shook his head and smiled. "Hell, I'm thinking I need to revamp mine if that shit works."

It worked all right.

And Miles couldn't wait to get started on some further in-depth cross-examination.

CHAPTER NINE

The plane touched down after too many hours in the air and CB Norris roused himself from his first-class seat and made his way through the Bucharest airport terminal. His ulcer was acting up, thanks to Carstons fucking him over. The multiple gin and tonics on the plane hadn't helped his stomach lining either, but goddamn. That girl drove a man to drink.

He was swallowing another antacid without aid of water when his cell phone buzzed. God, he hated the damn things. Fumbling to get to the phone inside his coat pocket, he finally got hold of it and wished he hadn't when he saw the caller ID.

"Norris," he answered.

"Where is my *posh ratt*?" Nico's heavy accent made his words nearly run together. "You have her, yes?"

In a manner of speaking. "She's on her way back to Romania."

His non-answer answer forced the stupid crime lord to think for a moment. Something he wasn't used to doing. "In what? A coffin? You promised her delivered to me alive."

"She's alive. She'll be at that old horse dealer's place within a day or two." The only way to get there was by all-wheel drive or on foot. The tiny cabin had long ago been abandoned. "I'll catch up with her there. Once I have the USB, I'll deliver the girl and you can tell me Blackwater's whereabouts."

"You said you would capture the bitch in America."

"Change of plans. This is better. I didn't have to transport her. I'll grab her at the cabin, get the USB, and then she's all yours."

"Renege on this deal and I will take pleasure in cutting off your balls, old man."

Yeah, like that was going to happen. "Trust me, I can't let Carstons loose after I get that USB anyway. You might as well have her. You still know Blackwater's location, right?"

"I have his daughter. He won't leave without her. Bring me my Gypsy girl and you can have Blackwater's. Then we are done."

Norris couldn't leave Carstons or Bourean alive after this. He would set it up so it looked like Bourean killed Carstons, then he would kill Nico making it look like he arrived a minute too late to save his beautiful, but pain-in-the-ass agent. Tragic, but with the video on that thumb drive Carstons had told him about and Blackwater's location, he'd be a goddamn hero.

He'd finally have closure. *Good time to retire.*

Norris disconnected, Bourean ranting in the background. *Little prick.* Bourean was nothing but a means to an end, but the world would be much better off without him when Norris put a bullet in his brain. It was too damn bad Charlotte Carstons had to go down with him.

The only problem was going to be the SEAL, Duncan. The real hero in this scenario, it appeared he was a standup guy trying to help a woman in distress and keep her out of trouble. Poor bastard had no idea just how much trouble Carstons was.

He'd have to find a way to take out Duncan. Not a job he relished. Too many loose ends, too much cleanup work to do afterward. Somehow, he'd have to make it look like Nico's handiwork. Orlo would come in handy for that.

With the way he'd set up Carstons to look like a traitor to her country, she was going to tarnish the good SEAL's reputation as well. With the piece of information Norris had in his back pocket, he could manipulate the truth of their time together in that cabin to look like they were both double agents, working together to screw over America and the United Kingdom. A Bonnie and Clyde duo that he would personally put an end to.

Taking the SIM card out of the phone, Norris stomped on it, busting it into a dozen little pieces, then tossed the plastic case in a nearby garbage can. He grabbed his carryon luggage and headed for Orlo waiting for him outside.

SERBIA

Fat Cat's, a pub and pool hall, sat in the middle of a low valley, a long, flat building with loud music and a dozen motorcycles outside in the parking lot, lit by the moon and nothing else.

"No cameras," Megadeth said, climbing the hill to stand at Charlotte's side. Miles stood on her other. "Sixteen men, four women, the bartender. That's it."

Frigid air cut through the layers of clothes Charlotte wore and made her teeth chatter. Snowflakes fell lazily, dotting the valley with white here and there.

They'd stopped in Switzerland to refuel, the hours onboard the plane eating at her. Miles had come back, like he'd promised, and insisted his boss was not to blame for MI6 showing up at the Van Nuys airport. They discussed possible other alternatives to how those men had found her, but not one of them seemed logical. Miles had disappeared into the cockpit again without touching her, kissing her.

During the flight, she'd read an entire Robert B. Parker novel, flipped through a dozen magazines showing fashion models, European architecture, and the latest NBA players, but her mind spun with scenarios about the upcoming journey to the caves. They'd finally made it to Serbia, along the Romanian border, Miles setting the plane down near an abandoned farmhouse behind an old barn. Inside the barn were two old Land Rovers and a Jeep.

Along with the motorcycles down below in the parking lot, a couple of beat up, but rugged trucks sat side by side. Neither was better than what they were driving, although both were better equipped than motorcycles for the terrain in these parts. The bikers wouldn't let a few snowflakes stop them, though. They'd ride all winter long.

They had a vehicle, but they needed money and supplies. "Miles, go inside the bar, start a tab, and work your way into a pool game. I'll join you and we'll make off with enough cash to get us where we need to go. Megadeth, you're the muscle in case something goes wrong. Stay outside and watch for trouble. When I show up, Miles, pretend you don't know me. Follow my lead. I'll handle the rest."

"I have money," Miles said.

"You have American dollars. We need euros, and we don't have time to exchange money." She shucked her sweatshirt, took the hem of the shirt underneath and tied it on the side, revealing a hint of her stomach. "I know a few tricks at the table. I can get all the cash we need."

Miles shook his head. "I don't like it. There has to be another, safer way."

Megadeth surveyed the area, his breath fogging in the cold air. "What exactly are you planning to do?"

She shook out her braid, ran some lipstick she'd taken from the safe house over her lips. "Lose a couple of pool games to Miles. Win a couple more from someone else."

Megadeth smiled. "Brilliant idea."

At the same time, Miles shook his head, more vigorously this time, and said, "Terrible idea."

"You put us down in Serbia," Charlotte countered. "It's ten miles to the border, another hundred to the mountains to the spot where we're going. We need supplies, a map, money for bribes. This is where we start."

Miles' voice was terse. "This was the best option for an airstrip that's not on any maps. We're trying to stay under the radar, remember?"

She didn't ask how he knew about the abandoned farm. He seemed to be quite familiar with the area.

A snowflake landed in his hair, sparkling under the moonlight. "You're calling attention to yourself if you cheat some guys out of their paychecks. This is not exactly low-profile."

"Who said I was going to cheat?"

"You're that good at pool?" Megadeth asked.

"Taught William a thing or two."

Both men looked at her.

"Prince William? Surely you've heard of him."

Megadeth chuckled. "You taught Willy how to play pool?"

"Don't be silly. He knew how to play pool, but he'd never played with me." Her bones felt so cold, she thought they might splinter if she didn't get inside where it was warm, pronto. "Need I remind you, this is my op. If you're a part of it, we do things my way."

"What if Bourean's men show up?" Miles said.

"I doubt Nicolae has men here in the backwoods watering hole. And all I'm going to do is give a couple of guys a funny story to tell down the road."

With that, she took off for Fat Cat's.

THREE HOURS LATER

Charlotte was laughing as she drove them back to the plane, her breath clouding in front of her. "Did you see that guy's eyes when I used his skull ring to divert the last ball into the pocket? Priceless."

They bumped over the rough terrain and around a curve. Her eyes shone from the dashboard lights, her hands gripped the steering wheel. She'd found a pair of fingerless gloves in the backseat and put them on, the extra-large gloves engulfing her small hands.

Jax had decided to stay at the bar after a pretty woman going in with some friends gave him a wink and come-hither stare. No one inside had seen him with Miles and Charlotte so Miles had okay'd it. They had plenty of euros now and the skull ring in question was on Charlotte's middle finger.

He didn't like it, but he had to give her props. Her trick pool shots had mesmerized the crowd, cheers ringing out whenever she sank a ball. Cash had piled up on the corner of the table, people giving her various props and betting she couldn't use them to make the complicated and difficult shots.

She was damn good at straight pool too. He hadn't had to fake losing to her the first few games.

While they were flush with cash now, what they didn't have was supplies. Stores in the town three miles away wouldn't open until morning. They were spending the night in the plane.

What was left of the night, anyway. It was 2 a.m.

Miles suspected Jax was giving him time alone with Charlotte as much as pursuing a Serbian hookup. Not the best thing to leave the man alone at the bar, but the former SEAL knew how to handle himself and understood the seriousness of staying under the radar.

Truth was, if he screwed up and called attention to himself, Miles was prepared to leave him behind and call in reinforcements to get him out of Europe. He wouldn't let Jax or anyone else take a fall for him, but he also wasn't about to let him jeopardize the mission.

The plane came into view as they crested a hill. "Where did you learn to do those tricks with the glasses and stuff?"

Her smile faltered. She cleared her throat. "My father. He was quite the pool shark. And a physics professor."

There was so much he didn't know about her. This tiny peek into her past fascinated him.

So did the idea of getting her undressed.

Later.

What he did know about her was a slim volume of facts in the file Beatrice had sent to his phone that he'd read in the air over Switzerland. "I thought your father was Royal Air Force."

Her eyes cut to him. "How did you know that?"

A woman like her would hate that he'd dug into her background. That he hadn't just asked her. Would she have told him the truth? He doubted it. She'd been a spy for so long, been keeping secrets for so long, she might *never* trust him with the truth.

But it was time to start being honest with each other.

His libido didn't agree. Telling her Beatrice had run a background check and gathered information for him would kill any possibility he was getting inside her before the sun came up. If he told her about Hardy and the fact he and his SEAL team had helped the operatives try to find her nine months ago, she would never speak to him again. "When I got back to the States, I dug up information on you." That was the truth. "Sue me, I was damn curious and pretty fucking determined to find you again."

"You didn't know who I was. How could dig up anything on me?"

"I sketched your picture, ran it through some fancy facial rec software Shadow Force owns. It told me who you were. The rest wasn't easy—MI6 guards your personal information like Fort Knox."

She slowed the truck. Her voice, and her eyes, softened. "You sketched me?"

That tone, that look, made his libido sit up again. He shrugged a shoulder. "Guess it was good enough to get a hit."

"Damn." She smiled, her shoulders relaxing along with the rest of her. Apparently that whole *Titanic* Jack-sketching-Rose thing worked on women. "You never told me you were an artist. That's so cool. And you must be quite talented if your sketch got a hit through facial recognition."

Yep, definitely working. Her tone suggested sex was a possible future option. "We didn't talk a lot about our talents and skills for those few weeks we were together."

"Mmm." She steered the Land Cruiser to a spot behind the barn and killed the engine. Moonlight bounced off the airplane's wings a few yards away in the field. Her fingers drummed against the steering wheel. "Look, I know things between us are complicated. It's not that I don't want to tell you about myself, I just can't. There's too much...rubbish...in my past. I don't like to rehash it. Some of it I can't tell you, or anyone, because it would endanger you. Just knowing me could get you killed, even before the whole Nico incident. It's a lot to walk around with day in and day out."

She twisted in the seat to face him, lifting one knee and laying it on the console between them. "I feel like I have two relationships with you—which is funny, since I have, like, *no* relationships with anyone else."

He was still thinking about getting her into the airplane and out of her clothes. After a pause, he realized she was waiting for him to catch up. "Sorry, *two* relationships?"

"I shared this incredible six weeks of fantasy life with you, and yet, I barely know who you are."

Fantasy life. That's what they'd had. And then real life had intruded, putting her at Bourean's mercy. "I'm the same man I was in the cabin."

"But I'm not the same woman. That woman...she only existed for those few weeks with you. Now, she's on the run, and I don't know how to start over with you when I have all of this hanging over me. I've had to play too many roles, be too many different people. Honestly, I don't even know who I am anymore. What I want."

He picked up a strand of her hair and rubbed it between his fingers. "We have time to figure that out."

Her fingers intertwined with his. "That's the thing, Miles, we don't. Until I clear my name and put Bourean behind bars, I can't have any kind of a normal life. You deserve better than that."

Wait. Was she blowing him off? Was this the "just friends" speech? "How about you let me decide what works for me and what doesn't?"

She leaned her temple against the headrest, and even in the shadowy interior, he could feel her stare, see the intelligence in her eyes. She was running him like she had the balls on the pool table tonight. Not just calculating one or two balls ahead, but playing the entire game out in her head before her cue touched the first ball.

As she stared at him, holding his hand, she was doing the same with their relationship. Running every option, figuring out every move she should or shouldn't make.

On one hand, it pissed him off. Why couldn't she be the carefree, spur-of-the-moment woman he'd worshipped in that cabin? Why couldn't she trust him enough to at least try at this thing they had?

On the other hand, he hadn't been completely honest with her. He'd never been good with long-term relationships. He had too many quirks, too much love for danger and the high that came from a successful mission. Mostly, he wanted to get in her pants and see if he could replay that time in the mountains. He needed to get her out of his system. Then she could go back to playing spy and he could forget this silly notion he was in love with her.

She squeezed his fingers. "After this is over, if I'm still...alive and not in prison...maybe we can start over."

After? *What about now?*

He tugged their combined hands toward his lips and kissed her knuckles. "Why wait? Hell, we could both die here tonight. I don't know about you, but I'd rather get started on the do-over asap."

For half a second, he thought for sure she was going to take him up on the offer right there in the front seat of the cab. She caught her bottom lip with her teeth and chuckled. Then ran her tongue over her lips and leaned forward over their steepled hands, planting those soft, moist lips on his.

He kissed her back, enjoying the way her lips parted, allowing him access. The way her tongue danced with his. The way she moaned...

But then she drew back—tongue, lips, even her hand,

leaving him. "I wish I could, Miles." Her face was in the moonlight now, brows furrowed, tears pooling in her eyes. "I do, but..."

"But what?"

She shook her head. "I have to finish my op. Period. My mission comes first. Otherwise, the death of your men, and everything I endured under Nicolae's hands will be for nothing. He and that terrorist will be free to keep hurting people. Please understand, I can't get distracted by an affair, and you are a *huge* distraction for me."

Once again, conflicting logic waged war in his head. She was wildly attracted to him—plus. However, she wasn't going to act on it—negative.

How could he convince her that they were on the same side, that they shared the same goals?

Grabbing her hand again, he forced it open and intertwined their fingers. "I have no intention of going home without nailing the bastard who brought that helo down and killed my team. I will help you complete your mission as well, but believe me when I say that I will never stop trying to seduce you. I've never wanted anyone more than I want you, Charlotte, and outside of seeing justice done for my men, the one thing I want more than anything is to get you back under me. I want to make you shudder and come apart under me, screaming my name when you do it. We will be together again, and I'm not allowing a timeline or anything else to get in the way."

She said nothing, leaving the keys in the ignition and bailing out of the Land Cruiser. He didn't go after her as she hustled for the plane, watching her sweet ass sway and her hair fly out behind her in the moonlight.

Oh, yes, darlin', you can run, but you won't get far.

He'd seen the lust flare in her eyes when he'd mentioned being under him. Seen the way she'd licked her lips again. Her mind told her to keep their relationship professional, but her body was betraying her. It wouldn't be long until that very female side of her took control.

He'd be ready.

CHAPTER TEN

Charlotte rustled around in the shot bottles, shining her tiny flashlight on the labels. Champagne, gin, whiskey...

There. She grabbed the bottle with the green and blue label, then felt a presence behind her.

She'd shed her coat even though the plane was cold. Warmer than outside, but the latent heat it had built up on the flight over was long gone. "I'm heading to Mexico," she said, lifting the tiny tequila bottle to show it to Miles. "Where would you like to go? Jamaica?" She held up the rum bottle. Then the vodka. "Russia?"

His eyes were heavy on her in the circle of light from her flashlight. "Why don't you get some sleep. I'll take first watch." He turned his back on her, walking away and tapping one of the overhead bins. "Blankets are up here."

She didn't need a blanket, his words from the cab of the truck pinging around inside her like tiny missiles, heating her from the inside. "Miles..."

He stopped but didn't turn.

She stammered. Truth be told, she didn't know what to say even if he did face her.

What if he was right? What if the op went sideways and this was their last night together? Their last few moments alone? Was she going to waste it sleeping?

Unanswered questions. *Hate them.*

Her silence finally made him look over his shoulder. "What is it, Charlotte?"

God, she sucked at this. Give her a cabal to infiltrate, a

mafia lord to bring down, a terrorist cell to take out. But this…

Her finger trembled as she shut off the flashlight, sudden darkness enveloping them. "I can't sleep," she whispered.

"Fine. You take first watch and let me sleep. I could use some."

His boots made a slight shuffling noise as he once again started for the front of the plane.

"My father," she started, clearing her throat, "was Tactical Intelligence in the Royal Air Force, but he was first and foremost a physicist. He had a lot of ideas about the mechanics of pool that he tested with me when I was a kid, including my 3D perception and stroke control. As I got better at 9-shot, he upped the ante with trick shots. I prefer domino setups, but since I didn't have dominoes tonight, I used other props."

The footsteps stopped. Charlotte put down the bottles of liquid courage and stepped into the main cabin. Enough light from outside seeped through the windows that she could see Miles standing there, a few feet away, all broad shoulders and long, lean planes, the grey shadows dancing over his body. His angled cheekbones came into view when he leaned forward slightly, propping his big hands on the seats flanking him in the aisle. "Go on."

He understood what she was doing—sharing a sliver of her past.

She wanted to rush him, to throw her arms around his neck and kiss him for his patience. "My mother was a homemaker. She made us matching dresses until I was ten and I insisted she stop. It was cute when I was a toddler, but the embarrassment when I got older was too much. Telling her that crushed her feelings. She was just trying to be a proper mother—her own had been less…conventional. Mum wanted to prove she was normal. I regret hurting her feelings to this day, but honestly, those dresses were dreadful. Purple and yellow gingham was her favorite. Every family picture we had made from the time I was a baby until that tenth birthday, she and I were dressed in matching gingham."

His chuckle was low and light. "Sounds horrible, but kinda sweet."

"Sweet, yes. After I refused to wear them anymore, I helped her turn the dresses into curtains for our kitchen windows to try to make amends. She was good like that. She covered her hurt and kept plunging forward, no matter the circumstances."

He moved a step closer to her. "Reminds me of someone else I know."

There was more, so much more that she wanted to tell him. About her mother, her father, herself. "My older brother, Landon, has autism. Mild, but still a strain on our family. This boy at school, Teddy Oostenrick, made fun of Lanny all the time and it really pissed me off. I finally punched him in the nose when we were seven. I got in trouble, of course, but it didn't stop me. All through primary and into elementary, I took on anyone who made fun of my brother, and there were a lot. My dad finally taught me how to fight more efficiently and not get caught. I'd wait for the bullies after school, off school property, and then I'd kick their arses."

Miles was chuckling now, slowly moving closer and closer. "Landon's lucky to have you for a sister."

"When we got older, he's the one who made me look at things logically, with less emotion. I learned a lot from him. How to think outside the box, how to run numbers and combinations in my head and look for different possible outcomes. His autism felt like a burden growing up, but it helped me in so many ways. All of my family—my mom, my dad, Landon—they made me the agent I am today."

He was close enough to touch her now. His fingers skimmed her hand, his thumb grazing her wrist. "When we're done here, I'll make sure you get back to them to tell them that."

The thought of seeing them made a lump form in her throat. She hadn't been home—really home—in years. Her mother was dead. An accident they said, but Charlotte knew better. She'd been there that night, had seen the blood on her mother's chest, the fire bursting from the shop's windows.

Insisting her mother had been murdered only resulted in her being put in a psyche ward, straps around her wrist, drugs pumping into her veins. She'd learned a lot since then. Her mother's killer was still out there. Her father still wouldn't speak of her death.

Miles brushed her face, stroking her cheek and jaw. "Out in the truck you said you didn't know who you were or what you wanted. I think that's bullshit. You know exactly who you are, Charlotte Carstons—a beautiful, intelligent MI6 agent on a mission—and I believe you know exactly what you want. You simply need to be honest with yourself."

Her cheeks heated, the memory of his words in the truck filling her brain again.

...the one thing I want more than anything is to get you back under me.

She could be honest with herself. That's exactly what she wanted too.

Looking up into his eyes, the night so dark and silent around them, she felt like she was back in her cabin. Snow fell outside, no one around for miles. Inside the plane, the air between them was charged with sexual longing. A craving so strong, she couldn't deny it even if she was the best liar in the world.

"There's more you should know about me, about my heritage. I don't think you'll care but some people do. My mother...well, I'm a *posh ratt*. That's slang for half-blood."

"Your mother is a Horvath. I know," he said, brushing his lips across hers. "She's a Gypsy and you have Gypsy blood in you." His hand circled back to rub her lower spine. "Probably put a curse on me, haven't you? That's why I can't get you out of my blood."

In Romania, she had to keep her half-blood status a secret. In the old country, they looked down on a Romani *rackli*—Gypsy woman—marrying a *gorga mush*—non-Gypsy man. The *chavvies*—kids from that union—were always outcasts and looked down on.

In Britain, standards among the Gypsy population were looser, although some still considered mixed blood a taint to the tribe. Like the Mudbloods in the fictional Harry Potter stories, she was ignored or even hated by those who felt she was beneath them. Her father's job had given her a certain amount of insulation in school, but she'd hidden her half-blood status from many Gypsies over the years.

She leaned into Miles, kissing him lightly and laughing. "A spell to keep you lusting after me. There's a dance that goes along with it. I can show you."

They chuckled together, and then he kissed her for real, bending her back and parting her lips with his tongue. She welcomed it, wrapping her arms around his neck and feeling the surge of familiar passion.

So long. She'd waited for this for so long, never believing it would happen. Now he was here, with her, and ready to pick up where they'd left off.

Heat prickled over her skin as his fingers went under her shirt and touched her gently on her back. His tongue wove around hers before his teeth nipped at her bottom lip.

Maneuvering her around, he guided her to the table, giving her a boost onto it. She spread her legs wide, allowing him access as he bent his head. Arching her own back, she let him kiss down her neck, across her collarbone, moaning as he licked the hollow of her throat.

His fingers still rubbed slow and steady up and down her back. Heady with lust, it took her a moment to realize he was tracing her scars.

Flashbacks of her time at Nicolae's hands suddenly filled her head, making her stiffen. She turned her head away from Miles, revulsion thick in her throat.

It wasn't only the awful memories of the beatings. She knew how to shove them deep into a mental hole. But she was full of scars, inside and out. Ugly scars that she needed to keep hidden.

As she tried to scoot away, he stopped her, his mouth brushing against her ear. "I'm sorry I wasn't there to stop the bastard," he murmured, "but he won't get away with what he did to you. To all of us. We're going to take him down, and whoever was working with him as well."

His warm breath on her ear, his solid hold on her—not constraining, only comforting—melted the unease flooding her body. Miles knew she had secrets and he'd already seen the physical scars. He hadn't run, hadn't told her to get lost. So why was she freezing up at the thought of him seeing those scars again, tracing them with his fingers?

Parting her lips, she let go of the breath she was holding. She looked into his face, the shadows making his eyes unfathomably dark. Her fingertips lightly touched his cheek. "You said earlier that I knew what I wanted. You were right. I want you. But I have to be sure...is this what you really want?"

His answer was a kiss, long and deep, his hand bracketing her face and holding her in place. He worked over her lips, then spread soft kisses to her cheeks, her forehead. He held her still as he broke away from kissing her and looked deep into her eyes. "I don't know what tomorrow holds, Charlotte, but tonight, this is exactly what I want. You. All of you. No holds barred, no secrets between us."

His hands caught the hem of her shirt and worked it up her arms, over her head, baring her to him. She let him slip her bra straps down, free her breasts, and once more lower his head.

As he used his skilled mouth on each breast, Charlotte closed her eyes and pretended they had a future.

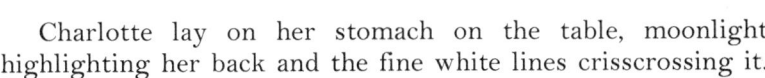

Charlotte lay on her stomach on the table, moonlight highlighting her back and the fine white lines crisscrossing it. They looked silvery in the light.

Miles kissed his way down the back of her neck, listened to her sigh. She hated baring herself in this manner, letting him see the scars, but he needed to. Hands working on getting her pants off, he took a moment to look—really look—at those damn scars.

He'd thought he'd seen it in the bathroom when she'd been exposed. Again when he'd removed the tracking device from between her shoulder blades. Now, with no towels or robes in the way, he was sure of it.

N-I-C-O. The letters were carved in the pale skin over her right hipbone.

The bastard had marked her as his.

Anger roared through him, sickening him at the thought she'd endured such torture. That Nicolae Bourean—or any man—thought he had the right to brand her.

Before he realized that his hands had stopped peeling off her pants, that his lips had stopped tracing her vertebrae, she jerked a look at him over her shoulder. He didn't shift his gaze fast enough and she caught him staring at those letters. She jerked, half turning and tugging her pants back up.

"Stop," he said, stilling her hands. "Let me look at you."

"What's there to see? Do hideous scars turn you on?"

"You're beautiful, scars or no." Did she even know Bourean had carved his name into her hip? "If you decide you want to remove them, I know a doctor who can help. She's had good luck with laser surgery. Helped me with a few of mine."

"You've had scars removed?"

He shrugged, unbuttoned his shirt to show her his chest. "More like refashioned."

The scar on his chest, courtesy of some shrapnel from the helicopter crash, had been smoothed out by Dr. Pasil. Over it, Miles'd had his favorite tattoo artist create a stylized wave and trident with the initials of his dead Team brothers on the tip of each of the trident's points.

She sat up and touched the tattoo, her fingers cool against his skin. "That's wicked. I can't see or feel the scar that was there at all."

"I'm lucky the shrapnel didn't do more damage and that the cream you treated it with healed the cut so well, but there was a decent scar there and the laser surgery reduced it significantly. Dr. Pasil can help you too. I'm sure of it."

Her hand fell away, traced the hint of hair that ran down his stomach and disappeared under his belt buckle. She looked up at him, leaned forward and kissed the trident on his chest, causing him to suck in his breath. "We're a mess, you know. All of our scars."

Her accent had thickened, her eyes pools of the deepest blue in the moonlight. They *were* a mess, but he didn't care.

He caught her mouth with his, laying her back down on the tabletop as he kissed down her neck, between her breasts, down her stomach. Morning was only a few hours off, and while he could have used the sleep, he needed Charlotte so much more.

Heart beating like a gorilla in his chest, he loved hearing her moan his name. Her hands were in his hair, the jeans sliding down her long legs and hitting the floor.

A buzzing came from his back pocket, his phone vibrating his ass cheek and disturbing the quiet of the plane's cabin. He ignored it, spreading Charlotte's legs wide and kissing the inside of her thighs.

"What's that?" she half whispered, half moaned. "Is that your phone?"

He trailed his lips up higher. "Don't worry about it," he said against her soft, smooth skin.

Her fingernails scraped against his scalp, her fingers tugging his hair, encouraging his lips to move even higher. "What if it's your friend? What if he's in trouble?"

Shit, Jax. She could be right. Pausing in his ministrations, he laid his forehead against the top of her right thigh, dug his phone out. Caller ID told him it wasn't Jaxon, but it *was* important.

Straightening, he still kept his body looming over Charlotte so she didn't get any ideas he was done with her. Far from it. "Don't move," he said to her as he punched the accept button and glanced out the nearby window. The landscape beyond the plane looked the same. Empty. "Yo. What's up?" he said into his phone.

Beatrice—thank God—was her normal self. No small talk; all business. "Rory and I found something. Check your messages."

Miles clicked over to his message app, saw a grainy, monochrome photo that meant nothing to him. Charlotte was giving him a curious stare. "What is it?"

"Can you see it?" Beatrice said in his ear. "Security camera at the safe house caught it."

He did another scan of the photo. Grey mass with a blob here and there was all he saw. Charlotte sat up, forcing him to move back. "Caught what exactly?"

"Upper left-hand corner. See the darker mass in the fog?"

A third look at the photo. This time, Charlotte leaned forward, scanning the photo as well as she located her shirt and tugged it on with one hand and hit the speaker button with her other.

Multitasking. She'd always been good at it. He smiled as he remembered just how good she was at it in bed.

Which made annoyance at the current interruption burn like acid under his skin. "Looks like a bird," he said to Beatrice. "Why do I care?"

"It's a drone."

Charlotte's eyes snapped to his. "A drone?" she said, grabbing her jeans from the ground.

Beatrice didn't miss a beat. "Yes, Agent Carstons. We believe it followed you from the house. Any clue who might have sent it?"

"No." Charlotte shook her head even though Beatrice couldn't see it. She pulled up her jeans and zipped them and Miles wanted to punch the table. "Nicolae, I guess. He traded in them on occasion, but I never knew him to use one."

A squeak from Beatrice's chair filtered through the phone. "I don't believe it was Nicolae Bourean. Whoever used this drone to track you had to be on your tail at the safe house. They're the ones who notified MI6 where you were headed."

"Nicolae's the one who embedded a tracking chip in her back," Miles argued. "That's the only way anyone could have found us at the safe house."

"Unless Bourean is working with MI6, Agent Carstons, I'd say there's another player in the mix. From airport footage, we can see that the drone definitely followed you to the airport, then disappeared right before the MI6 agents showed up."

Charlotte sank into one of the seats and stared out the window. "Nico is wanted by MI6. He would never work *with* them. Even if they cut him a deal in exchange for his help, he wouldn't give up the chance at killing me. There's no satisfaction in that. No revenge."

"Then I suggest you review your contacts and friendships, Agent. Someone has betrayed you."

The line went dead. Miles put the phone away and slid into the seat next to Charlotte. "At least we know now how MI6 found us at the airport."

"Yeah." She continued to stare out the window, but her mind seemed a million miles away. "You're sure there is no other tracking device buried under my skin?"

"Positive."

"And yet someone found us again." She pointed out the window and Miles' heart lurched into his chest.

A dark figured moved stealthily down the hill, disappearing behind a tree.

"Damn it." He rose and checked his weapon. He should have been paying more attention. The farm was long ago abandoned, but that didn't mean it wasn't ever used by criminals and vagrants. Or maybe even a spy or two when they needed a place that looked deserted to hide in.

Charlotte laid a hand on his. "Are you sure it's not Megadeth?"

"Hiding in the woods? Stay here. I'll take care of it."

"Bull." Charlotte rose from her seat, grabbing her coat from behind her. "We do this together."

Two minutes ago, he'd had her on her on her back, nearly naked. Now she wanted to jump into the line of fire with him. "I don't think you understand how this works. *I'm* protecting *you.* Now sit tight."

White teeth flashed in the shadows at him and he heard the click of her gun's magazine snapping into place. "I've never had a partner before. This could be fun."

Jesus. He was so screwed. "Charlotte…"

"Don't *Charlotte* me. I'm a trained operative, not some rich housewife who can't hold her own against an abusive husband. We're partners in this. Now get moving before that guy out there ambushes us."

Defeat wasn't in his vocabulary. *This is only a concession.* "Stay close and watch my six."

There was a teasing note to her voice. Excitement too. "You think *you're* taking the lead on this?"

Screwed, yessiree. He was one-hundred percent screwed. "Either that, or you sit your sweet ass back down in that seat. You're a Rock Star client, operative or not, and I'm your bodyguard. Take it or leave it, Carstons."

Her hand found his ass and gave one cheek a little squeeze. "Oh, I'm taking it," she said, her presence suddenly warm against his backside. "Lead the way, bodyguard."

WASHINGTON, D.C.

Beatrice Reese stared at the paper file on Charlotte Carstons and tapped her pen on her blotter. Paper files were so last millennium, but the SFI computer system was undergoing a complete virus scan like it did every Wednesday evening, and she preferred not to fight with her computer while the scan ran in the background. Rory assured her the scan didn't slow down her computer or the normal office intranet, but Beatrice didn't believe him.

Most places ran their full system scans in the middle of the night when no one was around. At SFI headquarters, there were always staff around. Much of their communication often happened at night when their Rock Star clients were more active, as were the criminals Shadow Force teams hunted.

Granted, several of her paramilitary teams were out of the country and in different time zones, but her and Rory's analysis of peak times confirmed that Wednesday evenings between five and eight p.m. EST were usually quite dead and the opportune time for him to babysit the scan. Beatrice relied on logic, data, facts. She still didn't understand why that particular time was so slow every week.

Security wasn't just important at SFI, it was at the top of the list. Client safety was a close second. Beatrice preached it daily to her staff and employees. Security and safety—sides of the same coin.

And that's why she was particularly worried about Miles Duncan.

Charlotte Carstons had a red X on her back. A target. Not just from a Romanian crime lord, but also by her employer. A bad combination if Beatrice had ever seen one. Since she had once been hunted by her own employer—the U.S. government—she knew all about that particular scenario. Things had been ugly for a while, but she'd lucked out. The assassin sent to kill her wanted out of the termination business…and he'd turned to her for help.

That's why Rory was now on the SFI payroll.

Carstons, however, wasn't going to get that lucky. Even if Beatrice found a way to get MI6 to back off—and she did have her ways—there was still Nicolae Bourean to deal with.

One problem at a time. She picked up her phone and buzzed Connor, her assistant. "Get Zeb Riceman on the line for me, please."

"Yes, ma'am."

A minute later, Zeb's rough, growly voice came over the line. "Whatcha want, girlie? I'm eatin' dinner."

Hmm. Maybe that accounted for one variable regarding the slow time in her analysis. "Do you remember an operative named CB Norris? George W. era. Left the CIA eleven months and thirteen days after 9/11."

She heard chewing, then Zeb sipping liquid. A former client, Savanna Bunkett, had told Beatrice the man had a fondness for strawberry pop and top shelf vodka.

"Norris?" Zeb growled. "Haven't heard that name in awhile. Righteous SOB. We crossed paths but not until he was high up in the Agency's ranks. He put together a couple of scrimmage runs into the hills of Afghanistan looking for bin Laden. I had the pleasure of deciphering intel his team uncovered, which was a bunch of nothin'."

"I haven't yet confirmed this, but it appears Mr. Norris may be involved in a current security mission SFI is investigating in Romania. Norris is running agents for MI6 and one of those agents is now our client. Is there anything pertinent you can tell me about the man? Perhaps why he was fired from the Agency?"

"Officially, the CIA said he retired and went to live in London. In certain circles I was kin to, they claim he got his ass booted after he said some nasty things to his commander-in-chief. He was told none-to-politely to take his opinions and his traitorous mouth and find a new country to call home. He was too smart and dedicated for his own good. He knew bin Laden was a serious threat to America before bin Laden knew it himself. I read a few of his missives back in the day, before 9/11."

"And?"

"I thought he was crazy, just like everybody else who read 'em."

Power could make a man stronger, bolder, more confident. It could open doors and give him deep reserves of leverage. Power was the strongest motivator Beatrice had seen in D.C. and the philosophers were accurate: it always corrupted.

What she'd learned since becoming pregnant was that true power had nothing to do with politics or ambition. Nothing to do with leverage, blackmail, or violence.

Creation, not destruction, was true power. Growing a child inside you, creating a company that took care of your employees and protected innocent people from the corrupt power mongers running the country, that was true power.

"When the towers fell and it was revealed bin Laden was behind it," Beatrice said, "Norris felt vindicated."

"Wouldn't you? He saw himself on a personal mission to go after that asshole and he thought with all of his previous intel gathering and predictions, he should be a shoo-in for a top slot in the intelligence world. He might have made it, too, if he'd played his cards right and been patient. He knew as well as anyone that Washington moves as slow as a snail, even when we're under attack."

"Why join MI6? They don't seem to appreciate his brilliance and skills any more than the U.S. did if he's stuck in Romania running operatives and assets. If he wanted fame and glory, he missed the jackpot."

"Rings true." A napkin rustled in the background. "Let me do some digging. Guy's got to have an ulterior motive."

"I would appreciate learning anything you find out."

They said their goodbyes and Beatrice rocked back and forth in her chair, rubbing her still-growing belly. Her analytical mind knew Miles could handle himself in any circumstance. He'd already proved that several times in the past few months. Even with his ankle injury, the Navy had offered him a position training SEALs. He'd rejected the offer and accepted hers instead. A quiet soldier, he'd learned the value of his own freedom. His perspective about what was important to him had shifted.

Love could do that.

Beatrice had known about the intensive searches Miles had done on Agent Carstons from the moment he'd come to work for the Rock Stars. As he transitioned to the paramilitary side, she'd suspected that was the biggest reason he'd signed on with SFI—he knew they had leading technology, sources for top-secret intelligence, a database of identities that rivaled everything Homeland, the FBI, and Interpol put together had, and a team that would have his back. The men working for SFI, whether bodyguards or full-blown paramilitary soldiers—might remind Duncan of his SEAL brothers who'd died in the Carpathian Mountains, but not nearly as much as seeing fresh, new recruits at the Naval Special Warfare Training Center in Coronado would have every day.

She'd helped him out here and there with his searches, but they'd lead to unwanted attention. At that point, she'd told him to stand down.

She had a soft spot for him—unusual for her. Her emotional quotient had always had a deficit due to her high IQ and she preferred not getting personally attached to the men who worked for SFI. In reality, she *did* care about each and every one of them—it wasn't that she was a cold-hearted bitch. She was loyal to them to a fault because of her own personal code of ethics.

But Miles reminded her of her husband, Callan Reese. A SEAL who'd lost his fellow teammates on a mission and lived to tell about it. The survivor's guilt still ate at him. He often spent hours in the gym beating on a punching bag or running miles and miles of D.C. landscapes in the pre-dawn hours. When she looked in Miles Duncan's eyes, she saw the same ghosts haunting him. The same questions the Fates would never answer. Why him? Why did he survive when the others died?

Luck? Destiny? God? Beatrice didn't believe in any of those pat answers. She did believe Charlotte Carstons was in the right place at the right time to save Miles' life and nurse him back to health. She only hoped he didn't lose it repaying the favor.

Her office door opened and Cal stuck his head in. His dark hair was freshly washed; his normal stubble gone. "You ready?"

"For what?"

He smiled what looked like a tolerant smile you'd give a child. "Dinner, remember? We're meeting Emit and Jeanie at the restaurant. Trace and Savanna might swing by, too, if she can bug out of the newsroom in time."

Dinner, right. She'd forgotten their date with the man who'd started it all. If it weren't for Emit, she might be dead. Cal, too.

Beatrice hefted her big belly and stood, Cal hurrying to help her. As he eased her out of her chair and grabbed her coat, she realized she was hungry. Of course, at this stage of her pregnancy, she was hungry all the time. And getting uncomfortable.

"I'm worried about Miles," she told him, trying and failing at buttoning her coat over her stomach.

"Worried? You?"

Cal's grin eased the tension between her shoulder blades. He enjoyed teasing her even when she didn't always get the joke. This joke was obvious… She wasn't a worrier. Period.

"He's off on this mission by himself. Well, Jaxon Sloan is with him, but not a full team."

"I thought this was a quick in-and-out."

"It should be."

He led her to the door, pacing his steps with her slower ones. "But…?"

"There are too many unknowns with this one. I don't like it."

His chuckle was low and, thankfully, nonjudgmental. "Afraid the Queen's going to blow a gasket? How about I help you do some intel gathering on these 'unknowns' after dinner? Jeanie wants to talk about a baby shower tonight. We shouldn't stand her up."

Beatrice had never attended a baby shower before but had heard horror stories about them. "I don't want one. Should I?"

Cal shut the door behind them, then put his hands on either side of her head and kissed her slow and soft. She melted a little, forgetting to worry about Miles or the awkwardness that always plagued her in social situations.

When he finally broke the kiss, he smiled down at her. "We'll keep it simple and invite everyone to our place. Just our SFI family. I'll grill and we'll cater the rest. Jeanie can throw up some decorations and figure out the cake and whatever else you want. It's our first kid and you deserve to be in the spotlight for a few minutes. You do a lot for the rest of us. Let us do something for you."

Cal, always coming to her rescue and making her feel special. Needed.

"I guess I can't blame Miles for running to Charlotte's rescue."

A frown creased Cal's forehead. "You lost me there. We were talking about dinner and baby showers."

Poor guy would never follow her train of thought when her brain was working out a problem. "You and Miles. You remind me of each other. Both good guys who would do anything for the woman they love."

Cal slid his hand into hers and gave it a squeeze as he led her to the elevators. "I promise...even if I have to go to Romania and save his ass, Miles will make it out alive."

The baby in her belly kicked, as if agreeing with his father. "Yep, definitely a boy," she said, rubbing her belly. "I stand by my prediction. He's just as bullheaded as you are."

Cal laughed. They'd forgone finding out the sex of the child in order to keep their wager alive. "Nope, gonna be a girl. Everyone says so."

The elevator dinged and the doors opened. Secretly, Beatrice hoped it might be a girl. Either way, she'd be happy. "I love you, Cal Reese," she said, stepping into the elevator. "But you're not going after Miles if he gets into trouble."

He swung in beside her and punched the button for the ground floor. "I'm not?"

"I have other men I can send, and if this baby comes early,"—she smiled at him sweetly—"I want you to be there in the delivery room so I can collect my hundred bucks when you see it's a boy."

CHAPTER ELEVEN

SERBIA

The temperature had dropped another ten degrees. Charlotte's breath fogged in front of her. The wooded area they'd seen the man disappear into smelled of frigid air and pine needles.

Gloves. She definitely needed gloves with fingers, not the too big ones she was sporting right now.

Two steps in front of her on her left was Miles, winding his way slowly, carefully through the darkness. Charlotte kept one hand on him, moonlight shivering its way down here and there through the trees, offering little illumination. The darkness was good and bad. It made it difficult to spot their quarry, but gave them excellent cover.

And any reason to keep her hands on Miles was a good one.

He held up a fist to signal her to stop as he slid in behind a large tree trunk. She pulled up next to him, eyes scanning the area, gun aimed at the sky. Underneath her hand, she felt the tight readiness of his muscles. He might have been known as the Evasion God in the Teams, but the predator in him was on the hunt on this early morning in a Serbian forest.

Working in tandem with a partner during a tactical engagement was a foreign experience for her. She'd been trained to do so, but that training was years behind her. She'd been a solo operative in the field for so long, she'd forgotten the nuances of having a partner. The advantages and disadvantages.

Having Miles for a partner definitely had both. Her body was still warm where he'd touched her, kissed her. The endorphins he'd created in her brain were fading, but they'd mellowed her anxiety while heightening her anticipation. Only a few days ago, she'd felt all alone in the world. A sad place to be. Now, her body tingled, her senses felt alive. As she breathed in the pine scent from the air and watched the broad back of her lover, she had the feeling she would never be alone again.

As misguided as the feeling might have been, she was going to believe in it.

She didn't believe in much these days. A hardness like a peach pit had lodged in her breastbone and she couldn't seem to shake it. She'd experienced the same feeling after seeing her mother murdered. The same feeling when her father had her committed to the mental hospital.

MI6 had given her purpose. Uncovered talents and skills and developed them. Made her believe in herself again. She wasn't going to let them down, even if they currently believed her a traitor. She wasn't and she was about to prove it. There were only two entities she was loyal to and both were in reach.

Trusting Miles with her body was easy. Trusting him with the necklace had been out of necessity. Could she trust him with her heart?

He lowered his fist and they stepped out from the tree, moving to their right. Who was out here? A random stranger or someone after her?

Charlotte hadn't seen or heard anything, but apparently Miles had. He honed in on a spot a few yards away, moving her in that direction.

Her pulse hammered. In the quiet of the forest, she heard a night creature stirring off to her left, heard her heart beating in her ears. Purposely slowing her breathing, she stepped carefully through the forest debris, hoping to avoid snapping a twig or twisting her ankle and going down. Her hand stayed anchored on his back. Since she couldn't see shit, she had to trust Miles knew what he was doing.

Another fist raise and he pulled up short. She felt, more than saw, him cock his head to the side, listening. Charlotte strained her ears too. The nocturnal stirrings were gone. It was so quiet, she thought she could hear the snow falling. What had alerted him?

A bead of sweat trickled down her spine. She held her breath, her mind ticking off the seconds. One...two...three...

An awareness came to her. The presence of the man, so close she could probably reach out and touch him.

Miles must have felt him too. He swiveled and grabbed her hand, nearly knocking her off balance. The next thing she knew, he pushed her down on the forest floor and cocked his gun.

"Dude, don't shoot," a familiar voice said a few feet away. "It's me."

The hot adrenaline pumping in Charlotte's veins whooshed out of her system and left her shaky. The hard-packed pine needles under her butt were cold. She let go of a strained laugh.

Miles lowered his gun. "You SOB. What the hell are you doing out here, skulking around in the woods?"

"Skulking? I wasn't skulking. I was making sure no one followed me from the bar," Megadeth said, "and you know, making sure you two were decent."

Charlotte used a tree to leverage herself back onto her feet. "Why are you back already?"

"My date with the redhead was going great until her husband showed up. Since I have to lay low, figured it wasn't a good idea to engage the asshole."

"We would have come picked you up if you'd called."

"Thought you might be...busy. You know, sleeping or whatever," he said. "Can we continue this discussion in the plane? It's fucking cold out here."

Charlotte agreed. The three of them wound their way out of the forest and back to the plane. She offered to make Megadeth something warm to drink, but he declined, grabbing a blanket from an overhead compartment and heading to the front. "Gonna grab some shuteye," he told Miles. "Relieve me in two."

He disappeared into the cockpit and shut the door.

Two hours. They had two hours to themselves. Charlotte smiled at Miles, but he didn't smile back. Instead, he kissed her forehead and patted her shoulder. "You need to get some sleep too. I'll keep an eye on things."

Jet lag was settling in. Even in the shadowy interior, she could see the tiredness in his face, his body. "I slept on the way here," she said. "I'll take first watch. You go lay down."

He started to argue, but she shut him down. "You have to trust me, Miles, and this is *my* mission. I know what I'm doing. I need you fresh and on the top of your game come sunrise, soldier, so get some sleep."

For a moment, he simply stood and stared at her. She could feel him wrestling with himself. He was used to being in charge; it was hard for him to relinquish that. His natural instinct to protect was even stronger.

Finally, he gave up, grabbing another blanket and, without a word, joining Megadeth in the cockpit. Why there when they had an entire plane, who knew? Maybe he wanted to be ready in case they had to make a quick getaway.

Or maybe because he was scared to be too close to her.

Charlotte blew on her fingers and set up her watch point.

Miles woke with a start. The sun coming through the window blinded him for a moment and he rubbed his eyes as he threw off the blanket someone—Charlotte, no doubt—had thrown over him.

Jet lag was a bitch. He never should have laid down. His arms hung like fifty-pound weights. His legs dragged when he tried to walk. He'd been in too many time zones over the past week and it had finally caught up with him.

He yawned and stretched. "Charlotte?"

She was nowhere to be seen. The plane was quiet.

Too quiet.

"Jax?" Miles called, not caring about using his real name.

No answer.

Adrenaline shot through his sluggish limbs, brain synapses fired in rapid succession. *Where are they?*

A quick sweep of the plane revealed it was empty. Jax and Charlotte's backpacks were still there. The magazines Charlotte had been looking at were on the floor where Miles had pushed them off the table when he'd gone down on her.

But their coats were gone. The blanket Jax had used was crumpled in a ball and left behind in his co-pilot's seat.

Miles scanned the yard outside the windows, the nearby woods. Nothing moved but some birds pecking at the snow for food.

Sunlight glistened sharply off the new fallen snow. Miles hit the top of the plane's stairs and looked around again.

There. He shielded his eyes with one hand. Footprints. Two sets leading away from the plane and toward the abandoned farmhouse a hundred yards away.

Checking his weapon, he did another visual sweep of the area, saw nothing to be alarmed about. Still, his pulse raced. The sun's placement told him it had to be mid-morning. A check of his watch, which he'd reset last night to local time, told him it was after ten. Why hadn't they woken him? Had something happened?

Snow crunched under his boots as he followed the tracks to the dilapidated house. The front steps were crumbling, the porch leaned to the south. Several windows on the front were broken. He stopped on the porch and heard the sound of voices. Muffled. He'd used this place before for shelter on other missions. It was out of the way and unobtrusive. The perfect spot to hide.

Cautiously, he moved through the screen door and into a living area. Following the voices, he stopped just outside what appeared to be the kitchen.

"So you two worked together before?" Jax was saying.

Silverware clinked, the sounds of someone rustling through a drawer met his ears. "Our paths crossed about a year ago, yes," Charlotte answered. "How long have you known him?"

Redirection. Typical Charlotte.

"We landed on the same Team more than once when we were both SEALs. Figured he'd end up running a team at some point. Would have if not for his bum ankle."

"And since he joined Emit's group? Have you worked with him much?"

"A few times. He's solid."

The clinking of utensils stopped. Charlotte must have looked at Jax for clarification. Miles moved slightly, catching a glimpse of Charlotte's back, her hair.

"You know," Jax said. He was across the room, out of Miles' view. "Once he trusts you, he's got your back forever."

Charlotte's voice was light, breathy. "Good to know."

"I say that because I like the guy. He's a valuable part of our team." The creak of a cabinet door opening and closing suggested he wasn't looking at her. Playing things casual. "Don't want to see him get hurt."

A pause hung in the air and Miles could almost see Charlotte's head moving in a slight nod. "Message received. It's not my intention to hurt him. Emotionally, I mean. The mission we're on, however, is a dangerous one. I can't guarantee he won't be harmed physically. All I can assure is that I'll do my best to keep him safe."

"Good luck with that. He's got a protective streak a mile wide. If bullets fly, he'll shove you out of the way and take every last one."

Her sigh echoed in the high-ceiling room. "It's rather charming, don't you think? Very manly, the way he tries to shield everyone. Safeguard them. I've never had anyone do that for me."

Jax snorted. "Charming? Never thought of it that way, but if you say so, Charlie."

Jax was calling her Charlie now?

Charlotte clasped her hands in front of her. "As long as we're being forthright, I need to explain to you how the rest of the mission will go."

Miles could hear the smile in her voice, but there was steel underneath it.

"Go on," Jax said. Wary. Miles felt a bit wary himself.

"As I'm sure you realize,"—her voice was spun sugar now—"a woman traveling with *two* men is rather...out of the ordinary."

Jax was quick on the uptake. Miles knew he'd worked with spies before and never had much use for them. Regardless of Charlotte's sugary voice and pleasant smile, he wasn't giving ground. "If anyone asks, you can say I'm your brother."

Her chuckle was light and conveyed that was the worst idea she'd heard in a long time. "I appreciate your dedication, but I'm afraid no one would believe us."

Jax tried the stepbrother angle and even threw in something about adoption. Charlotte shut him down on all counts.

Finally, he gave in. "You want me to hang back or bow out completely?"

"Could you stay here while we continue onto Romania? That way if we need help, you'll be close by."

She was good, he'd give her that. She didn't want Jax knowing where her cabin was, or the spot she'd hidden the USB. Like she'd told Miles, the fewer people who knew, the less chance there was that someone would end up in Nico's hands spilling their guts.

She turned her head slightly to look out a window. "Miles

and I will return here, if at all possible, and we'll all fly home together."

Was Jax buying this? Miles doubted it. Home to Charlotte wasn't the States. Once she had her file, she would head straight to her handler, or maybe back to Vauxhall Cross.

Sliding around the doorframe, Miles leaned one shoulder against it. "Am I interrupting something?"

Charlotte jumped. Jax gave him a chin nod. "Morning, Sleeping Beauty."

"Miles," Charlotte said. She'd braided her hair and her lips were shiny with pink gloss. She pointed to a bag on the floor. "We were just gathering a few extra supplies."

They had the truck, weapons, the clothes on their backs, and some food. They could use a map and a few other things, but he was curious. "Like what?"

"A map for one thing," Charlotte said, withdrawing a folded one from her back pocket and holding it up. She waved it toward the bag on the floor. "We also found some silver to sell or barter, extra batteries, and a couple pair of traction cleats to put on the bottoms of our boots for when we climb in the mountains. I think with our other supplies and the cash, we won't need to stop at any stores."

"I also grabbed a few tools I found in the barn," Jax said. "A couple of knives and some oil for the truck, just in case. There's a generator out back, but it's not portable."

They'd been busy. "Why didn't you wake me?"

"You kidding?" Jax snickered. "After you almost shot me last night in the trees, we figured you needed some sleep, man."

Charlotte walked to the kitchen table, spreading the map out on the linoleum top. "We have a long trip today. By my calculations we're here." She pointed to a spot on the map, then ran her finger along a winding line that crossed the border into Romania and skirted the mountains. "We're heading to this area. I've sent the route and coordinates to your phone."

She seemed chipper, ready to go. Almost excited. Miles wished he felt the same. He followed the line her finger had traced and mentally calculated the distance. A six to eight hour drive, depending on the roads and the weather. "We better get hauling then."

Charlotte gave him a smile that made his lower gut tingle as she refolded the map. "I'll gather some food from the plane's kitchen and be ready to go shortly."

She practically skipped out of the farmhouse, leaving him and Jax to haul the load of supplies back.

Outside in the bright sunlight, Jax broached the subject Miles had overheard him discussing with Charlotte. "Your girl wants to ditch me."

Up ahead, she was already at the plane, climbing the steps. "I heard."

"What's she up to?"

He wanted to say nothing. She was simply going after this USB. Or maybe, his ego said, she wanted to be alone with him to fuck his brains out. He could get behind that. "The mission is to get to the caves and retrieve an item of intel she left there, take it back to London and give it to MI6."

"So she says."

"Nicolae Bourean kidnapped and tortured her after I left here nine months ago. She may have some revenge in mind."

Jax shrugged, keeping his pace steady but slow so they could talk. "Can't blame her for that. You?"

"I'd like to take some revenge on his ass myself."

"As long as you know what you're getting into and you're cool with it." Jax hefted the supply bag higher on his shoulder. "You want me to do as she says? Hang back and wait for your call?"

"The spot we're heading to is pretty remote. If we get in trouble, I'd prefer you were a little closer."

"That old Jeep in the barn needs a tune-up but I used the Land Rover to jump start it this morning and it purred like a kitten. I found a battery charger and hooked it up. Should be ready to roll by now. I'll give you guys an hour head start, then I'll follow."

They neared the Land Rover and Miles nodded. "Let Beatrice know the plan, okay?"

"Damn straight. She scares the shit of me. It's like she can read my mind, man. No way I'm crossing her or pissing her off by not reporting in."

Smart man. Miles slapped him on the back and took the supply bag from him to shove in the truck. "You got any GPS trackers on this?"

"Two, and a couple on your girl. She doesn't know it."

His girl. The words made his pulse skip around. "You better not let her hear you call her that."

Jax grinned. "She's a hellcat, isn't she?"

She's something. "The 'girl' moniker will earn you a punch in the nose."

They headed for the plane. "If you run into that asshole Bourean, make him bleed for me too. Make sure he can never hurt her, or anyone else, again."

Miles bumped fists with him before he climbed the stairs. "Deal."

CHAPTER TWELVE

The Land Rover bumped over potholes, climbing the hill to the top as the farmhouse and barn grew smaller behind them.

Charlotte held onto the door handle, the rough terrain jostling her from side to side. Finally, they were on their way.

Even so, it had been ridiculously hard to watch Miles sleep and not wake him up and get him going. The light covering of snow on the ground was a harbinger of what was to come. Winter in these parts was harsh and any day now could bring a sudden and violent storm. She had no intention of getting stranded in those mountains again.

They crested the hill and headed west, Miles quiet. Was he still tired?

Watching him sleep in the plane had given her a sense of calm, reminding her of the nights when he was injured and she'd stayed awake to watch him sleep in case his fever got too high or he woke and needed a drink. He was normally restrained, quiet, except in bed. There, he was anything but subdued. Outside of sex, though, he kept things to himself. Behind his eyes, she could see the wheels in his head turning. Always analyzing, always planning his next move.

Of course, he'd insisted on driving today. *Such a man.*

They drove a good half hour or longer before he finally spoke. "You going to tell me what you're up to?"

"Up to?"

"Why'd you want Megadeth to stay behind?"

"You can stop calling him that. He told me his name is Jaxon."

Miles quirked one brow, his gaze never leaving the road. "He told you that, did he?"

"He may not trust me completely, but he trusts me with that. Also told me a bit about his childhood. We had a nice conversation in the farmhouse. He thinks quite highly of you."

"Why did you want him to stay back at the plane? The real reason you wanted to leave him behind?"

"I have a plan and it will work better if it's just the two of us."

"Don't you think you should share that plan with me?"

"When the time comes."

Miles braked. Hard. Charlotte flew forward, her seatbelt locking up. "For goodness' sake! What are you doing?"

"Tell me the plan now or we turn around and head back."

She stared at him, narrowing her eyes.

"Now, Charlotte. I'm not kidding."

Was it possible he knew her better than she'd thought? "I told you. We cross the border today, get to the cabin later tonight. Tomorrow morning, we hike to the caves, retrieve the USB, and start back."

"You're leaving out details. Why?"

So maybe she was. It was too early in the journey to tell him everything. "The details may change. No sense locking them into stone at this point."

"I know you're afraid Jax will get hurt if he's with us. That's why you asked him to stay behind, isn't it?"

Of course, she didn't want Jaxon to get hurt. "That's why I tried to talk *you* out of coming, if you'll recall. I've survived a lot in my life. I know how to endure pain and soldier on. And while I'm sure both of you can handle quite a bit of danger and such as well, I also know both of you have something to go back to. You started your lives over, found the right job for your skill set. You have a life in San Diego and a future with SFI."

"You have a life to go back to. Your parents, your brother."

She really didn't. "My mother is dead. My father and brother couldn't care less about me."

"Your file didn't state your mother had passed."

The whole thing had been covered up. Her father had forbidden her to talk about it. Not that that had stopped her. "She was murdered."

Miles' face clouded with concern. "Charlotte, I'm so sorry. I didn't know."

One of the conditions of her agreement with MI6 was that she could look for her mother's killer in her downtime. A lot of good that had done her. Four years later, she was no closer to finding the bastard than when she'd been eleven and strapped to a bed at the looney bin. "That's because someone doesn't want it known."

His brows furrowed. "What do you mean?"

She hadn't spoken of it in years. When you told people your mother had been murdered but there was no proof—and that your father had had you committed—they tended to look at you differently. She hated that look. Another reason she'd stopped talking about it a long time ago.

What would it hurt to do so now? It was a long story, but they had a long drive ahead of them. "Do you really want to know?"

"Yeah, I really do."

He thought that now, but once she told him, things would change between them. She was sure of it. It always did.

But the cat was out of the bag. At least he wasn't asking her to go into detail about her op.

Settling back in her seat, she motioned for Miles to drive. He took his foot off the brake and they once more started forward.

Only for Charlotte, she felt like she was being sucked backward, at least in time. "My mother was a good seamstress, as I mentioned. So good, in fact, she opened a small shop in a strip of businesses not far from Embassy Row that catered to the international community. She worked with everyone from Vietnamese to South Africans. Word got around, and soon she had some pretty impressive clients. Duchesses and other royal ladies. Everyday after lessons, I would go to the shop and help out.

"There were Gypsies, too, some from Romania, others from neighboring countries. They all knew each other, even though many didn't get along. The Roma women brought my mother business. One of the men—he was said to be a tinker from Ireland with some Roma blood in him—regularly stopped by to help her with maintenance on the building when my father was away. Dad was away a lot."

She told him a few of the little things, details that came back to her about her mom and the shop. Like how every Wednesday, the women would gather in the backroom to drink tea with rum and spices and *rokker*—talk. How she never liked the tinker even though he fixed the plumbing when it backed up and installed better lighting in the backroom where her mother sewed.

"One day, I was late getting to the shop. A violent storm had broken out right before the school bell released us and I stayed under some shelter until it was over. By the time I got to Mum's shop, it was dark. The front door was locked and the sign said closed. I thought she was angry with me and had closed up early. Or maybe the storm had scared her and she was hiding in the back."

In her mind, she saw the cobbled street, wet from the rain. The gas lamps springing to life. "I went around to the alley. A gunshot echoed from my mum's shop. I started running, but I slipped on the slick pavement and went down. When I looked up, there was a man hurrying out of the back entrance. He took off down the alley as I got to my feet and I saw black smoke coming out one of the windows. I ran to them and peeped in, saw my mother lying on the floor. Blood blooming on the front of her chest." Her words sounded dispassionate, but inside, she felt the enormous weight that had always been there, choking her. She had to swallow past it, past the peach pit lodged in her throat. "They said the explosion that followed was caused by a gas leak. It threw me back a couple of meters and slammed me into the opposite wall. It took out the shop next to hers. My mother's body was nothing but ash and bones when they finally dug through the debris and found her. I suffered a concussion and some scrapes and bruises."

"Who was the man you saw running from the shop? Did they catch him?"

"They told me I made it up, that my concussion caused me to remember the situation wrongly. I didn't see his face and couldn't make a solid ID, but I know it was him. The Gypsy man. I've been looking for him ever since that night."

"You think he shot her and then tried to cover it up with the explosion."

"Yes."

"Why?"

"I don't know. I think my father does, but he's always refused to discuss it. I wouldn't shut up about it and I caused quite a stir. My father had to be out of the country a lot and finding anyone to watch after me and my brother was challenging. Losing our mother, our father being out of the country so much, and me running around claiming our mother was murdered was too much for my brother. He retreated into his head, which caused my father to blame me. The doctors put me on drugs, but they messed with me to the point I was a zombie, so I quit taking them. I ran away from home, tried to find the man. Finally, my father had me committed. For six months, I lived in an institution. Drugs in my veins kept me zombie-fied. They strapped me down any time I raised my voice or asked a question because they said I was upsetting the other patients."

At least this time, when Miles slammed on the brakes, he'd already yanked the truck over to the side of the road. Before she could protest, he pulled her across the shifter and into his arms.

"Jesus Christ, what an awful life you've lived," he said into her hair.

One hand was on her back, the other on the back of her head. She took a deep breath, enjoying his scent and sunk into the embrace. It was good to be held.

"I'm okay," she said, chin on his shoulder. The quiet, forest road had been mostly empty, but now a car buzzed around them. "I'm not one of those people who dwells on the bad stuff, and like I told you before, my parents and my brother made me the agent I am today. That whole incident changed my perception of the world and how to live in it. I realized on the anniversary of my mother's death that I either had to become the daughter my father needed and the sister my brother needed, or I'd end up in a facility until I turned eighteen. By then, I'd be so brain dead from the drugs, I'd never be able to live on my own. I straightened out, and even though I secretly never gave up my quest to find out what happened that night, I quit talking about it. I righted the ship, as they say. I went back to school, learned how to manage my brother and his condition, and behaved myself when Dad went out of town on assignments and we had a live-in nanny.

Miles broke the embrace and brushed a strand of hair from her face. "Did you ever find the man?"

"No. I had several leads over the years from discreetly talking to my mother's backroom friends, but they were all dead ends. His name was Orlo Ayres, but that could have been one of many aliases the man had. He was what the Gypsy women called a traveller. No one knew precisely where he came from, who is clan was. He moved around a lot and kept to himself. An outcast. But he was the best plumber and electrician in the community. Like my mother, he was known for his skills and never lacked work. One of the women once told me he worked for the Romanian ambassador, that they were friends, but because of the man's past, he wasn't allowed inside the embassy. However, she'd seen him coming and going from there and the Iranian embassy at odd hours of the night. She suspected he was a spy."

"Did you ever contact the Romanian ambassador?"

"I didn't learn this until I was seventeen. By then, the man was dead. The Iranians wouldn't talk to me."

Miles chuffed the steering wheel with the heel of his hand. "Well." He stared out at the bright white landscape. "Looks like you and I will have another mission after this one."

"What?"

He shifted and gave her a grave look. "After we're done with Bourean, we're hunting down your mother's killer."

He believed her. Just like that.

Holy cow.

Something popped inside her chest like a helium balloon. A warm sensation flooded her heart. "We are?"

He pulled back onto the road and gunned the engine. "We are."

"What's the silverware for?" Miles asked. They'd been on the road for hours. Traffic had grown heavier as they joined the easterly flow of travelers even though they tried to stay on the back roads as much as possible.

Charlotte had the map laid out in her lap studying it. Her hair had worked itself loose of the braid and a few strands caressed her cheek. Throughout the afternoon, the sun had played tag with clouds in the grey winter sky. When it had shone through, the highlights in her hair had turned a pretty copper. "Bartering."

"And the ammo you threw in the bag that doesn't work with our guns?"

"Ditto."

After she'd told him about her family, she'd asked about his. He'd figured she already knew about his southern upbringing and his parents' forty-plus year marriage, but told her about them anyway. His mother was a Tennessee Farnwall, heir to the Farnwall whiskey empire. His father, a Texas cattleman who had built a highly successful dude ranch/vacation conglomerate throughout the South. The two had met at one of his father's first dude ranches when his mother vacationed there. They'd fallen in love during a whirlwind romance and had been going strong ever since. With two older sisters and a younger brother, there was plenty of family drama, but they all got along pretty well.

Didn't he want to join one of the family businesses, Charlotte had asked. He'd admitted he'd never felt the pull. He'd always wanted to travel, to do some good in the world. He liked a good whiskey but didn't much care how it was made and had no interest in ranching or catering to vacationers.

The sun was sinking fast in the rearview and traffic had slowed to a crawl. A medieval forest lined both sides of the road. There seemed to be a bottleneck up ahead, but he couldn't see around the line of cars to tell what it was. "What exactly are we bartering for?" he asked. "We know where the USB is, so we don't need intel on that. We have transportation, food, clothing..."

"You'll see," Charlotte said without looking up.

She'd switched the radio on and was humming along with some guy singing about 'The World Is Mine'. Even after the progress they'd made opening up to one another, she was still holding out on him. "I don't like surprises, Charlotte. Just tell me why we need the ammo and silverware."

She sighed and looked up. "The area we're traveling through is a bit of a no-man's land. On any given day, a crime lord may send some of his men to collect a toll, or there may be renegades and outlaws that stop you and go through your things looking for something they want in exchange for your safe passage. Some of them claim to be Gypsies, but the Gypsies here never bother anyone. Not even the tribes who live along the sides of the roads. They get angry about the outlaws and criminals pretending to be them and giving them a bad name, but there's little they can do about it. People are predisposed to think ill of them."

Miles' internal warning system kicked into high gear. "None

of these criminals happen to be associated with Bourean, do they?"

"They might," she said, staring straight ahead. "But it wouldn't be any of his normal men from the compound who've see me before. It's doubtful they'd recognize me."

"Why the hell would they want silverware instead of money?"

"Oh, they love money." She pulled the rubber band from her hair and started finger-combing the long locks, pulling bangs over her forehead. She also donned a pair of sunglasses. "But most travelers through these parts don't have much and ammo is worth a lot throughout Europe. The renegades and outlaws have plenty of guns, thanks to the fall of the Soviet Union, but never enough ammunition. Silverware, the real stuff like we have, can be bartered for something like ammo, or melted down and sold by the ounce."

They'd come to a full stop. Charlotte went back to her map and her humming. Miles beat his thumb against the steering wheel, running evade-and-escape scenarios through his mind as they inched forward.

Sure enough, as they rounded a corner, he saw exactly what Charlotte had described. A group of men that put the bikers at the bar the previous night to shame were stopping cars and collecting "tolls".

"Let me do the talking," Charlotte said as she calmly folded her map and tucked it away. "I picked you up at the bar last night and we're having a weekend fling. You Americans are always fascinated with Transylvania and the stories of Dracula, so that's where I'm taking you. A little sight-seeing and a lot of sex."

Honestly, it sounded like a sweet combination to him. If only they weren't, in reality, dodging homicidal crime lords and equally nasty, if more proper, government agents.

She withdrew ammo from the bag behind the seat and hid the rest under it. "They'll be rude and act inappropriately. Don't let it get to you."

Miles ground his teeth for a moment. The car in front of them had ponied up whatever it took to make the men on each side of the road happy and was jetting off. He pulled the car forward, eyeing the M4s and the ratty boots the men wore as they evaluated him and Charlotte through the windshield. "They touch you and they're all dead."

Her hand snaked out, fingers intertwining with his on top of the gear shift. She was smiling. "Remember, sex and sight-seeing. Happy, go-lucky. We don't have a care in the world."

The song on the radio ended and the news came on. The newscaster spoke in Romanian, his voice too loud for their close quarters. Miles forced himself to smile back at Charlotte as he shook off her hand, cut the radio, and rolled down his window. She did the same with hers, engaging the man on her side in what sounded like a similar dialect to the newscaster. She spoke loud enough for both men to hear, that smile of hers never wavering as she bounced her gaze back and forth and answered for Miles when the asshole on his side started asking questions. She handed each of the outlaws an ammo clip with a few euros strapped to it.

The man on her side leaned down, a lengthy beard combed and braided into two tails complete with colorful beads, dangling from his chin. His eyes were hard, unforgiving. He said something, ran a finger down Charlotte's cheek. She slapped his hand away, but laughed as if he were joking about something, then let go of a rapid string of words. For a few seconds, the man stared at her, and Miles tensed, foot hovering over the gas pedal.

Shit, shit, shit... He was reaching for his weapon when the man's laugh cut through the weird silence. Charlotte sighed and handed him the cross ring from her finger. Beaded Tails eyed it and put it on, then wagged a finger at Charlotte, straightened, and slapped the top of the Land Rover's hood. The universal signal to drive on.

Miles didn't breathe again until they were a mile down the road. Charlotte rolled up her window and turned the radio back on. "You did good, Duncan. I thought for sure you were going to open fire when he touched my cheek."

I was. "What did you say to him?"

"Nothing much."

She started humming again as she pulled her hair into a ponytail and secured it.

"Charlotte...? Tell me."

A grin split her face as she looked over at him. "I said I was going to dump you after Transylvania and I'd see him when I got back. That I'd take all of your money and have it for him when I returned. But if he touched me again without my consent, his balls would turn black and fall off. He got the message. Sometimes playing the role of Gypsy has its perks."

"Like back in San Diego with Ted."

"Yeah, like that."

The sun sank below the horizon in the rearview. A new song came on the radio. Charlotte sang along softly and, this time when she reached for Miles' hand on the gearshift, he didn't shake her off.

CHAPTER THIRTEEN

ROMANIA

The cabin was shrouded in darkness, difficult to see from this far away, even with their night vision goggles. Nestled into a bend halfway up a mountain, it was hidden from normal view by a grove of trees and overgrown vegetation.

Charlotte had a moment of deja vu. Everything looked exactly the same as when she'd left the old horse trainer's cabin nearly ten months ago except for a little more overgrown vegetation covering the barn and creeping into the main yard.

The locals didn't consider the spot where the cabin nestled a true mountain—not compared to the surrounding Carpathians—but it was still a dangerous trek up that winding road to where the cabin sat.

"No lights," Miles said, his face hidden behind his binoculars. "No tracks up that road that I can see. Looks deserted."

Hopefully, it had been since the day she'd left. "We should still be careful. If Nico figured out that's where I was living, he might have set up surveillance or a trap to catch me if I returned. My handler knew the place, too, so MI6 could have planted cameras and or listening devices."

"We'll initiate a full sweep when we get closer."

"I'll initiate a sweep." She handed him a handheld radio. "You stay here and keep an eye out for visitors. Warn me if you see anyone. Once I'm sure the place is clean, I'll let you know."

"Good idea, except you're staying here. I'll sneak up to the cabin and sanitize it if necessary. Then you can join me."

"Are you going to do this every time?"

He lowered the binoculars. The moon overhead gave her a clear view of his face, the planes and ridges, the light growth of beard along his jaw. "Do what?"

"Argue with me about taking the lead on my mission."

"I don't know what the big deal is."

Of course he didn't. "You kidnapped me from my motel room, then inserted yourself into my mission. You drove the boat, flew the plane, drove the truck. You insisted I stay behind in the plane last night when I saw Jaxon sneaking around outside."

His dark brows lowered. "You drove the truck back from the bar. I let you come with me into the forest last night."

"I got to drive for two whole miles. Yippee. And I only got to go into the forest as your backup after I insisted."

"What's the problem?"

"The problem is you're calling all the shots about everything. All I wanted was my necklace back. Now I have this full blown...I don't know what."

He shrugged. "You're used to working alone. I get that."

"It's not just that, Miles. I can't...I don't... Ugh!" Men. How to explain so he would understand? "I'm grateful for everything you've done, but I feel like I have to keep reminding you that this is *my* mission. I call the shots. I take the risks."

He grabbed her hand and pulled her close. "And I have to keep reminding you that I'm your bodyguard. My job is to keep you safe."

"Maybe that's the problem." She saw flecks of the moon reflected in his eyes. "This isn't a safe mission, no matter which way we look at it."

No, it was definitely not safe, not when he was standing so close the heat from his body engulfing her. Not when he was holding onto her and staring down at her under a silvery moon.

And not when the cabin where she'd fallen in love with him was only a few hundred yards away.

It was if he felt it too...that tug to get there, to see it again. "There were nights after I made it back to the States," he said, "when I wondered if I'd dreamed it. The cabin. If I'd dreamed you up and what happened between us in there."

His lips lowered and brushed across hers, their breath mingling in the night air. "It was no dream," she whispered.

He rubbed a thumb along her jawline. "Then let's do our sweep. The faster we clear the place, the sooner I can get those pants off you."

She rose on her toes and planted a soft kiss on his lips. "It still makes sense for one of us to be lookout while the other sanitizes. You're the Evasion God from all accounts, so you should be lookout."

He grinned down at her. "Is this the plan, then? To seduce me into doing things your way?"

"Is it working?"

"Hell, yes. Get your ass up to that cabin, Agent Carstons, before my hard-on makes it impossible for me to walk."

She laughed and started to take off on foot when he grabbed her and pulled her back. All the joking was gone. "Be careful."

She planted another kiss on him. "You too. No getting hurt or dying before I get you alone."

"Don't worry." His grin broadened. "I'm allergic to death."

The terrain was rocky, slippery, and her travel made more difficult because she was staying off the trail that led directly to the cabin's front door. The night vision goggles helped her see where she was going, but fog had moved in. The woods were so thick, little snow covered the ground. Dead pine needles crunched under foot, releasing their scent into the air as the maze of tree trunks forced her to serpentine her way up the mountainside. At times, the fog was so thick, the trees seemed to pop up out of nowhere, reminding her of the boat ride.

The idea that someone had used a drone to track her kept nagging at her brain. Nico liked his toys, but generally his toys were women. Not that he didn't enjoy big screen TVs and cell phones, but he was more likely to buy a case of vodka and a rocket launcher than a drone.

The gray market dealt in everything under the sun and so did Nico. Perhaps he'd branched out to drones or ended up with one after a bartering session.

Most likely, however, the drone came from her employer.

Who and how? How did they find her in America when they couldn't apparently find her in Nico's compound?

They weren't looking for you then.

She heard a branch behind her snap and she froze. There are things in these woods besides the occasional human. Bears, who should be hibernating by now, but some wouldn't until deep winter. Wolves. She didn't want to use a flashlight or her weapon. Either could give away her position. But if push came to shove, she'd rather give up her position to the bad guys than die from a bear mauling.

Peripheral vision was limited by the goggles. She stayed put, waiting, like she'd patiently waited when she'd been watching Miles. Counting her breaths and keeping her body pinned against a tree, she saw a faint movement off to her right a minute later. She waited, holding her breath, then saw the reflection of a mammalian retina as it checked her out before skittering away. The size and movement suggested a possum.

Hopefully there wasn't a big, bad bear chasing it.

The concentration of brown bears in these mountains was the largest in the world. Just her luck, she'd run into one. Nico and MI6 would both get cheated.

The crazy irony—or maybe the bone-deep chill spreading in her veins—nearly made her laugh out loud. Instead she took a fortifying, icy breath and continued her journey.

The cabin's nearly invisible footprint helped whoever was inside stay hidden. Sneaking up on it without being seen wasn't the easiest, but the overgrowth helped her keep her presence a secret. She scanned the area for trip wires or sensors of any kind. No cameras hanging in the trees, no appearance that any human presence had been there in a long, long time.

Nine months, perhaps?

Still, she took her time, retracing her steps around the place multiple times. When she was sure there were no security hurdles outside, she shimmied up to one of the cabin's windows, removed her night vision goggles and peered inside.

Squares of moonlight shone on the living room floor. The couple of pieces of furniture were right where she and Miles had left them, logs still stacked next to the fireplace. Because the cabin was little more than two rooms and a bath, the bedroom and living room were one. She could just make out the corner of the bed, the edge of a sheet draping down to the floor.

The last time she had been here, she had been with Miles.

Now she was back and he was with her. They couldn't climb the mountain and explore the cave until daylight. Thank God the cabin was still here so they had a place to warm up and sleep.

And maybe do a few other things.

She edged around to look in the kitchen window and saw the same tableau as the living room. Everything frozen in time. Mugs she'd washed out and left to drain on a dishtowel on the counter. A couple pieces of dried kindling piled on the floor near the wood-burning stove. It looked exactly the way it had when she left it.

The best part of this scenario was that she was almost done with this mission. Maybe, just maybe, unlike last time, she and Miles actually had a chance at a future together.

Charlotte jimmied the lock on the back door and let herself in. A quick survey of the rooms revealed no hidden cameras or bugs.

She grabbed her two-way radio and hit the button. "All clear, Miles."

She hoped that after this mission their future was all clear too.

All clear.

Miles heard the words but for him nothing was clear. The snow, the cold, the mountain towering over him...

He couldn't breathe. Memories flashed through his mind. The screams, the explosion, the fire. Men he knew and loved gone in a ball of flames.

SEALs didn't refer to each other as brothers for no reason.

His memories of that night were sketchy. He'd been positioned to lead his team, first man out of the helicopter. When the warning came from the pilot that a missile was headed their way, he hadn't had time to react before the helo tilted.

He was tossed out, his next memory that of falling, the snow below and the sky above becoming a single blur of white and gray. He remembered hitting the ground, bouncing, hitting again and rolling, eating snow as he went. Before he came to a stop, the helicopter exploded. Shock and pain roared through him, his vision blinded by the explosion, the sudden loss.

The memories continued in full blown high-def. Debris rained down, screams bouncing off the side of the mountain. His world had turned upside down.

"Miles?" Charlotte's voice woke him from his reverie, concern lacing her tone. "Are you there?"

The memories were still thick as the fog rising from the trees as he clicked on his radio. "Copy that," he said, his voice ragged. "On my way."

"There's a tree down across the lane that leads to the cabin. You'll have to leave the truck there and walk the rest of the way."

Nothing could be easy with this trip. Shaking off the memories of the past, he drove the truck to the spot, eyed the tree intersecting the lane. It wasn't your normal sized pine. This thing was an ancient behemoth that appeared to have toppled down the mountain. There was no moving it.

He grabbed his backpack and started hiking the last quarter mile to the cabin. Physical movement helped keep the memories at bay, but the sucking black hole in his chest burned with every breath. His ankle—the one he'd broken in his fall that day—ached with every step up the mountainside. At least his route to the cabin was more direct than Charlotte's had been since he didn't have to worry about avoiding surveillance.

She opened the cabin's front door upon his approach. She was smiling from ear to ear, like a 1950's housewife greeting her husband after he'd had a long day at work. "Everything is just as we left it. We can sleep in an actual bed tonight."

He nodded, following her inside.

She'd lit an oil lamp that gave off a soft glow, chattering about how much she loved the cabin. When he didn't respond, she turned to face him. "Is everything okay?"

"Yeah." Dropping his backpack next to the fireplace, he glanced around. The place seemed like it had been stuck in a time warp. It was smaller than he remembered, smelled less like Charlotte and more like musty linens and old wood.

His hands shook as he removed his gloves. "I'll get a fire going."

Which was the last thing he wanted to do. The cabin was freezing, so they needed heat, but the flashbacks had left him jittery. Starting a fire would only trigger the memories again.

He had to fight them. Had to remember the breathing

techniques Beatrice, of all people, had taught him to calm his mind and his emotions.

Long inhale, hold it for three counts, long exhale.

Repeat.

Charlotte disappeared into the tiny kitchen in the back. "No humans have been in here since we left," she called, "but the mice have had a merry time of it."

The wood chunks were as dry as the cold air outside. All he needed was some kindling to get things started. A stack of old magazines sat on the floor next to the bed. He grabbed one and started ripping out pages, crushing them in his hands and stuffing them under the logs still sitting in the grate. When he had enough, he opened the flue, lit the kindling, and watched the glossy magazine pages curl in on themselves. Flames inched higher, catching the logs that hadn't finished burning the last time he'd been here.

He still remembered dousing them, Emit Petit waiting patiently for him outside. It was the second worst night of his life. Leaving Charlotte behind. Not understanding why she'd abandoned him.

The note.

He whirled around, gaze locking on the bookshelf near the window. He'd left a note stuck in her favorite book, *Harry Potter and The Chamber of Secrets*, knowing she would find it after he was gone. But she'd never read it because she hadn't returned to the cabin.

The book was tattered, well-worn from Charlotte's readings. She'd rarely let a day go by without reading something from it. He fumbled it open, searching for his note. Pages flipped under his fingers.

Where was it?

He turned the book upside down and shook it.

Nothing. The note was gone.

"There should be oil for the generator outside," she said. "Do you think it will still work?"

He looked up. "What?"

"The generator. Do you think it will still work if we prime it? I've got soup heating on the wood stove but I'd love some actual light and running water."

The generator. Right. He thumbed through the book one more time. Why did his brain feel like he was moving through quicksand? One wrong move and he'd be sucked into a pit of shit he'd never be able to climb out of. He'd left a note. Where was it? Had he placed it in a different book by mistake?

Charlotte touched his arm. He hadn't even noticed she'd moved to stand beside him. "Harry Potter. I've missed these stories."

He handed the book to her and watched her slender fingers flip through the pages. Maybe his note was in a different book.

No. I put it in that one. I know I did.

"Miles?" Charlotte was staring up at him. "Are you sure you're okay?"

"Yeah." He shook off the brain freeze, ran his gaze over the bookcase. He was losing it. It had been nine months and he'd been through a traumatic experience. Hell, he still couldn't remember everything that had happened when the helo was blown from the sky and he'd passed out afterward. His memory was simply faulty, no way around it. The note had to be in one of the other books. "I'll go check on that generator."

Escaping outside, he took a deep breath. He needed closure, resolution. He couldn't go through the rest of his life with this guilt hanging over his head.

The only way to find resolution in what had happened was to hunt down the bastard who'd killed his teammates.

He would. He would find the man and bring justice to his friends. First light, they'd get to the caves and retrieve the USB. He'd get a copy of that video, figure out who the terrorist was. Beatrice and Rory could run face recognition on him. Something. Miles would find him before MI6. He had to.

This was personal.

For now, he needed to compartmentalize. The physical work required to prime the generator and get it running helped. He noticed Charlotte's portable satellite nearby and considered rigging it up and seeing if he could connect to the outside world. But that would send a signal out and he couldn't risk the wrong person seeing it. So he left the satellite alone and gathered wood from the pile stacked near the back door.

Stomping the snow off his boots inside, he heard Charlotte humming from the living room. His mind flashed back to another memory...this one a good one. One that made his body ache with longing.

He stood in the archway between the rooms, listening to her clear, soft voice and a low throbbing set up shop in his groin. She sat facing the fire, a heavy mug in her hand. The same mug she'd fed him from dozens of times until he could sit up and hold the damn thing himself.

The song she hummed haunted his dreams. The flickering light from the fire played across her features. She'd removed her coat and sweatshirt, the thin material of the cotton shirt she wore outlining her heavy breasts and flat stomach.

He remembered waking one cold night when he was still half immobile and in pain from his numerous contusions and broken ankle. Charlotte was bathing herself by the firelight, the tiny bathroom so cold she probably couldn't stand to undress in there. She'd thought he was sleeping, and as she hummed that tune, she peeled off one section of clothes at a time and washed from the hot water in a pot over the fire.

The luscious skin of her neck and shoulders came first, the washcloth rubbing, circling, running over her body like the hand of a lover. Then her breasts, her rosy nipples tightening in the cool air.

The scent of her soap mixed with the smell of the burning wood and the salve she had spread on his bruised ribs and hips. She'd moved delicately down her ribs, over her stomach, back up. Once finished, she'd drawn on a soft flannel pajama top, then went to work taking off her pants, socks, underwear.

He shouldn't have watched. He barely knew her then, barely understood why he was in her cabin and his teammates were all dead.

Her skin, her movements, her sheer beauty mesmerized him. He couldn't look away as she'd run the washcloth down her long legs, between the juncture of her thighs...

"Miles?"

Once again, Charlotte was close to him and he didn't know how. He hadn't seen her move.

She held out the mug. "Are you ready for some soup?"

Dropping the logs, he knew he was ready for more than that. "Smells good," he said, taking the mug. For half a second, his mind tried to derail again and get lost in flashbacks. He shoved them away. He was here, with Charlotte, now. Their past didn't matter. Only tonight did.

So he set down the mug and reached for her.

CHAPTER FOURTEEN

Charlotte wasn't expecting Miles to grab her.

He reached out, wrapped a hand around her wrist and tugged her to him. "I don't really want soup," he said.

She let out a little "oh", and fell forward into his chest.

He smelled like fresh air, pine tree sap, and Miles. His lips came down on hers, demanding, needy, like a man who'd been trapped in the desert for too long without water and had suddenly found a well full.

She relished it, sighing into his mouth as she parted her lips and granted him access. She wrapped her arms around his neck, dug her fingers into his hair, gently tugging.

He growled low in his throat, just the way she remembered from their last stint in the cabin. That sound made everything in her sit up and give a cheer. This was what she'd been waiting for, dreaming of, not realizing it would ever actually come true.

She'd worshipped his injured body the last time they'd been alone here. Took her time—what else did they have, being snowed in?—and enjoyed the equal amount of attentiveness he'd given her. Those memories had helped her survive Nico, but had left her oh-so-hungry for more.

Heat and desire rushing through her veins, she couldn't wait a second longer. She wanted Miles, needed him. Every. Last. Drop.

Tugging at the buttons on his coat, she worked them loose and shoved the coat off his shoulders, never breaking their kiss. His hands were busy, too, massaging her breasts through her shirt, lifting the hem and touching her bare stomach with his fingers.

"I'm not really interested in soup right now, either," she said on a fast exhale.

His return grin was wolfish, possessive. "How about a little dessert first?"

They took turns undressing each other. She had to release his lips when he pulled her shirt up and over her head. She did the same to his.

Pants went next, then underwear, all the while their hands, lips, tongues, touching, stroking, teasing. Charlotte was panting like a runner when Miles backed her up against a low buffet—an antique mahogany piece that held quilts and pillows. The only article of clothing she still had on was her socks, refusing to put her bare feet on the cold wooden floor.

Miles, on the other hand, didn't seem to feel the cold. He stood before her completely naked, that feral, wolfish look darkening his eyes as he let his gaze travel over her. The cross necklace hung between his pectorals and his arousal left no doubt in her mind of his need. "I've waited a long time for this," he said.

He stepped between her legs, hooked his hands behind her thighs and lifted her onto the top of the buffet in one fluid motion. Candleholders and a bowl of pinecones went flying.

Charlotte laughed, wrapping her legs around his hips as she gripped the edge of the buffet. "Your patience is about to be rewarded."

But instead of plunging into her, he slid a finger down her throat and placed his hand on her heart. "I barely know you, but I've never wanted any woman the way I want you."

Her skin warmed under his hand, her heart beating solid and sure in her chest. "I'm sorry to bring you back to this place. I know it must call up memories you'd rather not think about. That's one of the reasons I wanted to come alone. Not just to keep you out of danger, but to keep you from having flashbacks about the crash."

He closed his eyes, his hand falling from her heart, and the shadow she'd seen earlier passed once more over his features. For a moment, she was afraid she'd lost him again. That he was reliving what had happened to him and his SEAL team.

But then he opened his eyes, the haunted look disappearing. "I will find the terrorist who ordered the helo blown out of the sky, and I will take justice for my men."

She should tell him she knew the terrorist's name, that

Madeena was the man's daughter and knew his hiding places. But putting Madeena in danger, making her give up the goods on her father, wasn't fair to the girl. "When I take down Nico's crime ring, we'll get the info from him."

"Yeah, maybe," Miles said. "For now, I don't want to think about the past or the future. I want to focus on you, right here, right now."

Charlotte didn't want to wait any longer. She gripped the hair at the back of his head and drew him to her. His erection pressed against her wet folds, parting them slowly, inch by inch.

Groaning, she widened her thighs and arched her back, her nipples brushing against his chest. "God, stop teasing me," she said, barely able to find her breath. "We've waited too damn long already."

He grinned and then thrust into her in one, long, singular motion.

Finally! She gasped, closing her eyes and enjoying the sensation, his hands on her hips holding her still.

When he didn't move, she opened her eyes. His head was tipped back slightly, eyes closed, as if he, too, were enjoying the perfection of their joined bodies.

She smiled to herself. His head came back to center, eyes half-lidded as he met hers. He drew back slightly and drove into her again, building a rhythm as she clutched the buffet.

His rapid fire thrusts rocked the furniture, scooting the feet backward on the floor until it was pinned up against the wall. She met him thrust for fierce thrust, reveling as he pushed deeper and deeper. He reached back and gripped her ankles, raising them higher and tipping her upper back against the wall.

Leaning over, he brought his mouth down and kissed the scar that crossed her collarbone, let his tongue trace the line. His thumb found the sensitive spot between her folds and she jumped at the dual sensations. He was attacking all her vulnerable spots at once, making her feel beautiful, wanted.

Safe.

Just when she thought she couldn't take it a moment longer, he slid his hands under her buttocks and lifted her hips another inch. At the same time he pushed into her, pleasure ripping through her veins as everything in her cried out. "Oh, God, Miles. *Yesyesyes!*"

He drove inside her one more time, and she sank her nails

into his back, arching into the mind-blowing explosion of her orgasm. As her body pulsed and quaked around him, he froze for a moment, every inch of him hard as stone.

He threw his head back and cursed as he came in a rush, her name spilling from his lips.

"I've got you," she whispered, squeezing her legs around him and tightened her core, milking him and drawing out the aftermath of their furniture-moving sex.

He pinned her to the buffet with his last thrust, then dropped his head onto her shoulder.

"And I've got you," he said, holding her tight.

⌐————••————⌐

Miles slept late again.

He didn't mean to. The plan was to get up with the sun and take off for the caves. After a night of nonstop sex, though, he was exhausted.

Charlotte murmured next to him, curling into his chest. Sunlight shone through the window, spotlighting their abandoned clothes on the floor. The fire had gone out and the cabin was chilly.

Miles pulled Charlotte closer, tucking his arm around her and kissing the top of her head. He wished he could stay there with one of her legs thrown across his, the real world kept at bay.

They were good together. Had been from the start. A part of him wished Charlotte didn't care about her mission. That he didn't feel the driving need to hunt down a terrorist. The two of them could stay at the cabin, tucked into the mountainside and live unencumbered lives.

A pipe dream, that was. Nothing but a fucking pipe dream.

Charlotte shifted, waking and stretching. Fingernails trailed over his chest and he went rock hard again.

God, how many times had they done it? It was like they couldn't get their fill. The sheets smelled like sex. Charlotte's hand glided down under the sheet and tickled his morning erection.

"Hmm. Look what I found," she giggled.

And that was all it took. He flipped both of them over, pulling her underneath him. Her legs parted without hesitation and she cupped his ass cheeks, slamming him home with no warm up. Didn't matter. She was wet and ready.

Although she wanted him to take her fast and hard, he slowed things down, keeping the rhythm smooth and steady. She begged him to speed up, but he wouldn't. He wanted the moment to last this time. To etch fresh memories of her under him in his mind.

When they were done, panting and boneless once more, he collapsed on top of her. She wound her hands through his hair, down his shoulders, and traced the line of his spine with her cool fingers. "I don't want this to end."

Relief that she felt the same way he did flooded his exhausted body. Relief plus something more. Something he didn't want to name that had hit him during the night. No matter how many times he fucked her, it wasn't enough. He would never get her out of his system.

His chest felt tight and he distracted himself by nibbling her ear and listening to her lighthearted giggle. "We'll come back after you clear your name and Nicolae Bourean is behind bars."

They stayed tangled in each other's arms for a few more blissful moments, then got up. Miles stoked the fire. Charlotte heated water for them to wash with. He enjoyed her graceful movements as she cleaned herself, then went to work on him. She'd removed the blue contacts during the night and her brown eyes glittered with flecks of gold in the morning sunlight coming through the window. He tried not to stare at the scars on her back, tried not to let anger work its way back under his skin.

He failed.

When Charlotte finished washing him and he was hard once more, she went to her knees and took him in her mouth. His vision went white from the sensation. As she expertly worked him over, he tangled one hand in her hair and used the other to grab onto the fireplace mantel. He mentally vowed he wouldn't lose her this time.

Never again.

They eventually managed to dress and repacked their backpacks. Breakfast was protein bars and coffee they'd brought from the plane. "We'll need the bag of silverware from under the truck seat," Charlotte said, washing out the mugs that had worked for soup the night before and coffee that morning. "Could you grab it?"

They would be heading to the caves on foot since the truck was stuck halfway down the winding lane. From what he understood, they wouldn't have gone far before having to ditch the truck anyway. There was no other way to get into the mountain that deep except on foot.

"What do we need the bag for?" he asked.

She rinsed her mug and set it on a towel to dry next to his. As if they would be back in a few hours. "The same reason we needed it on the road into this area."

"For bribes? There are outlaws in the caves?"

"Not exactly. There are Gypsies who travel the tunnels and can make passage difficult if you don't pay their security fee." She made air quotes around the last two words. "They're harmless, really, but they're also the caretakers of the caves we're going to. They protect the property left there, sort of like the goblins at Gringotts Wizarding Bank in Harry Potter."

Fictional goblins seemed almost preferable. "I'll get the bag."

When he returned, bag in hand, Charlotte was sticking *The Chamber of Secrets* in her backpack. He glanced at the bookshelf. He'd forgotten to look for the note in the other books there.

"Just so you know," Charlotte said. "I now believe someone was here in the cabin after we left."

"Who?"

"I'm not sure, but possibly my handler."

"You said everything was the same as when we left it."

"It is, almost." She pointed at her backpack. "That Harry Potter book? It's not mine."

"What do you mean it's not yours?"

"I didn't notice it until now." Her gaze darted to the window, back to him. She grabbed her coat, suddenly all business and making Miles' internal radar go on high alert. "Let's get out of here. I'll tell you on the way."

CHAPTER FIFTEEN

Beatrice was half a mile into her walking workout in the SFI training center when her playlist was interrupted by an incoming call.

"Zebulon," she greeted him. "Any update on CB Norris?"

"I ain't calling you to give you an update on my hemorrhoids, girlie."

Zeb's coarseness made him infinitely likable in her book. "Good, because I'm not interested in those."

He laughed. "Norris could be trouble, but then you already knew that, didn't you?"

"Correct. That's why I asked you to look into him. What did you find?"

"Nothing."

Beatrice slowed her pace. Her walks were becoming increasingly more challenging with the weight of the baby. "What do you mean nothing? You just said he could be trouble."

"Exactly. He's being a good boy, doing the Queen's bidding, and keeping his nose out of trouble in Romania. He only has one operative, but from my calculations, he has over a dozen assets he's running in that area. Lots of HUMIN, not a lot of action."

Human intel. Old school spy craft, but important even in this day and age.

Zeb went on. "His mission is to take out Nicolae Bourean,

but in two years, he's done little more than keep an eye on the POS."

"What do you believe he's doing? Is Bourean bribing him off?"

"Possibly, but my guess is, he's biding his time with the little fish while he goes after the whale."

Beatrice stopped, and used the towel around her neck to wipe perspiration from her forehead. "The ulterior motive you mentioned the other day?"

"Bingo. He likes big game. Terrorists. One of the men who came up through bin Laden's ranks was a guy known only as Blackwater. The kid joined bin Laden when he was fifteen, became one of his commanders. Norris had a boner for him back in the day too."

"Blackwater. I remember his file crossing my desk at NSA. He's a recruiter now, correct? Setting up terrorist cells all over Europe, with no single affiliation to any group."

Zeb coughed and cleared his throat. "You got it. The man's allegiance isn't to al Qaeda or anyone else. It's simply to destroy the West, America. Any group who agrees with that mission, any radical who believes in that cause, he helps them."

"Norris missed bin Laden," Beatrice mused. "He wants Blackwater."

"Bet you can't guess where the latest human intel suggests Blackwater is hiding out?"

Beatrice started walking again, but this time, she was headed to the locker room. "Romania," she sighed. "The Carpathian mountains."

"Give the lady a gold star."

"You might want to clear your schedule, Zeb."

"Oh, yeah? Why's that?"

She hit the locker room door. "I'll be in touch."

ROMANIA

The forest was primordial, ancient. Like the magical forest in a fairytale.

The Southern Carpathian Mountains were often referred to

as the Transylvanian Alps. The entrance to the cave Charlotte sought was only a few miles away, but required a steep, uneven climb up the mountainside through a forest that had been untouched by man. There were no hikers here, no tourists, or castles turned into day spas. Only virgin forest, wild animals, and the leftovers of the Ice Age.

She'd added a layer of clothing from her trunk at the cabin; found a pair of woolen socks for inside her boots. Miles had brought hand warmers from the plane and they'd broken them open and slid them inside their gloves.

He walked behind her, letting her lead the way. She put her foot up on a rocky outcropping, grabbed a tree trunk to help her leverage over it. "There's a harmony here, don't you think?" she asked him. "A sacredness, pure and beautiful."

A bird trilled in the canopy of trees hanging over them. "Sure," he answered, not sounding like he cared much. His hand landed on her lower back, steading her as she climbed onto the outcropping. "Tell me about the book."

"Ah, yes, the book." She tried not to sound out of breath, but it was difficult. The cold air, mixed with the high altitude and the difficult climb, left her feeling winded and they'd only been going a mile or so.

"It was my cheat sheet for a code system CB Norris and I used to communicate."

"A cheat sheet?"

"The closest village is small but has a solid tourist base coming to see their castles and old-world charm along the river. It's part of Nico's chain of towns where he runs his business dealings all the way down to Bucharest and where I first made contact with him." She crossed the rocky plateau and hopped off the other side. "There's a library inside one of the restored castles that has a sizable collection of books and documents dating back to Medieval times. They carry classics as well. No one checks the books out, mind you, but you can go in and sit at the tables and read whatever you like. Modern classics, like the Harry Potter series, are also on their shelves."

A black squirrel chattered at them from a nearby tree. Another sat off to their left, digging in the snow, probably looking for an acorn he had buried. "When I had a message for him, I would leave it in that library's copy of *The Chamber of Secrets* by circling letters inside the book with a pencil very lightly, thus creating my message. I would leave a bookmark inside the book containing the numbers of the pages where the message was. He would go to the library and retrieve it by finding the letters I'd circled. It was slow, but effective, since I never knew when he was in town and cell service was so unreliable. Plus, he's very old school. Doesn't like cell phones or in-person meetings. Someone is always watching, according to him. Always listening."

"Slick," Miles said, jumping down from the outcropping as Charlotte continued on toward the next one. As they gained elevation, they also gained more snow. "So you would create the message in your copy of the book first, then use it when you got to the library to transfer it."

"It was much more efficient that way. He would erase the marks in the library's copy after he read the message, and I would do the same in mine to prep it for the next one."

"So how do you know the book in your backpack isn't yours?"

"The contact information—a phone number—for Emit Petit is missing."

"You wrote that in the book?"

Her fingers were stiff. She stopped and cupped her gloved hands, blowing on them for a moment. "In code. After the initial time I had to call him, I coded the number into the book just in case I ever needed it again, using page numbers and number references in the manuscript. In this copy,"—she patted the backpack—"those marks are missing. I didn't notice it last night when I thumbed through the pages, but the book felt different. I couldn't put my finger on it, and then we got a little…sidetracked…before I had a chance to really go through it. This morning, I took a closer look. I've had the same copy of *The Chamber of Secrets* since my, uh, incarceration as a young girl. I know my book; the weight of it, the feel of the pages I've read hundreds of times. The copy that you pulled off the shelf is worn like mine, and I can see past pencil marks on the pages that have been erased, but this copy is not the one I've owned since I was eleven."

Miles caught up to her, took her gloved hands and rubbed them between his. The sun was bright overhead, but filtered where they stood underneath the canopy of trees. "You think it's your handler's?"

"That's exactly what I think, only I don't know why. Why he would change them out? He probably came to the cabin looking for me when I disappeared, but why exchange the books? And why didn't he tell me when I contacted him after I escaped Nico?"

Miles looked up. Sunlight and shadows dappled his face. He hadn't shaved in a couple of days, dark stubble lining his jaw—stubble that had tickled her skin last night in the most erotic ways.

He stopped rubbing her hands, but still held them inside of his. "I don't know if this has anything to do with it, but..."

A tightness crept into Charlotte's stomach as his voice trailed off. "But what?"

He sighed, tilted his head back down to look at her. "I left you a note in that book before Petit took me away."

"A note?"

His eyes shifted to the right. He released her hands. "I didn't understand why you'd left me there without saying goodbye. Petit gave me the song and dance about how I should just be grateful you'd saved me and contacted him. That people, especially my family members, were going to be thrilled to know I was still alive. They all thought I was dead. He said you weren't coming back to the cabin—that you'd told him little, only that you had to leave and wouldn't be back. It was time for me to go home."

Snow crunched under his feet as he took a step away, stared up at the mountain they were climbing. A few miles farther east, on the other side of the ridge, was the spot his helicopter had gone down. "I didn't think of America as my home so much anymore. I didn't want to go. I was angry, confused. I wrote you a note and stuck it in the book, believing if you ever did come back, you'd find it."

The tightness in her stomach moved up to her throat. "What did the note say?"

"That I... I hoped you'd change your mind about us. And if you did, to call me. I left my contact information in the note, along with some details about our time together. What it meant to me. How I didn't want to lose you, and, well, you get the idea."

A love note? He'd left her a romantic, if upset, love note?

Had he told her he loved her? Her heart thrummed in her ears. "I'm sorry I never got it."

He met her eyes. "Me, too."

They stayed that way for a moment, lost in the quiet of the forest and each other's gazes.

The moment passed too quickly when a bird overhead squawked at them and a shadow moved over the sun. "We better keep moving," he said.

She wanted to call him back, to hold onto that moment. Her heart hurt inside her chest watching him walk away, and she put a hand on a nearby tree trunk to steady herself.

The tree trunk was solid, enduring. She looked up at the leaves fluttering overhead. *You should have said it. I love you. It's three words.*

Three words she hadn't said to anyone in years. The last person had been Lanny, her brother.

Patting the tree trunk, she wished something in her life would endure with the same tenacity these mountains had. Hauling herself up the embankment, it was hard to think about her missing book and why CB would have taken it when all she could think about was the words Miles had written in that note. He couldn't bring himself to say he loved her now, what made her think he'd actually said it then?

Words, she learned a long time ago, didn't matter. Actions did.

They trudged on, the snow beginning to slow their steps as it got deeper, but they were close to the cave entrance. She checked her map again. The tunnels went through this part of the mountain from one side to the other, but they also went deeper down, where the safe was hidden.

"My younger sister, Cricket, is a Harry Potter fan," Miles said a few minutes later, breaking the silence between them. "She grew up on the books and movies and was totally in love with Harry. She dressed up as Hermione every year at Halloween and slept in robes."

An invitation to talk about something except their current situation—an olive branch? Charlotte wasn't used to talking about the past, but talking passed the time and made the climb less daunting. "When I was in the mental hospital, I dreamed Hagrid would show up and break me out. I wanted to believe I was special, like Harry, and someone somewhere would see the good in me like my mother had always done before she was murdered. That they would take me away to a new life."

He grabbed one of her hands, clenched it as they climbed side by side. "You *are* special."

If only that were true.

"The magic of Harry Potter is in that belief," she said,

enjoying his steadying presence on the rocky path. "That each of us is the chosen one, and no matter what happens in the real world—the Muggle world—we know there's another enchanted world out there where magic is real. We want to believe we've been chosen for a great purpose, and that love will keep us safe in the end, no matter what evil we face. I clung to that idea all through my childhood."

The forest thinned and they walked into a clearing. Her teeth were chattering and her toes felt numb. "There." Charlotte pointed.

Miles followed her outstretched finger, squinted, and sounded baffled. "There what? I don't see anything but brush and rocks."

Her lips were cold, but they could still form a smile. "Exactly," she said, a buoyant feeling invading her chest. There was still the next daunting obstacle to get over, but she had a plan to ensure success. "That's the cave."

CHAPTER SIXTEEN

He'd never realized when they were snowed in at the cabin, just how far it had been from the helicopter's crash site. "How in the world did you get me through these tunnels all the way down to your cabin when I was unconscious?" Miles asked.

Charlotte was a few steps ahead of him, her flashlight's beam bouncing over the walls. The tunnels curved and twisted, intersecting here and there like snakes slithering over each other. At points, veins of ice ran through the walls and stalactites hung down, while at those warmed by nearby hot springs, moss covered the walls.

Even with his extensive training, he couldn't make heads or tails of them, yet Charlotte seemed to have no trouble at all.

Every once in a while, Charlotte's light would land on a notch in the cave wall or a cleft or scratch on the floor and she would say, "this way" and take him off into another tunnel. They'd been going downhill for the past fifty yards or so. "I had a little help," she said.

Help? Her soft voice seemed at odds in the harsh, rocky environment. He heard the trickle of water up ahead, but the low-hanging ceiling played havoc with sounds. The caves had a different type of quiet than the forest. A tight, airless quality that resonated with the earth and what was long ago buried here. Even the sound of his own breathing seemed to echo back at him.

He kept his own flashlight beam on the floor so he didn't trip from the stalagmites that seemed to pop up when he least expected them. They hadn't met up with any of the cave dwellers she'd told him about and that was just as well. The fewer people who knew they were in these parts, the better. "What kind of help?"

Knowing her, she'd built a travois to carry his bruised and broken body, but navigating these tunnels and then the forest outside while pulling him behind her couldn't have been easy. In fact, he'd wager it was downright impossible.

She rounded a bend without answering, disappearing out of his sight momentarily. "Come on," he heard her call. "It's up here."

Well, that had been easier than he'd thought if they were already to the spot she'd hidden the USB. Once they had that, he'd get Charlotte back to the plane, send Beatrice a copy of the video and see if she could get a positive ID on the terrorist and his last known location. With any luck, the man was still somewhere in these mountains. Either way, Bourean would know. Once Miles had Charlotte safely back with Jax, Jax could take her to London and let her clear her name. Meanwhile, Miles was going back for Nicolae Bourean and his accomplice. He had a score to settle.

Miles went around the bend and nearly conked his head on a stalactite hanging down from the ceiling. The tunnel grew smaller so that he had to scrunch over to keep going, the echo of Charlotte's footsteps shepherding him forward.

He caught the slightest whiff of fresh air. Light flickered on the ground, stronger than what Charlotte's flashlight could give off. As Miles went down on his hands and knees, hunkering down even tighter to squeeze through another, even smaller opening, he wondered if there was a hole in the ceiling far above them, allowing light and air to circulate.

Which meant he just had to hold his breath, squeeze a little tighter, shift his shoulders to the left, and...

He dug his heels in and gave a push, angling his body at the same time. With a grunt, he popped through the tunnel hole and landed on his right shoulder.

Light met his eyes as he rolled over. Above him, Charlotte's face appeared as he sucked in a deep breath and let his chest expand to normal size again.

"Hi." She smiled down at him. Her face was bathed in a golden glow, not from an overhead skylight, but from sconces burning on the walls that had opened up. "Glad you could make it. You looked like Santa trying to get down the chimney."

"You didn't tell me I'd have to squeeze through a pin head."

One of her gloved hands reached down. He grabbed it and let her help him up. He stopped short when he saw a man with a scraggy beard, long hair, and a tattoo on the left side of his neck, staring at him.

The guy was a giant, at least two-fifty, his arms and legs the size of tree trunks. He stood with arms crossed over a massive chest and belly. He wore a scraggly beard and his long hair was pulled back in a ponytail.

Miles automatically went for his gun. "Who the hell is that?"

"The help I told you about earlier?" Charlotte said, a quirky smile dancing over her lips. "This is Moose. Moose, you remember Miles. You two have already met, but Miles, you were unconscious at the time."

The man's gaze was on Miles' hand where it hovered over his weapon. The name Moose fit him, but Hagrid might have been a better one. "Do you need the silverware?" he said low under his breath.

She patted his arm. "Not yet."

Moose spoke to her, but it was in a language Miles didn't understand. There was Romanian and broken English mixed with what he suspected was Gypsy *jibs*, a dialect of words Charlotte had told him about.

Charlotte replied, also in a mix of languages. Then in English, she asked, "How is Renalda?"

The man's gaze bounced away, back to Charlotte's face. He swallowed hard, his Adam's apple bobbing up and down sharply. His voice fit his body. "She is…unwell."

"She didn't have a change of heart about the chemo, I take it?"

He shook his head, looked down at the floor.

"Renalda is a distant aunt of my mother's," Charlotte explained. "She has lung cancer. Her whole clan lives in the caves during the winter when it's too harsh to live outside."

Although the caves were interesting, why anyone would want to live in them was beyond him. "She's related to you?"

"I knew when I took this assignment I would have the chance to return to my mother's birthplace, to possibly find a part of my family's history. The whole time I was here, I never got anywhere with my research until the day I hid in this cave and watched Bourean's men shoot down the plane. Renalda and her clan heard the crash, came to see what had happened and discovered me. They started to chase me away, but Renalda recognized something of my mother in me. My aura, she says, but I'm guessing it was my eyes. I have my mum's eyes. They look like Renalda's own. I told her I was a mixed blood Gypsy, who my parents were, and explained my situation. She and her clan are the guardians of the safes inside this cave. The family has been entrusted for centuries with the wealth and valuables hidden down here. The cross necklace you're wearing belongs to her. The USB is in Renalda's own personal safe."

The secrets this woman had. "And why didn't you tell me this before?"

"Would it have made a difference?"

He supposed not. "Why not just call her and ask her to send you the USB?"

Charlotte chuckled. "There are no phones here. No electricity. This section of the cave is heated by a natural spring not far away from where they get water. It's said to have healing properties, and Renalda believed it would be enough to heal her." She glanced at Moose. "Apparently, it wasn't."

"Why not come directly here after you escaped Bourean?"

Moose grunted and said something in that hybrid language that made Charlotte smile. "Yes, he does ask a lot of questions, but he has the right to know." She spoke to Miles. "I needed the key."

"She's your great-aunt. Are you telling me she wouldn't open the safe unless you gave her the cross back?"

"There is only one key that fits the safe." She pointed to his chest. "That one. It's been in the family all these centuries and is hailed as having both a blessing and a curse as part of its makeup. It protects those who are worthy and protect it in turn. Anyone who misuses it or doesn't respect it is cursed with bad luck."

"You don't really believe that."

Another grunt issued from Moose, his belly jutting out at the sound.

"It doesn't matter what I believe, Miles. It's the Gypsy way. Renalda is leader of this clan and she bestowed a gift on me. She set your leg and gave me the salves to heal your cuts and bruises. She hid my valuables in her own personal safe and trusted me with a family heirloom to open it. I owe her a great debt. Now that we're here, we can return the necklace, retrieve the USB, and I can try to talk some sense into Renalda about the chemo. If she doesn't go to the doctor, she will die."

A man emerged from the opposite wall near Moose. Seeing Charlotte, he yelled and swept Charlotte up in his arms. Once again, Miles' hand went to his weapon, but Moose stepped forward as if to shield them.

"Timothy! Put me down," Charlotte said, but she was laughing as the man swung her in a circle before depositing her on her feet.

He was a smaller version of Moose. Just as tall, but lanky, with the same beard, long hair, and tattoo. The man looked Miles over from head to toe with beady eyes. "This is him? The man you rescued?"

At least Lanky spoke decent English, even if his accent was thick.

"Miles Duncan." Miles kept his hand loose and ready to reach for his gun. "And you are?"

Charlotte adjusted her jacket. "This is Renalda's son, Timothy. My second cousin."

Timothy picked up Charlotte's backpack and cocked his head toward the entrance he'd emerged from. "Renalda said you would honor your family and come back. We mustn't keep her waiting."

As Timothy disappeared into the tunnel, Charlotte looked at Miles and smiled. "I'll try to keep the family reunion short, but they *are* Gypsies. Prepare to be fed and take part in some dancing before we get out of here."

Dancing? Miles hesitated before following her, Moose's beady eyes watching him every step of the way.

The party was in full swing. Charlotte wiped sweat from the back of her neck, accepted a drink from Timothy. The up-tempo music echoed between the caves and Charlotte laughed as Miles tried to learn a dance step from a group of teen girls.

Renalda, a hundred pounds of jewelry on her frail body, sat next to Charlotte and laughed along with her.

"Your man is very serious," Renalda said, clapping her hands to the beat. "He has a long face."

Long face was Renalda's way of saying someone was somber and un-smiling. "He's been through a lot."

Miles glanced over, shooting Charlotte a *help me* look.

She gave him a thumbs-up.

Renalda smiled. "His face brightens when he looks at you."

Full of good food and enjoying this reprieve from the real world, Charlotte smiled back. Here, she could be herself. She could admit truths she couldn't outside these cave walls. "I love him."

"He did right, coming back with you. His aura is strong, bright."

Was Renalda giving her blessing? Her great-aunt believed she was gifted with the Sight and could predict outcomes, especially with love matches.

Charlotte humored her. "Are we compatible?"

Renalda stopped clapping. "You have difficulties to overcome."

True enough. Didn't answer her question, though. "If we succeed with those, do we have a chance?"

"His heart has darkness in it. Be careful, or he will pull you into that."

Miles had survivor's guilt and wanted revenge for the death of this men. Charlotte understood both. The darkness that lived inside her seemed a thousand times worse.

Miles had given her the cross earlier. She removed it from a pocket and held it up for Renalda to see. "Can we open the safe now?"

Renalda touched the cross as if it were a long, lost friend. Her rheumy eyes closed for a moment as she held it to her chest. Then she opened her eyes and took Charlotte's hand. Together, they stood, and Renalda lead her deep into the cave, leaving Miles behind.

CHAPTER SEVENTEEN

Heavy clouds rolled over the Transylvanian Alps as the sun dropped behind them. A storm was brewing—a bad one from the look of those clouds—and the hair on the back of Charlotte's neck stood up from the electrically charged air.

But she couldn't keep the smile off her face. She had the USB.

During the dancing and feasting, Miles had tugged her away from the festivities for a few minutes. In the shadows of the cave, he'd kissed her mindless and ran his hands under her shirt. They'd stayed that way, making out like a couple of kids for a long time. She'd wrapped her legs around his hips and he'd thumbed her through her pants until she cried out from an orgasm. Luckily, the music was loud and he'd smothered her mouth with his to keep their make-out session against a cave wall a secret.

They'd danced and ate and sang along with the songs even though they didn't understand the words Renalda taught them.

As she threaded her way down the mountain now, Miles a few steps behind her, she felt an undeniable lightness. Happiness she hadn't felt since their six weeks alone in the cabin.

From the look of the storm moving in, they might end up stuck in the cabin again.

"We need to get to the truck and get out of here before that storm hits," Miles called to her.

"We could end up driving right into it," Charlotte called back. The wind was picking up, the pine tree limbs above her head lifting and falling on the breeze. The creaking sound they produced was ominous. "I need to see a weather report. Maybe we can connect my portable satellite at the cabin to one of our phones and check the radar."

She paused as they crested a small ridge and saw the cabin down below, the last of the sun's rays peeking between the clouds and the mountain range and bathing the cabin in a soft peach glow.

A part of her wanted to stay in the cabin another night. One more night of just the two of them alone.

The practical part of her knew they could end up stranded here again. Storms here could dump multiple feet of snow in a matter of hours. They often came one right after the other with no let up in between.

Would that be so bad? a tiny voice inside her head asked.

It would, she mentally answered. She had the USB, but Madeena was still in Nico's possession. Without Charlotte there to buffer his attacks, Madeena was being subjected to all of his brutality, his sick appetites.

Miles stopped next to her, scanning the area around the cabin. She wondered if he, too, considered spending another night there.

He wasn't going to like it when she told him the second half of her plan—where she sent him on to hook up with Jaxon and get the USB to authorities while she went back for Madeena.

But no one was going anywhere until she checked on this storm system.

"Area looks clear," he noted as he started down the incline.

She followed. Once they reached the backside of the cabin, he handed her his backpack. "Go on in, see if you can copy what's on your USB to my laptop. I'll work on setting up the satellite."

Making a copy of the USB contents was a good idea, and since she planned to send Miles back to the plane while she went back for Madeena, he'd have a copy of the video while she hung on to the original. "I'll make some coffee."

He nodded, already working on standing up the satellite base.

Charlotte dumped the backpacks on the kitchen counter and filled the tea kettle with water. She lit the wood stove, and while the water heated, set up the mugs with a couple of teaspoons of instant coffee. Then she unloaded a very cold laptop from Miles' backpack and laid her gun on the counter.

She walked into the living area to set up the laptop and came to a dead stop.

The man sitting in front of the fireplace tapped a gun against his thigh. "Hello, Agent Carstons."

"CB?" Charlotte laughed out loud, the sound too loud in her ears. "Oh my God. What are you doing here?"

His bald head was covered with a black, knit stocking hat. The rest of his outfit was all black, too. "Looking for you, of course."

"But how did you know I was here?"

"I followed you. At least for awhile. You're a slick fish to catch, Carstons. Almost had you in San Diego, then again at the airport. But you evaded me." He chuckled. "I knew you'd come back here. It was only a matter of time."

This didn't make sense. "You...? I'm sorry, did you say you followed me to San Diego?"

He nodded, the cat who'd swallowed the canary.

A scary sense of understanding snaked across her mind. "You sent the men at Van Nuys."

A wink. "You catch on fast."

"But why? Why would you turn me into MI6 when you know I have to clear my name."

He held out a gloved hand. "The USB. Hand it over."

It was in her pocket. She had no intention of giving it to him.

Her head felt heavy, a new kind of cold seeping into her system. Resentment, disbelief. He'd betrayed her.

Hurt, sharp and brutal, stung inside her chest.

The only question was, in how many ways? "What do you want with the USB?"

"I promised Nicolae he could have it."

Charlotte kept herself from glancing at the gun in his hand. "You're in cahoots with Nico?"

Another smug smile.

"You set it up to look like it was me in order to cover your own arse."

Norris dropped his outstretched hand and smiled. "Surprised you didn't figure that out before, but you were a little busy, weren't you? Fucking the SEAL, being tortured by Nicolae, going on the run from MI6."

Hysteria rose inside her. She needed to get that gun away from him. *Keep him talking.*

"Why sell out to Nico?" Covertly, she adjusted her grip on the laptop. Thoughts settling once more, she figured she might have to use it as a shield or whip it at his head to create a diversion. "You're a patriot through and through. You hate scum like Nicolae Bourean."

"He's the key to tracking down the man I've been chasing for years. The one that got away. The one whose capture will put me in the history books."

"What are you talking about?"

"The terrorist you said you have on the video. He's mine."

Madeena's father. "Why do you want him?"

"I didn't get bin Laden. He's second on my bucket list."

He was nuts. If she kept him talking along enough, Miles would come in. Two against one, they could take him. "I'll help you take him down."

He laughed as if this were the best joke he'd heard in forever. "You're helping all right, but not like that." He raised his gun. "Give me the USB."

Where was Miles? "I'm sorry, I can't do that."

"The hell you can't."

Time to lie. "I don't have it."

She could see in his eyes that he didn't believe her, but he played along for a moment. "And why is that? Your boyfriend has it?"

She could tell him they'd lost the key. That the Gypsies wouldn't allow her to get to the safe. That someone had stolen the USB. Anything to throw him off.

But even if he did believe her, she couldn't put her relations in jeopardy or risk him seeing the necklace around Miles' neck. Renalda had given it back to him as a keepsake. CB would shoot first, ask questions later. "I lost it in the woods."

"Bullshit. Hand it over Carstons or I'll kill your boyfriend."

At that moment, the kitchen door flew open, banging against the wall. Charlotte turned, ready to yell a warning at Miles, when she saw a man crowd through the opening and drop Miles to the floor.

Eyes closed, body limp, he lay unmoving. He was bleeding from a cut over his temple. A lump was forming around it.

"Oh, my God." Charlotte ran to his side, setting the laptop on the floor as she knelt next to him. Cold air rushed in around them from the open door.

Miles was unconscious. She touched his neck, felt a pulse, saw the slow rise of his chest. "What the hell did you do to him?" she said to the man blocking doorway.

MISTY EVANS

And then she looked up and her heart stopped beating for a second.

He was older than in her memories, but still wore the same mustache that curled at the ends. His dark hair was shot through with gray now, his skin leathery and wrinkled.

But his eyes. She saw the same dead look in them that she'd seen when he'd fixed the plumbing and lighting in her mother's shop...

Charlotte couldn't breathe, couldn't think.

"You remember Orlo," CB said.

"You." She jumped to her feet, hands curling into fists. "You killed my mother."

"Your mother was a beautiful creature." CB strolled over to the counter, his gun trained on her as he snagged hers and stuffed it in his coat. "It was a shame she had to be disposed of."

Wait. Charlotte whirled to face him. "You knew my mother?"

"She was an asset I cultivated back when I was with the CIA. Her gaggle of Gypsy women gathered a lot of information for me working as maids and cleaning ladies for the embassies on the Row. They generously shared it with your mother during their weekly visits to her shop. She, in turn, passed on certain tidbits to me."

There was no way her mother had been a CIA asset. He had to be making this up.

But his eyes told her he wasn't lying. The gun he had trained on her was no joke.

Her fingernails bit into the palms of her hands as she clenched them tighter. "I trusted you. You were like a father to me."

"I treated you better than your father. What he did to you, put you in that mental hospital. You weren't crazy, you know."

Her glare switched to the man standing behind Miles. His face showed nothing—no emotions, no worries, nothing. "I know."

"Orlo here was following orders, that's all," CB said. "Good old Mum let it slip to your dad that she was working for me. She wanted him to leave the air force, wanted the whole family to go the U.S. of A. because she'd heard about some new facility in Maine for high-functioning autistics like your brother. I'd told her that once I had bin Laden, I'd do my best to help your family move and become U.S. citizens. She was impatient, told

160

your father, and he hit the roof. We'd known each other back in the day. Crossed paths in Serbia a few times, which is how I met your mother. Your dad knew I was obsessed with the Middle East. Bin Laden. Blackwater. He thought I was nuts, that I was wasting my time worrying about them. When he found out your mother was helping me, he wanted to kill me. Of course, I was in Khartoum at the time and he was in India on a mission. Your mother called and warned me that he was gunning for me."

Charlotte couldn't believe what she was hearing. She wanted to cover her ears, block it out. Gritting her teeth, she stood straight, tall. "I wish he'd gotten the job done. My mother would still be alive."

CB held up his empty hand in a gesture suggesting he'd had no choice. "I didn't want to do it. I loved your mother. She was sweet and elusive and quite cunning under all that silly Gypsy shit. But when Orlo went to talk to her, scare her a little, she fought back. That woman had a temper, let me tell you. Things got out of hand. She tried to kill him. He fought back."

"You expect me to believe that?"

"You saw him leave the building. My little Charlotte, the only witness. But he let you live on my orders. I'd told him from the moment I hired him to keep an eye on your mother, that he was never to touch you. And then the irony of all ironies, you and I ended up both working for MI6. Small world, huh?"

Small world. Did he really think she bought that excuse? He was too smart, too calculating, she realized now, to let chance dictate his life. "How long have you been working with Nico?"

"Long enough. He's been doing deals with terrorist groups for the past couple of years, trying to get in good with them and keep a steady flow of income by supplying as many of their needs as possible."

He stepped toward her and held out a hand. "I need that video and he wants you in exchange. Kinda pissed him off when you ran away." CB smirked. "You should have seen his face when his men told him you were missing. Classic moment."

"You were *there*?"

He caressed his gun a moment, wiping at nonexistent dust. "I was trying to cut a deal for your life, and then you blew that by escaping minutes before I would have rescued you. You never told me where the USB was, so I had no choice, really, other than to try to save your ass so you could show me. Nico knows where Blackwater is hiding out, but he wanted something in exchange. Once you escaped, that thing became you."

Think, Charlotte. "I'll give you the USB if you help me rescue a girl Nico is holding. Blackwater is her father. She knows where to find him. You'll have the video and his location. You can take down Nicolae Bourean and Blackwater in one swoop."

"I get the girl and Blackwater. Don't worry about that. But leave you alive?" He shook his head. "Sorry, that won't work."

A soft groan from Miles drew all of their attentions, but he didn't open his eyes. She had no idea how badly he was injured, so she fished the USB from her pocket and held it up. "I'll give you the USB and you can take me to Nico—if you leave Miles out of it."

CB eyed the USB, then gave a jerk of his head to Orlo. Before Charlotte could react, the assassin shoved her sideways, ripping the USB from her hand and sending her to the floor.

Landing on her stomach, her breath rushed out of her chest as Orlo shoved a knee in her back. He yanked her hands behind her and zip-tied them.

"Kill the SEAL," CB said, stepping over her, "and leave him in the woods for the wolves."

"No!" Charlotte shouted, bucking under Orlo and knocking him off balance.

He smacked the back of her head with something heavy, causing pain to explode behind her eyes. She blinked, but saw two of Miles lying on the floor in front of her instead of one.

"No fires this time." CB picked up the laptop. "We don't want to attract attention. Throw the girl in my trunk so I can get going. Nico's waiting. You can follow in their truck after you take care of the SEAL."

"No!" Charlotte yelled again and Orlo's boot connected with her side.

Her ribs cried in pain, her breath once more lodged in her throat.

CB ignored her, glancing around at the cabin as he hugged the laptop to his chest. "But shoot the SEAL in the woods. I like this place. I might come back here. Blood stains would be a pain in the ass to get out of these wooden floors."

Orlo grunted and yanked Charlotte to her feet, shoving her out the door even as she fought to get back to Miles.

Miles' eyes fluttered open as he woke up to a pounding in his head and pine needles in his nose. One side of his face lay buried in snow, his body shivering against the ground as he blinked his eyes and tried to focus.

The forest floor stretched before him, dark tree trunks, ghostly white snow. Storm clouds blanketed the moon and stars, and with the thick canopy overhead, their light wouldn't have reached the forest floor where he lay anyway.

Light from the cabin twenty yards away did reach him. Barely. He groaned as he rolled over and blinked up at the tree branches over his head. The pain was instant, agonizing.

Where am I? What happened?

Head screaming, he forced his body up to a sitting position, touched the side of his head where the pain drilled into his temple. The last thing he remembered was lifting the satellite dish onto the base outside the cabin. A blow. Lights out.

Sifting through the fog in his brain, he wondered if he'd lost his grip on the satellite dish and knocked himself out.

No. That didn't seem right.

Whatever had hit him had done it from behind.

Charlotte.

Miles squinted through the darkness, zeroing in on the cabin. Curtains hid the interior. No sign of where she was or where his attacker might be. Was she okay?

Who had knocked him out and dumped him up here in the woods? The outlaws Charlotte was always talking about? Had MI6 caught up to them?

MI6 wouldn't have knocked him out and left him in the woods.

Shit. Had to be a criminal. How had the guy snuck up on him? What was he doing to Charlotte?

Miles used a nearby tree to gain his footing, fighting a wave of nausea and dizziness as he stood. He had to get to her. Keep her safe.

Over the pounding of his head, he heard the distant sound of a car engine idling. The sound cleared more of the fog in his brain.

He must have been drifting in and out of consciousness after the blow. Vague snippets of memories—Charlotte's voice arguing with a man—trickled through his mind. He couldn't remember what the man had said, but Charlotte's voice still echoed in his head.

You killed my mother.

How long have you been working with Nico?

Miles!

A gust of wind came up, causing the branches overhead to bob up and down. Snow rained down on him and he had to wipe it from his face.

Drawing in a lung-filling breath of cold air, he shook off the last of the brain haze and started forward, then bent at the waist when another round of nausea cramped his gut.

Breathe, he told himself. *Don't pass out.*

Charlotte had recognized their attacker. *Was* it the man who'd killed her mother all those years ago? He was alive and working for Bourean now? That seemed like one big fucking coincidence.

How had the killer found them? Why had he come after them?

Because Charlotte can ID him.

Between the pounding in his head and the wind, he almost didn't hear the crunch of footsteps approaching from the west. West, where the trail led away from the cabin and the Land Rover was parked by the fallen tree.

Narrowing his eyes, Miles forced his double vision away. He could just make out a shadow moving near the tree line, headed toward him.

He reached for his weapon, came up empty. Whoever had blindsided him and dumped him in the woods had stripped him of his gun. The only reason the guy would come back was to finish him off.

Hell if he was going to let the bastard kill him with his own firearm. Ignoring the pain in his head, Miles slid around to the backside of a large tree and ran scenarios through his mind.

Evade or engage? That was the question.

He was the evasion god, after all. Disappearing into the forest would be easy, even if he had to cover his tracks in the snow.

No way. Leaving Charlotte behind wasn't an option.

Engage it is.

Miles saw a fat branch about the length of a baseball bat lying in the snow a few feet away. A tree branch wasn't much of a weapon against a gun, but it was better than nothing.

Diving for the branch would alert his attacker to his location. Of course, in a few more steps, the guy was going to see that Miles was no longer lying on the ground in a heap anyway.

The footsteps stopped. Miles heard a gun cock.

Yep. *Bad guy alert.* The killer was onto the fact his quarry was no longer unconscious.

Holding his breath, Miles listened. The wind continued to blow, increasing its speed and whistling through the trees. The car engine in the distance began accelerating. Christ, could there be more than one attacker? Was someone driving away with Charlotte?

Now or never, Miles told himself, and dove for the tree branch.

Gunshots echoed through the forest. Bullets ricocheted around his head, notching the tree trunks and raining wood chips on him as he grabbed the branch and rolled. A second wave of gunshots rang out, bullets ripping through the snow a hair's breath away from his shoulder and spraying snow into the air like a halo.

He spit a wood chip from his mouth, gained his feet, and whirled behind a massive trunk. Between the monochrome landscape and his head injury fucking with his vision, his eyes didn't want to focus. But he didn't need to see to know his attacker had also moved to a more secure hiding place.

With the snow under their feet, if either moved they would make a noise. The tree branches above him groaned as another gust of wind hit them. In the distance, a wolf howled.

He was losing time. He had to get to Charlotte. Had to get out of the woods before the storm hit.

Need a distraction.

Bending down, he released the tree branch and started scooping snow, packing handfuls into tight little balls.

He heard something behind him and stopped dead. Had his attacker snuck up on him? He held his breath, slowly grasping the branch again, as long seconds ticked by. He peeked an eye out and looked toward the last place he'd seen the killer.

Movement on his left caught his attention. Something small, sprinting at full speed across the forest floor was kicking up snow and snapping twigs as it bolted toward him. The rabbit was in an all-out panic, which meant only one thing.

Either the storm had unnerved the animal...or something bigger was chasing it.

Miles waved the branch, startling the rabbit into veering right, heading toward the man. He picked up one of his tightly packed snowballs and threw it as hard as he could at the tree next to where the man had taken cover.

Sure enough, shots rang out as the man thought Miles was coming for him. Miles lobed another snowball off to the man's left, and while the man turned and fired off several rounds, Miles pocketed his hard-packed snowball and ran behind the tree closest to his attacker.

Before he could swing to the side and charge the guy, however, a pack of deer emerged from the same direction the rabbit had emerged from, their hooves sounding like thunder on the snow-packed ground. Four does and one buck, tearing up the ground as they dodged trees and ran like their lives depended on it.

Whatever is coming is big, and I sure as hell don't want to be here when it arrives.

Miles used his last snowball to keep the man's attention on the direction he'd come from, throwing it hard and nailing a tree high up in some branches. A bird gave a distressed cry, lighting off the tree, apparently done with all the commotion. As the thing flapped and continued screeching through the canopy above them, Miles stepped out from behind his cover and attacked.

The man was under six foot, but solid. He turned at the precise moment Miles swung his make-shift bat.

Crack. The bat connected with the man's gun hand, knocking it from his grasp. The gun went off, a bullet whizzing past Miles' head as he let the bat's momentum carry him around for another swing.

The man lunged at the same moment Miles' swing came back around, the bat glancing harmlessly off the his back as he locked his arms around Miles waist and took him to the ground.

They both let out a grunt, the air was knocked out of them. The man landed a blow to Miles' ribs; Miles smacked the end of the tree branch bat into the guy's forehead.

The hit should have sent the guy into Loolooville, but the bastard was tough. They continued to scuffle in the snow, trading blows and wrestling to the death.

The storm broke open, the wind driving pellets of sleet into them as they rolled down hill. Miles lost the bat after banging into a trunk, his attacker's body pinning his arm against the rough bark. The sleet was forming a layer of ice on the snow, creating a skating rink effect. As the two slid down the hill, Miles managed to knee the man in the groin, causing him to go fetal.

Still sliding, Miles came up onto his knees, grabbed the man's shoulders, and used the momentum of their slide to whirl him around and slam his head into a rock outcropping.

The force of impact caused Miles to lose his grip and sent him heading straight for a huge tree, ice balls stinging his face like buckshot.

If he hit the tree going this fast, he was going to do some damage. He tucked and rolled, barely missing the trunk as he sped by, bark scraping against his backside.

He spun like a top, finally coming to a stop a few feet from the cabin's back door. For a second, he lay there, breathing hard and looking up at the angry sky as the sleet turned to snow.

He needed to know the killer was dead. He could really use the gun, too. But hiking back up the hill would take too much time and might be somewhat impossible considering the ice.

Slowly, Miles rose to his feet. The fight hadn't improved his headache, but at least his guts were no longer cramping.

Find Charlotte.

Miles scanned the back door, the windows. No sounds came from inside, no activity. He made his way inside to double check, bracing himself in case her dead body was waiting for him.

Empty.

Dammit. On the one hand, Charlotte wasn't dead. Not yet, anyway. On the other, she was gone.

The killer in the woods had had an accomplice and they must have driven off with Charlotte.

Miles' backpack was on the kitchen counter, sitting next to Charlotte's. His laptop was gone, however. Snatching up both backpacks, he headed for the door, praying the Land Rover, or whatever vehicle his attacker had been planning to use to get away, was still by the fallen tree.

Outside, the storm had officially gone into blizzard territory. With any luck, if the man in the woods was still alive, he wouldn't be for long in the freezing temperatures.

As Miles started skating down the lane toward the Land Rover, he heard the roar of what sounded like a bear echoing down from the hillside. On the heels of that came a man's strangled scream.

The scream ended abruptly and Miles paused for a second to look back. The forest was coated in snow, the trees standing like sentries staring down at him.

Miles turned away and continued his journey down the lane, fighting to breathe in the heavy, blinding snow.

It seemed like an eternity before he reached the fallen tree, a good, thick blanket of snow now covering the ice. He hefted himself over the massive trunk, the Land Rover still sitting in the same spot where he'd hidden it. The tire tracks from the other vehicle had all but disappeared under the new carpet of snow.

Nearly giddy with relief, he hoisted himself into the Land Rover. Tossing the backpacks into the passenger seat, he noticed a big duffel bag stuffed in the foot well.

Dragging it up to the seat, he pawed through it. Extra clothes, a couple of guns, a satellite phone.

"We are in business, kids," he said to the quiet interior. "Let's rock and roll."

He got the motor running and drove as fast as he could considering he didn't want to slide off the mountainside in the storm. The wheels on the Land Rover were heavy duty and ate up the snow covered lane without many issues.

Once he'd made the bottom of the mountain, he pulled out his cell. No service. Not that he'd expected any, but a man could hope.

Now what? He needed help and in a big way.

The sat phone.

Stopping for a moment, he jerked the thing out of the duffel bag and found the cord to hook it into the lighter. A minute later, he had Jax on the line.

"You *lost* her?" Jax said after Miles told him an abbreviated version of what had happened.

"I didn't lose her. The jackwagon snuck up on me and knocked me out."

"Jesus, man. Is she still wearing her Rock Star bracelet?"

"Yeah, I think so." The bracelet had a GPS tracking device in it. "Can you trace it?"

"I'm on it."

Jaxon called him back on the sat phone three minutes later. Which was good since Miles couldn't sit still and had come to the end of the mountain lane. He needed to know whether to go left or right.

"Southeast," Jaxon said. "She's headed for Bucharest."

Bourean's mansion. "How soon can you meet me there?"

"Actually, we're already here. In Bucharest, I mean."

"We?"

"I've got a team, sort of. They just flew in from the States and we're at the airport. Apparently Beatrice thought we might need backup."

Beatrice was always right. God Jr. ate logic for breakfast, but she had a keen sense of intuition as well. He owed her big when he got back.

If he got back.

He was probably a hundred miles from Bucharest. Maybe he'd overtake whoever had Charlotte before they got to Bourean's. If not... "We're going to need blueprints for Bourean's compound and a plan to get Charlotte out without staring World War III."

"On it."

The line went dead.

CHAPTER EIGHTEEN

Charlotte came awake slowly, her senses coming online one at a time. First she heard a loud whirring, like a giant bee buzzing under her. Next she smelled tires and damp carpeting. Mud, too. Her eyelids were heavy, but she forced them open, only to find herself in darkness.

She was lying on her stomach, her cheek resting on the damp carpeting. Her side ached, as did her head. Everything in her body felt sluggish, as if sludge was in her veins. Her tongue felt thick, her mouth dry.

I've been drugged.

She tried to reboot her brain along with her senses, but the neurons that were successfully firing were slow to come online and wake their counterparts.

For a few minutes, she just laid there and forced herself to breathe steadily and evenly. Her body bounced around and jarred a couple of times. She tried to bring her hands to her face, but found them handcuffed behind her back. That woke up more brain cells, a steady flood of memories coming to her.

The cabin. Norris.

Orlo.

Miles.

Lifting her head, she took a deep breath and looked around. The droning bee was a truck of some kind—a Jeep—and she had been tossed into the back. The second row seats had been put down to hold cargo—her. The windows in the back were blacked out, but up front, she could see CB driving, his knit cap still on. Driving snow rammed the windshield, the wipers working furiously.

How far were they from the cabin? She had to figure out a way to stop Norris and get back there.

Was Miles even still alive? Her stomach roiled at the thought of him dead in the woods, wild animals shredding his body.

Dammit, she knew something like this could happen.

Well, not *this* specifically. She'd never dreamed her mentor would turn on her and deliver her into the hands of a monster.

But then, her own flesh and blood father had put her in a mental institute to shut her up. Why was it such a far cry for her handler to betray her?

Stupid. I've been so stupid.

No wonder MI6 believed she was a traitor. CB Norris had made that happen, covering his own traitorous activities.

At the cabin, she'd fought Orlo with all her might, trying to save Miles. After she'd landed a solid kick to Orlo's shin, the assassin had hit her in the head with the butt of his gun. She'd gone down like a pile of bricks. Two hits to her head in one night was probably the reason her brain was having trouble rebooting. The drugs in her system, courtesy of CB no doubt, were making her body sluggish and out of sync with her head.

How long had she been out? How far down the road to Nico's were they?

And how in the hell was she going to get rid of Norris and turn this Jeep around?

He was so focused on driving in the crappy weather, he wasn't paying attention to her. The front seat was a bench, so the high back made a divider between them and gave her some cover.

Keeping an eye on him in the rearview, Charlotte slowly shifted to her side, working her zip-tied hands down and around her butt and legs. Her boots were an impediment, but she loosened her shoulders as much as she could. Stretching her arms for all she was worth in a fetal position, her arms finally had enough length to get her hands under her feet. She let out a silent breath and brought them forward.

Norris glanced up into the rearview, and Charlotte froze, closing her eyes. He didn't seem to notice her change in position, probably because she was in the shadowy back.

After the truck didn't slow and he made no comment, she peeked her eyes open and saw he was once more hunched forward and focused on the road.

Carefully, she turned her head in an arc, searching the backend for a weapon.

There was a spare tire near her feet, wheel chains for climbing mountain roads in the snow. Those chains would be an excellent weapon if they wouldn't make so much noise when she grabbed them.

Where was a tire iron when you needed one? Hell, where was a gun when you needed one?

She felt the zip tie around her wrists, the Rock Star bracelet clanging against the hard plastic ties. If she could sneak up behind CB, she could throw her cuffed hands over his head and use them as a noose to strangle him.

But he'd be armed, and while strangling him would give her great satisfaction at the moment, his hands would be free and he could grab his gun, shoot her, and call it a day.

Of course, he needed her alive for his bargain with Nico.

Even if he didn't go for his weapon, strangling him would send the Jeep skidding off the road. Jeeps were notorious for rolling and if they were on any type of mountain, she could end up dead along with him. That would not help Miles…if he was still alive.

He's alive. I know he's alive.

The rest of the inventory in the back of the Jeep consisted of a bag that probably held extra winter clothes, but maybe there was a weapon or something in it as well. If she could at least threaten the son of a bitch, he might pull the Jeep over and get out peacefully.

Who was she kidding? Her handler wasn't the type of operative to go peacefully into the night.

It was going to be a fight. One where she might die.

So be it. Better to go down fighting than end up in Nico's hands again.

Charlotte shifted slightly, hooking the duffel bag's handles with a boot toe and scooting it up toward her hands. All the while she kept an eye on CB.

In the distance, she saw lights on the horizon, shining through the blinding snow. They were getting close to a town, a village. Already going slowly because of the weather, CB would have to slow down even more.

That's my chance. Flat ground, slow-moving vehicle. Even if they did roll, she'd survive.

And then she'd do whatever it took to get back to Miles.

And kill Orlo.

Suddenly, clearing her name with MI6 didn't mean as much. Stopping Norris, his assassin, and Nicolae Bourean meant more. Between the three of them, they'd taken her mother from her, caused her dad to turn against her, and tried to carve the very soul out of her. If Miles *was* dead...

She gulped. Then they had succeeded in taking everything.

She felt around the duffel but found nothing more than clothes and a blanket. Norris didn't slow down as they winged through the village. No one else was out, not even snow plows, so his drive was free of everything but the snow.

With no gun to hold to his head, she couldn't force him to pull over. There was only one way to stop the Jeep and that meant attacking him. She really needed her hands free.

Charlotte ran the scenario through her mind. How she would scoot so she was directly behind him. How she could pop up on her knees, swing her arms over his head, and yank backwards, effectively pinning him around the throat.

She worried the bracelet's charm with her fingers.

Shinedown had said it held a GPS tracker, which was why Miles had insisted she wear it, but who would find her out here in time?

What else had he said it contained? A wire saw, a lock pick. She nearly banged her head against the seat. Of course. Why hadn't she thought of that earlier?

Blame it on her fuzzy head. Charlotte fiddled with the charms, the lock, her cold fingers struggling with the catch. Suddenly, it popped open and she tried to catch it, but it fell to the muddy carpet.

She ran her fingers over the carpet, keeping her upper body still. *There.* She felt metal.

Like a blind person, she stroked the large center gold plate that read 'Rock Star' on it, then ran her fingers around the edge underneath.

The woman in charge of SFI was one smart cookie. The former NSA operative knew a thing or two about secret tools.

Around the inside edge of the bracelet, Charlotte's fingers found the tiny, thin saw blade that popped out of the metal when she pushed on the charm. She'd seen similar tools hidden in rings and other jewelry that agents wore in case they found themselves in a situation like hers with plastic zip ties around their wrists.

Laying the bracelet down, she went to work sawing through the plastic.

"I know you're awake, Carstons." CB didn't even bother to look in the rearview as he remained hunched over the steering wheel. "You can stop playing possum."

Okay. So surprising him and strangling him might be out.

Sawing through the restraints wasn't easy when she could only move her hands so far. Still, she sawed faster. "Why did you do it? Sell me out?"

"It wasn't about you, Carstons. None of it. It was about getting to Blackwater."

Nothing personal? Was that what he was saying? "You killed my mother, which destroyed my relationship with my father. You made MI6 believe I'm a traitor, and you killed the only man I've ever loved. But you're saying it's *nothing personal?*"

"Exactly." He only had one hand on the wheel now. Probably had his other on a gun. "Your mother was an unfortunate accident that led to that situation with your dad. I tried, believe me, to talk sense into him about putting you in that institute, but he wouldn't listen. It was serendipity that brought you to me as a fresh recruit for her majesty's secret service. You have to admit, I turned you into one hell of a good spy. But the big picture here is Blackwater. Not you, not Bourean, certainly not some former SEAL with a hard-on for you."

A part of her felt totally gutted by all of it, but especially by the idea that Miles was dead. Her stomach cramped and her head swam for a moment. "How did you find out about him?"

"You told me about the video footage and that you'd hid it. Once I knew Bourean had you, I went to the cabin looking for it. You forgot to mention that you'd saved one of the SEALs from that helo. I found the book with Duncan's note in it so I did some digging. Sure enough, what do you know? One of the SEALs classified KIA was actually alive."

"You did take my book. I knew it. I never saw the letter Miles left me."

"Ah, jeez, that poor bastard. He really poured out his heart to you. Hard on a guy's ego, you know, the way you up and left him without a goodbye. Such a wuss, confessing his love and leaving a contact number anyway, in case you changed your mind. Said he'd keep the cross around his neck until you came back to him. The man needs some balls."

"He's more of a man than you'll ever be."

"It wasn't hard to put two and two together. You rescued the SEAL and he fell for you. But you knew your job wasn't done. You had to go back to Bourean and try to find out who the terrorist was so you could stop him too. Your job came first, not that SEAL. I admired that in you."

Miles was the only man she'd ever loved, and what had she done? Left him behind to finish her mission. She'd thought she was protecting him, allowing him to go back to his real life because life with her would never be marriage and family. Never be normal.

Yet, he was the only person she'd ever let herself feel anything for since her mother's death. She should have never walked away. "You've never been in love, have you?" she asked quietly.

"Love?" The windshield wipers beat to the sound of his laughter. "No, I never have, and thank God for that. Duty, honor...those things are worth fighting for, Carstons. They mean something in the big picture. The only thing I've ever been in love with is my job—something I thought you, of all people, would understand. Soon, I'm going to look Blackwater in the eye and kill that bastard. My life will have meant something. The greater good will prevail. I'll be a hero."

Anger rallied. She'd known this type of betrayal in the mental hospital, this torrent of emotion overriding good sense. Someone she trusted had pulled the safety net out from under her. Someone she had believed in had taken her respect and squashed it under their foot like an insignificant bug.

Since the night her mother had died, she hadn't put faith in anyone. She hadn't trusted anyone enough to love them and believe they wouldn't hurt her.

But she had respected this man, thought she understood him. She'd thought they were on the same side.

Funny thing was, they still were. They both still wanted to take down Nicolae Bourean and stop a terrorist at the same time. Only, Norris wanted her to sacrifice herself and everything she'd worked for and believed in, to help him do the job.

Her time in the mental hospital hadn't been a total waste.

She'd learned how to shut down the flood of emotions and be the good little soldier. Her time under Nico's control had fine-tuned that. She knew better than anyone how to detach from pain and fear and never lose sight of her ultimate goal.

And her ultimate goal right now was to get back to Miles.

The zip tie snapped. Her hands were free.

"Look, Carstons." CB turned a corner. "You want Bourean, I want Blackwater. I'll make sure they both die. All I need is a little help from you."

A little help, like sacrificing herself for the greater good. "What village is ahead?" she asked. The lights were closer now; they were almost there. She needed to calculate how far they'd come, how far she had to go to get back to the cabin.

"Village?" Norris met her gaze in the rearview for a moment. "This is no village."

"What is it, then?"

"Don't you recognize it? The castle beyond the gates?"

She squinted through the snow pelting against the windshield. "Should I?"

"It's the compound. Bourean's compound."

Her chest seized for a moment. They'd come farther than she'd thought.

With a deep breath, she willed the sharp edge of her fear to recede. *No emotions. Only action.* "I do understand your commitment to stopping Blackwater, to making a difference in the world." This was no longer about him selling her out to MI6. Oh no, this was much more personal. "So I know you'll understand my commitment to helping you. I'm in."

A flash of a grin showed in the rearview. "I had hoped you would come around."

She returned his smile, rubbing her thumb over the Rock Star bracelet before sliding it back on.

Then, sending up a prayer to her Gypsy ancestors, she propelled herself forward and went for his jugular.

⌒━━━━◦⊪◦━━━━⌒

Back roads in Romania were nothing to mess with. Especially in a winter blizzard.

Miles checked his watch's coordinates again, the red beeping dot signaling he was near Jaxon's meeting place. The mountain range and the snow had played havoc on the GPS system, but he'd taken a moment to hot wire the watch to the satellite phone and had been receiving a fairly steady signal since. He'd wanted to keep on Charlotte's trail, but the reality was, he knew where her abductor was headed. What he needed before he busted into Bourean's compound was a plan.

Bourean was smart enough to use a fortress that had stood for centuries, enduring wars and attacks from countless armies. Out by itself, the castle compound was still close enough to the city to support his business. Jax had found a spot that on a normal night would have offered the team the best vantage point. Unfortunately with the snow, visibility was slim to none.

Miles saw the meeting spot through the snow and pulled the Land Rover in next to a large cargo van. The van was totally kitted out with oversized tires, a lift kit, a satellite dish, push bar and spotlights.

Miles unhooked his watch from the sat phone and put it back on before securing the hood on his parka and pulling on gloves. Visibility might be low for them, but it was also nonexistent for security guards and cameras. They could use that to their advantage.

He knocked three times on the van's set of double doors at the rear and was admitted by Jax. Jax and Miles did their normal handshake-slap on the back greeting and Miles surveyed the interior.

A surveillance and security computer hub was built into the van's side, the desk littered with headphones, files, and blueprints. Morris "Moe" Bouchard was hunched over a computer screen, headphones on. Jax tapped his shoulder and Moe startled, looking up and giving Miles a nod. "Poison," he said in greeting.

"Henley." The two of them had worked together on the Savanna Bunkett case and were used to using each other's Rock Star code names, although no one understood why the Brit-sounding operative had chosen the Eagle's front man as his. Everyone knew the Eagles were country, not rock. "How ya doin', man?"

"Freezin' my arse off. You?"

"Been better." His temple pounded and his side ached from his fight with the assassin. "We have to find missions in warmer places. I thought D.C. was bad. This is worse."

"Second that, mate."

Miles dropped into a chair near Moe and looked at Jax as he flipped his hood back. "Just the three of us, then?"

"Nah, man. Beatrice sent us a whole crew. A couple of newbies, but they're solid."

Moe leaned forward and grinned at the computer screen, slapping the desktop. "She's in!"

"Who?" Miles studied the screen, seeing nothing but a lot of falling snow. "Charlotte?"

"Parker, mate. I freakin' love her."

"Parker Jeffries?" He cut his attention back to Jax. "Savanna's sister?"

Jax shrugged, pouring a cup of steaming liquid from a thermos and handing it to Miles. "CIA, NSA, the girl's got a resume longer than any of ours."

"She's an expert sniper," Moe added. "Sneaky little minx, too."

"She's part of our team?" Miles was still trying to wrap his head around it as he accepted the cup from Jax. The scent of fresh coffee filled the air. "But she's not SFI."

"She is for now," Jax said. "And she's inside Bourean's compound."

Three knocks sounded on the van's back door before it flew open. A man in full winter gear, including a ski mask, jumped in and slammed the door behind him.

Snowflakes skidded off his hood and coat and landed on the van floor. "Dirty ass weather out there, boys," he said, flipping off his hood and peeling the ski mask up. "Ah, Duncan. Glad you made it."

"Zeb?" Miles couldn't contain his shock. The man was old enough to be his grandfather. He shot Jax another look. "Seriously?"

Zeb reached out in the close quarters and smacked Miles upside the head. "Show some respect, boy."

"Ow." The lump over his temple wasn't ever going to go down at this rate. He set his cup down, the liquid untouched. "You're part of this rescue team? You and Parker Jeffries."

"Parker's in," Moe told Zeb. "Piece of cake."

Zeb nodded to Moe, spoke to Miles. "Yes, Duncan. For your information, I'm in charge of this sad little team, so pull your panties out of their wad and deal."

In charge? *In charge?*

Zeb shed his gloves, dug out a phone from inside his coat.

"Your girl caused quite a distraction in front of the main gates. Gave Parker time to breach the southeast wall and get inside the compound."

He punched the screen of his phone a couple of times and held it up for Miles to see. "This is her—Carstons—ain't it?"

The photo was grainy but it made Miles' heart drop into his stomach. A Jeep lay on its side, a couple of men—Bourean's, no doubt—extracting two bodies from the interior. One body was a man in black clothes and a knit hat. The other was Charlotte.

"Is she...?"

"Alive?" Zeb grunted and flipped through a few more shots showing Bourean's men hauling Charlotte and the man onto a couple of four-wheelers. "From all accounts, I'd say yes. My Romanian's rusty and it was hard to hear the discussion over the wind, but sounded like she was breathing. Norris, too."

"Norris? Wait. CB Norris, her handler?"

"You know the guy?"

"No, but I take it you do."

Zeb grabbed Miles' cup and downed the coffee, then wiped his mouth off with the back of his hand. "We brushed shoulders back in the day. He was CIA until he rubbed their noses in their own shit and they kicked him out. Guy's cagey but damn smart. Obsessive, too. Give him an assignment and he locks onto it like a gater on fresh meat. He likes hunting people, and once he knows his target, he'll use anyone he has to in order to get to that target and take it out. But I'll tell you boys something. If Norris had been in charge before 9/11, those towers would still be standing."

"Why's that?" Moe asked.

"He knew more about Osama bin Laden than Osama himself. I saw some of the guy's reports, heard talk about his 'crazy' ideas. Given the right tools, Norris would have found bin Laden and taken him out long before 9/11. He's one hell of a mastermind."

Jax leaned against Moe's workstation. "What's he doing in Romania running an MI6 agent?"

Zeb shook his head. "He's not after Bourean, I assure you. Small potatoes. Bourean has to be a stepping stone to a bigger player. Someone Norris believes is on his level. A mastermind like himself."

"The USB," Miles said. "Charlotte had video of the plane

crash and the helo attack. Bourean was working with a terrorist to supply him with RPGs. They were testing the equipment."

"That's Norris' target then. He was using Charlotte and Bourean to get to that guy, and I have a hunch I know who he is. This is big, boys."

Big or not, Miles wanted that terrorist. No way was Norris getting the man before he scored some revenge.

"It's gotta be Blackwater," Zeb said.

"Who's Blackwater?" Jax asked.

Zeb handed him the empty coffee cup and Jax poured him a fresh cup from the thermos while Zeb filled them in. "Blackwater was just a teenager when bin Laden planned 9/11. The guy has blood ties to him, some distance cousin or something, but he was destined to take over the bin Laden empire down the road. Asshole taught the kid everything he knew. In the ten years after 9/11, Blackwater grew up. His fingerprints were on a lot of small, subversive jobs all over the world. Some say he's the one behind ISIS, and that's probably true, but he's behind a lot of radical groups all over Europe. He's been in the wind for years, recruiting, setting up cells everywhere."

A crackling noise came from the computer along with a woman's voice. "Control, this is Jett. Do you read? Over."

"It's Parker," Moe told Miles. He was grinning again from ear to ear. "She got to pick her own Rock Star name and she's got a thing for Joan Jett."

He went back to the computer, tapped a key on his keyboard. "Jett, this is Control. Go ahead."

"Heat signatures suggest our target is on the ground floor of the main building, northwest side of main castle turret in the rear. Room contains at least four other heat signatures, two appear to be guards. Interactions have the appearance of an interrogation."

Interactions? As in beatings? Miles' stomach tightened.

"Roger that. Security?" Moe asked.

Parker rattled off intel on how many warm bodies she'd seen, where cameras were located, and the best places to breach. "Orders?"

"Tell her to sit tight," Zeb said. "We have to give Coldplay a little more time."

Moe relayed the instructions. Miles looked at Zeb. "Coldplay? He's here too?"

A knock sounded on the door and Jax opened it, allowing Trace Hunter—Coldplay—to enter. It was like the guy had heard his name and simply materialized out of thin air. "Colder than a sow's tits out here," he complained as he squeezed into the van.

The quarters were tight on a good day. With five of them—four former SEALs—crammed into it, they were shoulder to shoulder.

Trace nodded at Miles. "You owe Savanna flowers and a nice chardonnay when we get back. She's very unhappy I'm here."

"Not too happy about it myself."

Zeb chuckled. "Wait till she discovers her sister is on this mission. Then you'll really have hell to pay."

"She doesn't know?" Miles asked.

Zeb gave him a *don't be a dumbass* look, then said to Trace. "Did you get the stash?"

Trace blew on his hands through his gloves. "Eleanor is outside. She'll do you proud."

"Eleanor?" Miles almost hated to ask.

Zeb threw open the door and Miles peered over his shoulder. A long black case lay in the snow. "One?" Zeb looked incredulously over his shoulder at Trace. "That's it?"

Trace lifted his palms skyward. "What? I may be Superman, but breaking into a crime lord's compound, stealing an RPG, and lugging it through enemy territory back to you is not exactly easy. Damn thing weighs a ton."

Trace had gone in and stolen one of Bourean's own weapons to use against him? Miles just shook his head. The former SEAL had been part of a secret government project to enhance the natural abilities of soldiers. Since Trace's natural abilities had already been close to superhuman, it was no surprise he was now nearly unstoppable.

Good thing he was on their side. "Eleanor, huh? You name your weapons?" Miles asked.

"Of course." Trace looked at him as if he was a moron. "Don't you?"

Zeb pulled the doors closed. "Guess one will have to do."

"Oh," Trace pulled something from his coat pockets. "I picked up a few of these too."

He held up a handful of grenades.

One side of Zeb's mouth quirked. "Nice."

"Shouldn't they be taking Charlotte and Norris to a doctor?"

Miles tapped his thumbs against his thighs. He wanted to get moving. Get into that camp and pull Charlotte out. But if she was severely injured, her evac would take finesse and timing. "No telling how many injuries she and Norris have if the Jeep rolled."

"It rolled, in fact, three times." Zeb unzipped his parka. Even with the doors flying open, the van was warm from all the bodies. "I saw it. Both of them could have broken bones and internal injuries, but Bourean won't care about that. Why did Norris kidnap Charlotte? She still have that video?"

Miles nodded. "We had just returned from the mountains— she'd hid it there with some Gypsies—and we were on our way to clear her name when we were jumped."

"Clear her name?"

"MI6 thinks she's a traitor. That she went dark side with Bourean."

"Right. Beatrice mentioned that." Zeb sipped his coffee. "It's Norris. He set her up."

"Sorta figured that out."

Zeb gave him a hard look. "Injuries aside, Charlotte was unconscious when they picked her up, and we have to assume she may still be when we get to her. An exfiltration from behind enemy lines with a conscious subject is difficult enough. An unconscious subject is dead weight and no help at all."

"Parker's a doctor, right?" Miles said to Moe. "Is there any way she can get to her and give us a status report on her state of consciousness?"

"She's a brain scientist, dude." Moe looked away from the computer screen. "Not a medical doctor."

"She ran Project 24." Miles glanced at Trace. Parker had been the scientist who developed the drug concoction for Project 24, not realizing what the president wanted super soldiers for. Trace Hunter was the only survivor of that little experiment. "She must have some familiarity with medical evaluations."

"I'm a doctor," Jax said from the corner. "Sort of."

All eyes swung to him.

"I left my residency to join the Navy. Ended up in SEAL training, and the rest is a clusterfuck. I always planned to go back to the medical field. Never got it done."

Zeb nodded, touched Moe's shoulder. "Tell Parker to hold position and keep eyes on Charlotte. Jax and Miles are going in."

Finally. Miles was about to crawl out of his skin. "What's the plan, old man?"

The remark garnered him another swat upside the head, but Zeb was smiling. "We're going to do a little thing I like to call the Zeb Special."

"And what is that?" Jax asked, exchanging a worried look with Miles.

"Gather round, boys." Zeb motioned them to the blueprints lying on the table next to Moe's elbow. "This old man is about to teach you young'uns a thing or two."

Chapter Nineteen

BOUREAN COMPOUND
SANSA CITADEL

"Wake up, bitch!"

A sharp slap to her cheek snapped Charlotte's head sideways. Her whole body ached and her brain was fuzzy again. Not like in Norris' truck. This was a different fuzziness. Like she'd been spun in a dryer.

Or rolled over a couple times inside a Jeep.

Her eyelids fought against her opening them, but the sting in her cheek radiated through her jaw and up into her temple. An already pounding headache beat there, like someone was using a hammer against her skull.

Her body felt twisted, broken. She tasted blood in her mouth. Her eyelids fluttered a couple of times, bringing the man hovering over her into view.

Narrow face. Beard. Dark eyes filled with cold, calculating acumen. His black hair was tied back in a high man bun, his skin pocked. Light from the overhead chandelier glinted off the knife in his hand.

Charlotte moaned and closed her eyes. *Nightmare. This has to be a nightmare.*

Maybe if she kept her eyes closed, the nightmare would disappear. She'd wake up back in the cabin with Miles, not lying helpless under Nicolae Bourean.

Miles had to be dead by now, left in the frozen forest on the side of the mountain. No one would find his body. No one would ever know what happened except her.

And she wasn't going to last long at the hands of the man standing over her. *I'm so sorry, Miles. I should never have asked for your help.*

"You've got what you wanted," another voice said. Norris. "Now give me the girl."

From the corner of her eye, Charlotte saw CB leaning on a nearby table. He was holding a handkerchief covered in blood to his nose, his pants ripped at the knee where more blood dotted his skin. He'd at least had the airbag when they'd rolled. She hadn't.

Nico nodded at a man standing guard at the door and the man slipped out. "You kept your bargain. I keep mine."

He turned his attention back to Charlotte. Grabbing her by the top of her head, he yanked her hair straight up and gave her head a shake. "Did you think I wouldn't find you?" he sneered. "I own you, *posh ratt.*"

Her neck cried out in pain, her scalp too. Spittle landed on her cheek. Charlotte had sworn she'd never lay underneath Nico again. Never let him hurt her. Yet, here she was at his mercy once more. Her body battered and bruised, her heart shredded.

It was tempting to just lie there and let him do his worst. Torture her. Kill her. Whatever. Without Miles, she just didn't give a damn.

But then Nico gave her head another shake and cursed her in his native tongue and something inside Charlotte snapped. Rage ripped through her limbs, caused her eyelids to snap open like she'd been prodded with a branding iron.

Nico raised her head up off the floor, bringing her face close to his as he towered over her. When her gaze met his and she narrowed her eyes at him, he smiled.

"There she is. My Gypsy half-breed. Come on, bitch, fight back. You know you want to."

She did, in fact. She suddenly wanted to twist his balls off and stuff them down his throat. Her hand felt heavy, but she made a fist and punched straight up.

Her fist connected with Nico's balls but lacked force when he shifted at the last second. He lashed out with the knife, still holding her head in place, and Charlotte's next swing deflected it from cutting across her nose.

Her arm caught the blade though, cutting through her coat.

She grabbed Nico's wrist, the one holding her hair, and used it as leverage to kick up, nailing him in the buttocks. He toppled over her, releasing her hair, and rolled up to his knees.

Charlotte came to all fours, breathing heavy, waves of pain keeping her riding the edge of adrenaline. Nico smirked, jiggling the blade in his hand.

He lunged.

Charlotte tried to whirl out of the way, but the knife caught her other arm as Nico drove it into her flesh. His body weight took her flat to the floor.

He flipped her over, his knees coming down on her abdomen and forcing the air out of her. His laughter echoed through the room as he slapped her face again.

When you had nothing left to live for, you might as well go down fighting.

So she smiled back, blood pooling on her tongue. Her bottom lip was swelling; she hadn't noticed until she'd spread her lips to smile. Ignoring the tightness, she spit in his face, spraying him with blood.

He jerked back, cussing, and released her as he stood. Continuing his string of curses, he used his forearm to wipe the blood and spit from his nose and lips. He shook the knife at her, that cruel, calculating smile of his spreading his lips as he laughed without humor. "It is good to have you back, half-breed. You know I like strong-willed women who like to fight."

He liked women—girls, really—tied to a bed, begging for mercy. Charlotte swallowed the bile in her throat. "Oh, I'm ready to fight you, you worthless bastard."

His hand shot out to slap her again and she caught his wrist with one hand and punched him in the nose with the other.

He howled, more from surprise than pain, she imagined, and fell sideways. At the same time, the door opened and the guard came back with Madeena.

"Sarah!" The girl rushed forward, crying Charlotte's alias name as Charlotte forced herself to sit up. Madeena threw her arms around Charlotte's neck, her hug nearly taking Charlotte back down to the ground. "I thought you were dead."

I am.

A backhand from Nico sent the girl to the floor before Charlotte could whisk her out of the way. He screamed obscenities at Charlotte, or maybe his vitriol was for both of them. It was hard to tell.

He caught Charlotte with a kick from his booted foot, hitting her in the side. Her angry ribs roared. Orlo's kick had already left them sore; the roll in the Jeep hadn't helped. With Nico's kick, she crumpled forward and found it hard to breathe. Blood from the stab wound in her arm warmed her skin and ran down to her wrist.

She lifted her head and pinned Norris with a glare as she crawled toward Madeena, who cried softly on the floor. "I won't let you take the girl."

He smirked at Nico's bleeding nose and then at her. "How exactly do you think you're going to stop me?"

Good question. She had no idea. If only she had a wand and the Avada Kedavra spell was actually a real thing. She'd *avada kedavra* his arse all over the place.

She did know a couple of Gypsy spells. They were more for shriveling up someone's balls or giving him hives, but what the hell?

Nico kicked her in the back this time, sending her into Madeena. She lowered her voice—she could barely breathe anyway—and whispered in the girl's ear. "Be ready to run when I give you the signal."

The girl stopped crying, and Charlotte mumbled under her breath, nonsense words, but what did she care? Norris didn't know the jib, the language of her mother's people. Just like she had with Ted in San Diego, she let the darkness of her soul shine forth as she moved her mouth and pinned her eyes on Norris.

Nico was still blustering about his nose, one of his men rushing to get him an ice pack and something to stem the flow of blood.

Norris narrowed his eyes at Charlotte. "Speak up, Carstons. I can't hear you."

At that moment, Nico's man returned with the ice pack and a box of tissues.

Charlotte replicated the smirk CB had given her earlier. "That's because all the blood in your system is hardening. I just cursed you using a very old, very powerful Romani spell. You won't be able to hear or see in a few minutes and your balls will shrivel up and fall off."

The guard's eyes widened and he took a step back, shooting

a nervous glance at Norris and sliding covertly behind Nico as if his boss could ward off Gypsy curses.

"You're so full of shit," CB said, rolling his eyes. "Just like your mother. No one believes in that crap, Carstons. Stop demeaning yourself with hocus pocus nonsense."

But everyone in the room was watching him as if they were afraid *not* to believe it. The mind was a powerful thing. Madeena, the guard at the door, Nico and his man. All of them were staring at CB Norris as if watching a lab rat for signs of disease.

He shifted under everyone's scrutiny and waved his bloody handkerchief around. "What the fuck are you looking at?"

"Your nose is no longer bleeding," Nico said.

"So what? It finally stopped bleeding. *On its own*, not because some stupid ass curse is making my blood harden. Jesus, you people are gullible."

He strutted forward and reached out to grab Madeena. Charlotte ignored the fire rippling through her body and kicked a foot out, connecting with his knee.

Her movements were slow and labored, giving him time dodge to the side, her kick barely brushing his leg. Maddy grabbed onto her and Charlotte hugged her tight. "Touch her and you'll regret it."

Nico stepped forward and grabbed Charlotte by her hair again, yanking her back. At the same time, Norris grabbed Madeena by the arm.

"No!" Charlotte yelled, swinging a fist backward in Nico's direction as Madeena was wrenched from her, crying out and reaching out her hand.

Charlotte's fist struck Nico in the shoulder, but he only laughed and jerked her hair again.

A loud boom went off, far in the distance. The men all paused and looked at each other. Commotion arose outside in the courtyard. Nico jerked his chin at the guard. "Go see what the trouble is."

The man ran out.

Charlotte scrambled, reaching forward and grabbing Maddy's hand, but Norris' pull on the girl was too strong. He yanked her away.

Tears in her eyes from the stinging in her scalp, Charlotte continued to fight, punching and kicking at Nico as Norris shoved the girl toward the door.

"You won't get away with this," Charlotte yelled, her ribs on fire, her hair being pulled from her scalp. "If it's the last thing I do, I will make you pay for everything."

CB looked back at her and shook his head as if she were a sad, pitiful sight. "And how do you think you're going to do that, Carstons? With magic? Some stupid Gypsy curse?"

She was just about to tell him to go to hell when the side wall exploded.

SEAL missions were usually quiet, covert affairs. Stealth and accuracy was the name of the game. No guns blazing warfare. No calling attention to themselves.

SFI missions were the same. Most were rescue missions. Get in, grab the target, get out.

Tonight, the unofficial SFI gang going after Charlotte was on a rescue mission, but not all of them were going in quietly.

The Zeb Special involved a three-tiered approach. Distraction, diversion, and division. While Miles would have preferred the covert SEAL way of grabbing Charlotte and getting the hell out of Romania, Zeb's plan to take Bourean's compound by surprise attack had merit. Parker tallied twelve minions, four security cameras—one in each corner—and little to no one out and about because of the storm.

Zeb had laid out the parameters; Miles had taken lead by putting his own spin on the infiltration.

For one, Bourean was going to eat shit if Miles had anything to say about it.

Two, Norris was going to join Bourean at the shit table.

Miles put Trace Hunter in charge of activating the first layer of the Zeb Special, walking right up to the front gate and unloading the RPG.

Hunter was a machine. As he calmly set down the case, unlocked it, and readied the weapon, the guards at the gate went crazy. They yelled at him, demanding to know who he was, guns drawn.

Once they saw the long, black rocket and Hunter loading the warhead on the end, they started shooting.

Hunter never even flinched. He set that puppy on his shoulder and took a wide-legged stance, all the while bullets dancing at his feet in the snow.

Men dove off the guardhouse. Others ran screaming away from the gated entrance. Some managed to get away, but most weren't lucky enough to escape the explosion that tore through the front of the compound. Miles had a nice view of the action from his spot on the west parapet after Parker had given him the exact location where to breach the southeast wall.

"Wish I had popcorn," Parker said, her breath fogging the air.

"Wish I had another RPG," Miles replied.

Before stealing out into the night to take up their positions around the compound, they'd had a group chat with Beatrice back at HQ. She'd been in touch with MI6, informed them of the situation, and pulled a few strings. A team of SIS would be there soon to back up the Shadow Force squad. Andy Hardy, no longer in the States, was prepared to arrest Bourean and take Norris into custody.

Of course, Miles' gun might accidentally go off and shoot both men in the ass before the Brits got their hands on them.

"Get me proof that Norris set up Agent Carstons," Beatrice had told Miles over the video connection in the van. "Otherwise, I can't help with her MI6 issue."

There was no proof that Miles knew of. Only a confession from Norris would get Charlotte off the hook. Good thing Miles knew a few tricks for getting bastards to talk.

But if that didn't work...

With Parker covering him, Miles made his way down a secret passage that connected the parapet to the ground floor. He emerged, keeping his hood up and hanging low over his forehead as men ran past him on their way to the destroyed gate and guardhouse. A fire had started in a far section of the courtyard, thanks to Jax who was a whiz at flammables and the fact that a large portion of the castle was made of wood. With Parker's voice in his ear guiding him, Miles found the section of the main castle where they believed Charlotte was being held. One grenade later, he'd blown a hole in a wall.

Debris rained down, shouts went up. Someone inside started shooting at the opening. "That's right guys," he muttered under his breath. "Keep your eyes on that hole."

From the front of the compound, Miles heard the distant sounds of alarms and more gunfire. He worked his way around to the arched doorway to see who might be coming out. Bourean wouldn't stay in a room under siege. He wouldn't leave Charlotte in there either.

Sure enough, there was a man tugging a woman out of the room when Miles peeked around the corner. But it wasn't Bourean and Charlotte.

Norris. The guy's bald head had a few scratches on it, one of his pant legs was torn. He had hold of a young girl, who was sobbing and crying, and he shoved her out of the room toward an exit. "Go!" he was yelling. "Move your worthless ass."

Miles needed to stop Norris, but all he could think of was Charlotte, still in that room.

He was about to move on Norris when Charlotte bolted from the room, chasing after the girl. "You can't have her!"

Miles' heart froze inside his chest. "Charlotte!"

She was hurt, lurching to one side. Blood had soaked through her coat on her upper arm, her hair was dirty and wet. He called her name again over the din of noise from outside, but she didn't hear him as another man emerged on her heels, gun drawn and pointed at the back of her head.

Miles moved without thought, instincts firing into full throttle.

Charlotte hit Norris from behind, shoving him away from the girl. The girl threw herself at Charlotte and Charlotte grabbed her, hugging her to her side as she tried to run with her. Bourean launched himself at Charlotte, swinging his gun and catching her at the base of her neck.

Charlotte's body seized and then crumpled.

"No!" Miles was on top of Bourean before the man knew what hit him, his vision white with rage. He wrapped his arms around the guy's neck and took him down to the ground. The gun went off, the bullet ricocheting off the plaster ceiling before they landed.

The guy was scrappy but Miles had the superior strength and training. He broke his wrist, freeing the gun, then banged his head into the floor until the man went limp.

When he looked up, Charlotte was still on the floor, unmoving. Norris and the girl had disappeared.

"Bourean's down," he said into his comm as he crawled over to Charlotte's body. "Norris is on the run. Has a young girl with him. Don't let him get away."

"Roger that," came the replies, and then a question from Zeb who was watching and listening from the van. "What about our asset?"

Blood ran freely into her hair from a cut on the back of her neck at the base of her skull. Miles turned her gently so she was lying on her back. She was as pale as the snow outside, her bottom lip swollen. He checked her pulse and felt it thready under his fingertips. "Alive, but in serious condition."

Gunfire off to his left had him crouching farther over her body to protect her. A moment later, Jax came running into view. "What happened?" he said, kneeling beside her and brushing Miles' hands away. "Was she shot?"

Blood pooled on the floor, coating his fingers and seeping under his knees. "She took a hit to the back of her head. Cut open her scalp. She has a bleeding wound on her left deltoid. She came out of the room holding her ribs and dragging her left leg."

Jax pulled some supplies from his deep coat pockets and started wrapping her head. "We need a gurney to haul her out of here."

"A gurney's not viable," Zeb said in their ears. "Stabilize her and get the hell out of there. Coldplay and Jett can't cover you much longer."

Alarms were going off all over the place, probably from the fire Jax had started. In all the commotion, no one seemed to realize their leader was down for the count.

"Roger that," Miles said, wondering how the hell he was going stabilize Charlotte and haul ass in the next few seconds.

Jax wiggled his fingers at Miles. "Give me your hat."

Miles handed him the knit hat and watched as Jax put it over Charlotte's head, strapping it down tight with wide gauze. Miles held her hands, trying to warm them. They were so cold, they felt like ice cubes. Bright red marks showed on her wrists as if she'd been cuffed.

"Get me a blanket," Jax said. "Something sturdy that we can roll her up in."

Miles didn't want to let go of her hands, but he did, giving them a hard squeeze before he released her and headed for the room. He was three steps from her and Jax when a guy with an M4 came barreling around the corner.

Instinct took over again, and as the guy pulled up short at the sight of Bourean on the ground, Miles pulled his gun and shot him in the chest.

Man down.

With no time to lose, he scooted into the room, spotting an expensive wool rug with a fancy design on it in the center of the wooden floor.

Shoving the coffee table off, Miles jerked on the large, heavy rug, but got nowhere. It was anchored under a couple of chairs on one side and a couch on the other. Frustration burning through his veins, he did a linebacker move, hitting the couch full force and toppling it over. Then he turned and kicked each of the chairs off the rug.

Flipping it up and over, he folded it a couple of times and hauled it out of the room.

"Does anyone have eyes on Norris?" Zeb said in their comms.

Hunter and Parker both responded with nos.

Fuck. Miles would have punched the wall if he hadn't been concentrating on helping Jax position Charlotte on one end of the rug. Slowly, they began to roll her up.

When they finished, Jax helped him lift her up onto his shoulder, fireman-style. "Asset is secure," Miles told the group. "Now find me a clear path out of here."

"Go back to the secret passage," came Parker's reply. "Take a left instead of a right and you'll come to the back entrance I snuck you in through earlier. I'll have you covered."

"Roger that," Miles said and patted Charlotte's unconscious body. "Let's get you out of here, Agent Butter."

CHAPTER TWENTY

Charlotte fought through the heavy waves of pain and darkness. She was so damn cold again and a part of her just wanted to let go. Let go of the pain, let the darkness swallow her.

Nico. The castle. The images came in fits and starts, making her gasp. She'd been here before. She'd sworn she'd never let him do this to her again, and yet here she was, body broken, spirit crushed. Why not just give up? What was there to live for?

Miles.

She'd heard him call her name, hadn't she?

Had to be a trick of her mind. Miles was gone. She would never see him again.

Tears ran from the corners of her eyes. Hot and messy and she hated the world for a moment.

Pressing through the darkness, she tried to remember more. Madeena had been there, calling her Sarah, but in her mind, she heard Miles again. She was sure she had heard his voice calling her name.

In fact, through the pain buzzing in every cell of her body, she thought she could hear him saying her name right now.

Maybe I've already died and gone to heaven. Miles was there to meet her. A lovely thought, but surely heaven, or whatever afterlife there was, wasn't filled with so much cold and pain.

"Charlotte."

There it was again, the voice she loved with its slight southern accent.

"Charlie, can you hear me?"

Charlie? Miles never called her that, only her friends back in school had ever used that nickname. Friends, who one by one, deserted her after she claimed her mother was killed. Friends who treated her like she had a disease after she came out of the mental hospital.

This afterlife was really screwed up if this was some version of heaven.

She felt someone take her hand. Life seeped into her fingers, warmth, support.

"Come on, Charlotte. Wake up for me."

She wanted to wake up, but her eyes refused to obey the command to open. What if this was all a trick? What if the voice she was hearing wasn't real?

It can't be Miles. Miles is dead.

Man, God had a wicked sense of humor.

If she kept her eyes closed, maybe the voice would keep talking to her and she could pretend Miles *was* alive. She wanted more of that voice, more of the heat warming her hand. She could forget about the pain and the darkness if she just had those two things to anchor onto.

She'd never told him that she loved him. So many missed opportunities. What had she been waiting for? She, out of anyone, knew how easily a life could be snuffed out. How someone you love could be taken away in the blink of an eye.

Parting her lips, she took a deep breath. A fresh wave of pain shot through her ribs and she winced. "I love you, Miles," she said on a tremulous exhale.

Fingers brushed across her cheek. "I love you, too, sweetheart. Now, open them pretty eyes for me."

A surge of hope smothered her doubts. She forced her eyelids to crack open. "Miles?"

Her vision was crap. She was on a bed, under some blankets, but the person next to her was a giant blur.

She blinked rapidly, trying to bring him into focus. Every blink brought a clearer picture.

Dark hair, flannel shirt, a wide smile. "There's my girl."

He turned his face and called over his shoulder, "She's awake."

"Miles?" She couldn't seem to stop saying his name. He leaned closer, the features on his face becoming distinct. The beautiful eyes she loved, the angled jaw, the broad nose. "Did I die and go to heaven?"

In her peripheral vision, several fuzzy figures appeared.

Miles chuckled, rubbing her arm. "Close, but no. We're at an abandoned church not far from the compound. You're in the parish."

Despite the pain, despite the weakness and her blurry vision, Charlotte reached out and grabbed him. "Oh, my God. I thought you were dead."

Clumsily, she pulled him into an embrace, fighting through the sluggishness in her body. A tug on her arm made her glance at it. She was hooked up to some kind of homemade IV.

"Easy, easy." Miles held her tight but with care. After a too-short minute, he forced her to let go of him and lie prone again. "I killed the guy who got a jump on us at the cabin and then I came after you."

One of the fuzzy figures on the edge of her vision moved closer. "You took a serious hit to the back of your head, Charlie." As his features materialized, she recognized Jaxon. "I didn't want to give you any pain medicine in case you have a concussion, which I'm pretty sure you do."

Head concussion. Try three. "I'm pretty sure you're right."

Light laughter sounded from everyone. "How do you feel otherwise?" Miles asked. He held her hand and she had to keep squeezing it to make sure he was real. "You have a couple of bruised ribs, and it looks like you sprained your ankle. You took a stab to your shoulder."

Were the ribs only bruised? The pain was substantial. Didn't matter. *Miles is alive.* "I feel like I took a horse kicking," she said.

Another round of chuckles.

"Everything is wrapped up good and tight," Jax said. "I think you avoided any internal injuries, so the thing we're most worried about is your head."

"Not the first time someone's been worried about that," Charlotte mumbled. Although the last time anyone had worried about the condition of her head, they'd been more worried about her mental state than her physical one. "Nico? Did he get away?"

Miles exchanged a glance with an older guy. "A team of SIS showed up right as I carried you out. Nico was down for the count. They picked him up and have him in custody, but..."

"They don't have the video proving he and his men shot down the plane." Charlotte sighed. "CB Norris, my handler, has the USB. I don't suppose you nabbed him? The guy in black? He had a girl with him."

The older guy spoke. "He disappeared on us."

"Sorry." Charlotte squinted. "But who are all you people?"

A round of introductions ensued. Zeb, Parker, Trace, Moe. She repeated the names in her head three times to make sure she didn't forget.

"We assume Norris took the girl with him," Zeb said.

Madeena. *Have to find her.* Norris would use her for the same reason Miles would if he knew her identity—to find her father.

Charlotte tried shifting into a sitting position. The room spun, a fresh wave of pain exploding behind her eyes and inside her ribs. "Damn, that hurts."

"Whoa." Miles stopped her and forced her back down. "Where do you think you're going?"

"Madeena, the girl. She needs me." She rolled onto her side and pushed herself up on her elbow. The floor seemed to roll like a wave under the bed and she closed her eyes for a second, then blinked them open. The rolling stopped, the room didn't spin.

Better. "I didn't tell you this before, Miles, and I hope you don't hate me." *Especially after you told me you love me.* "But..."

Miles narrowed his eyes, his lips firming slightly before he spoke. "But what, Charlotte? Spit it out."

Should she tell him? Come clean?

God, she was tired. Tired of the lies and the secrets. She had to protect Madeena, but she couldn't lie to Miles any longer. She had to make him understand. "The girl? She knows the man responsible for shooting down your helicopter last year."

"The terrorist?"

"He goes by Blackwater," Zeb interjected.

Charlotte licked her dry, cracked lips. "Yes, I know."

Miles' voice rose. "You know?"

"That's what Madeena called him. Blackwater."

"Your handler, Norris, has been after him for almost twenty years," Zeb said. "How does the girl know him?"

Sweat broke out along the back of her neck. Everyone was staring at her, their faces now distinct and every one of them clouded with worry. "Nico made some kind of trade with the man. He got the girl as part of the payment for the RPGs."

"Who is she?" Miles asked.

Charlotte swallowed against the lump in her throat. "She's Blackwater's daughter."

Zeb's bushy eyebrows lifted. "Blackwater has a daughter?"

Charlotte nodded, keeping an eye on Miles. His face was tight, his body completely still. "From what Madeena told me," she said, "he has several sons whom he put into his training camps. She's his only daughter, no better than a dog to him. Her mother died and Blackwater wanted her gone. He sold her in the trade."

Miles' gaze was hard. "She knows where her father is hiding out, doesn't she?"

Charlotte nodded.

"You were going to tell me this, right? At some point, while we were still in Romania, you were going to tell me that you actually knew the identity of the bastard who killed my teammates and that this Madeena could help me find him. Right, Charlotte?"

She needed to sit up and face him straight on, make him understand. She didn't think the pain in her ribs could get much worse, but it did as she forced herself into a sitting position. Grabbing his hand, she held it tight. "I couldn't tell you. I knew you'd want to go after her and force her to tell you where Blackwater is hiding in the mountains. I couldn't do that to her."

His hand was slack in hers. "Couldn't do what?"

"Miles, she's fifteen. If she gave up her father's whereabouts to you and you killed him, think of the guilt she would live with for the rest of her life."

"Her father is a murderer. He gave her away like a piece of property to a man who's done despicable things to her. Why wouldn't she want to see him brought to justice?"

"It's a complicated situation, but believe me, she would never betray him willingly, even after what he's done to her." She knew the feeling well. No matter how badly her father had betrayed her, she still felt some loyalty to the man. Some love. "You might have had to...force it out of her, and she's been through enough. Nico is a master at torture."

"Wait." Miles jerked his hand away. "You think I would hurt some young girl to get what I wanted?" He jumped up and fell back a couple of steps. "Jesus Christ, Charlotte. I want revenge, but I'm not Nicolae Bourean. I don't get my rocks off on hurting women."

"I never said that. I just didn't want you or her to be put in such a position."

Zeb rubbed a hand down his face. "But Norris will do exactly that. Force her to tell him where Blackwater is."

Charlotte nodded. "He will use violence and torture if he has to. That's why I have to find them. Not just for the proof that Norris set me up and that Nico was working with Blackwater. I have to save Madeena. Besides, my beef with Norris is personal." She looked down at the blanket covering her legs, picked at a lint ball. "He had my mother killed."

It seemed strange to say the words out loud. To know that she'd been right all along, even when everyone else had been telling her she was wrong. Deep down, she'd believed what she saw that night was real, but after so many years of people telling her she was confused, she'd started to doubt herself.

"What?" Miles was back at her side. "Norris?"

She gave him the brief details, Miles sitting on the edge of the bed as she relayed the story CB had told her. "I was right all along," she said with a sad smile. "And all that time, I played right into his hands."

Miles pulled her into a gentle hug and it felt so good to be held, comforted. She wrapped her arms around him and closed her eyes.

Zeb interrupted the moment. "Norris is a borderline sociopath, Agent Carstons. You shouldn't feel bad about being dragged into his master plan."

But she did feel bad. Some operative she was. How flippin' stupid and gullible could she be? She broke from Miles' embrace and looked at Zeb. "You seem to know more about him than I do."

"I've been around a whole lot longer than you, missy." Zeb smiled at her. "Been in this game a lot longer too."

He was too old to be a current operative. Maybe a handler? "Are you CIA? NSA?"

He winked. "Let's just say I came out of retirement to help some friends."

She gave him a nod. "I appreciate that."

Parker, the woman, grabbed a coat off a nearby chair. "Norris will have to take Madeena somewhere to torture the information out of her. Where would he go?" she asked Charlotte.

Charlotte scanned her weary brain for an answer. "I don't know where he was staying, and he wouldn't take her back there, anyway. He didn't want Orlo to shoot Miles in the cabin because he said he was going to go back there. It's remote, it's close to the mountains…?"

"He said that, thinking we'd both be dead by now," Miles said. "We know about the cabin. He won't take her there."

Memories of Nico's torture flooded her mind. A fresh chill slipped over her skin. "Did anyone see him leave Nico's compound?"

Zeb's head came around and he zeroed in on her. "SIS cleared the premises but found no trail."

The man named Moe spoke up. He had a tablet in one hand. "Satellite imagery of the past few hours shows no vehicles leaving the compound except for those the SIS guys arrived in, and they didn't report any missing, so he didn't steal any of theirs."

"He's still in the castle," Zeb said.

"Probably took one of those secret passageways to disappear into," Miles added.

Charlotte fought the terror the memories of Nico's torture chamber invoked. The chamber of secrets she never wanted to see again. "I know where they are."

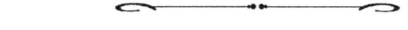

"What?" Miles shook his head at Charlotte's ridiculous idea. "You can't go. You can't even walk."

Charlotte shot him a look that said, "watch me", then yanked out the makeshift IV Jax had carefully put in her arm. "You guys don't know how to find Nico's torture chamber. I do."

Jax made an unhappy grunt at Charlotte undoing his handiwork. Charlotte threw back the blanket, swung her legs around and sat up.

"How would Norris know where it's at if it's that hard to find?" Parker asked.

"Who says he hasn't been in it before?" Charlotte swayed slightly and Miles grabbed her arm and plunked down on the bed next to her. She didn't pull away, but stiffened. "If he's been working with Nico all this time, I'm sure he knows more about that castle and its secret passages than any of us."

"I've already been in the secret passageway." Charlotte's earlier statement was still rocking Miles to the core. How could she believe he would hurt an innocent girl? He grabbed the set of blueprints from the nearby table, held them out to her. "I can find it if you tell me where it is."

She shook her head, made to stand. "I'm going. That's final."

God, she was so stubborn. Miles stared at her as she wobbled on her feet. Dark circles bruised the undersides of her eyes. Her hair was limp, her bottom lip swollen. She teetered precariously for a second, staring back at him, and in her eyes, he saw the raw determination propelling her to her feet. The driving intensity, not for justice, or revenge, or to clear her name, but to save a girl she barely knew. For the first time since they'd met, he wondered if he was finally seeing the real Charlotte Carstons.

"I won't ask her about Blackwater, I swear," Miles said, blocking her from moving away from the bed. "Just stay here with Jax. Let him give you some pain meds, get some more fluids in you. Please, for me, Charlotte."

She lifted a hand and touched his face. "I know you won't ask her about her father, but it has to be me who goes. She doesn't trust anyone, with good reason."

He gripped her hand, squeezed it. Madeena wasn't the only one who didn't trust anyone. "I'll bring the girl back, unharmed. I promise."

"It would be easier for her and for you, if I go. She'll come with me without question. She'll fight you."

Her point was valid if that were the truth. He could see in her steady gaze it was. "You're not healthy and you're in terrible pain."

"I'm breathing and upright. That's enough."

So stubborn. He let his forehead fall forward and rest on hers, lowering his voice. "I can't lose you again."

"You won't," she murmured. "I'm stuck to you like glue, mister. You're never getting rid of me after all we've been through. Renalda said we have some difficulties to overcome. Let's go overcome them and get on with a new life together."

Zeb cleared his throat. "I hate to break up this romantic moment, but we need to get a move on. A fifteen year old girl won't hold out long against a man like Norris."

Parker handed Charlotte her coat. Miles helped her get it on. Jax dropped a couple of white tablets into her hand, and held up a glass of water. "This won't do much, but it's better than nothing."

Charlotte swallowed the pills and gave Jax a grateful look. "Thank you."

Her boots were next. Charlotte sat on the edge of the bed as

Miles helped her pull the first one on. The others were already outside, readying themselves and the van. On his knees at her feet, he laced the ties.

"I can do that, you know," she said, sipping the water.

He double knotted the first one. "Those bruised ribs might say otherwise."

"Thank you for everything." She sighed. "You're the first person to take care of me since my mother."

He glanced up and saw tears in her eyes. Finishing up the second boot—he had to leave the ties loose because of the wrap job Jax had done on the ankle to stabilize it—he slid up to sit next to her. "I'm always going to take care of you, Charlotte, whether you like it or not."

A slim smile crossed her lips. "You don't have to do this—go after Norris and Madeena. Your team...I don't like putting them or you in danger."

"I don't like it either, but we're finishing this mission. Together. Nico's in custody, Norris is going to pay." He patted her knee. "And we're going to clear your name."

"As long as you and Maddy make it out of this okay, none of the rest matters to me."

"Yeah, well, it matters to me." He stood and helped her to her feet. "Come on, Agent Carstons, we've got some butt to kick."

CHAPTER TWENTY-ONE

BOUREAN COMPOUND

There were multiple secret passageways throughout the castle and its fortresses. Inside walls, under ground, behind fireplaces and bookshelves. Stone crawlspaces sometimes gave way to wood, acknowledging different centuries, different reasons for disappearing from the main areas of the castle. There were complete rooms off of some, others once led under and out of the castle grounds, escape routes in case of siege. As far as Charlotte knew, all of those had caved in long ago.

The stone walls she was now leading Miles and Jaxon through seeped with cold and frost. Charlotte hobbled on her bad foot, shivering deep in her bones.

Parker and Trace were keeping an eye on the entire compound, which was quite a feat considering the place took up ten acres of ground. Each was stationed in a tower, scopes and rifles in hand.

Zeb was in the van, monitoring their movements and giving verbal instructions when needed over their comm units. Moe was on standby, ready to assist with nabbing Norris or running interference should anyone unexpected show up.

The fires topside were mostly out, thanks to the snow, the castle grounds quiet and deserted when they'd arrived. The SIS had left with Nico and a handful of his men an hour ago. Charlotte counted herself lucky she wasn't with them.

The blizzard howled and blanketed everything in white, but

Charlotte, Miles, and Jax were too deep underground to hear it. Flashlight in hand and gun at the ready, Charlotte wove cautiously through the tunnel, praying her hunch was right, but hoping it wasn't at the same time. There was no good outcome for Madeena—tortured and left to die here, kicked out in the blizzard, or forced to watch Norris hunt down and kill her father. At least if she was here, Charlotte could help her.

The gun felt too heavy in her hand. An H&K P30, it was made for a bigger person, a wider hand. The hammer had no spur and there was no de-cocker button. The only way to release the cocked mainspring was to pull the trigger.

She'd never fired one of these before, but beggars couldn't be choosers. It was Zeb's gun, the only extra weapon they had unless they wanted to go clear across the grounds to break into Nico's weapon room. Charlotte didn't want to waste the time.

Noise at her feet startled her and she jumped. Caught in the flashlight beam, a rat skittered away and Charlotte shivered with revulsion. The rats. Those were the worst. Madeena, the poor girl, had made pets out of several of them. They were, of course, always after food, and the kindhearted girl would break off small pieces of her rations and feed them. More than once, Charlotte had woken up to one chewing on her hair, her clothes.

It hadn't always been that way. Before Nico had found out she was an MI6 agent, she'd practically had the run of the castle. He'd valued her as an asset because she brought him solid intel. He liked her because she was aloof and flirty but would never let him cross the line sexually. She was a challenge.

The second time around here, she'd been his slave.

The room was a typical medieval torture chamber. Chains, knives, punishment. One wall held implements, a long steel table under them with more assorted tools for inflicting pain.

The brutality she'd endured, and watched Madeena endure as well, infuriated her. It would be priceless to see Nico given a dose of his own medicine, but, right now she had to save the girl and stop Norris.

"How much farther?" Miles asked from behind her.

He'd been right at her side the whole way, a touch here and there, steadying her. The pain pills had kicked in and allowed her a certain amount of relief, enough to let her focus on finding the right tunnel and getting down to the torture chamber. She saw the familiar T in the passageway ahead. It looked like a dead end as her flashlight beam caressed the rock wall, but the illusion disappeared once you were up on it and could see the door encased by stones. "Almost there."

Rocks crunched under their feet. Debris from the explosions that had rocked this side of the grounds earlier, most likely. She slowed, not wanting the noise to warn anyone behind that door in case Norris was still in there.

A tiny sound met her ears and she raised her hand to signal Miles and Jax to stop. Slowly easing her way up to the door, she turned her head and listened.

Stifled sobbing filtered through the wood and stone.

A girl's sobs.

Relief stripped her of strength for a moment, her knees wobbling, her head going light. Gripping Zeb's gun tighter, she looked back at Miles and Jax and gave a nod. "She's alive," she mouthed.

Quietly, they slipped up beside her. Miles signaled her to stand back. She took one side of the door, Jax the other. Gun in hand, Miles reared back and kicked the door in.

Wood splintered. Miles raised his weapon, disappeared into the room, Jax on his heels.

Charlotte raised her gun and swung in behind Jax as Miles called, "Clear!"

His voice echoed off the high ceiling, the stone walls. No Norris. None of Nico's men hiding out. The only person inside was Madeena.

The girl was gagged and tied to a chair, wrists bound to the chair arms with wires. Her head was tipped forward, long, stringy dark hair cascading over her face as she sobbed. A thin cotton dress hung down past her knees. Her feet were bare and dirty, ankles tied to the chair legs with more wire.

She didn't even look up.

Blood ran from both of her wrists, covering her forearms and hands, running down the chair to pool on the floor.

"Oh God" Charlotte rushed to kneel in front of Madeena, brushing the stringy hair out of the girl's eyes and pulling the gag from her lips. "Maddy, it's me, Sarah. You're okay now. We're here to save you."

The girl's head wobbled on her neck as she tried to bring her chin up and look at Charlotte. She couldn't seem to get the job done. Her eyes were half-lidded as if she were drugged. Her words slurred. "Sa... Sarah?"

So much blood. "Yes, baby. It's me."

"I knew you...would come ba...back...for me."

Miles brought out a knife and started sawing the wires from her wrists. Jax shrugged off his backpack and let it fall to the floor, unzipping it and hauling out first aid items.

"I'm sorry it took me so long," Charlotte said. She accepted some gauze pads from Jax and began wiping blood and dirt from Madeena's face. "Did the bald man do this to you?"

Madeena's chin dropped to her collarbone as if her head were too heavy to hold up. "He said I had to tell him." A sob wracked her thin frame. "I didn't... I couldn't..."

"Hey, Charlie?"

Charlotte swung her attention to Jax. He met her eyes, then dropped his gaze to Madeena's arm.

She looked down. Jax was holding a wad of gauze to Madeena's forearm, and he lifted it for a second. Charlotte involuntarily gasped. Norris hadn't just sliced Maddy's wrist. He'd ran his knife up her forearm, laying it open.

"Same here," Miles said quietly, putting pressure on Madeena's other arm.

No wonder there was so much blood. Maddy hadn't been drugged. She had nearly bled out.

"Control, this is Poison," Miles said. "Target has been acquired. As you can see, target needs medical assistance before we evac."

Each of them had a tiny camera attached to a button on their coats, relaying information back to Zeb in the van. "Roger that," Zeb came back over their comms. "Can she walk?"

"I'll carry her," Miles said.

Charlotte's heart flooded with love. Being alone had been her modis operandi for so long, it felt uncomfortable to lean on others. To let someone like Miles—so strong and brave—into her world, even though that's what she wanted most. Keeping people at a distance was how she'd survived since her mother's death. She'd learned not to need anyone.

Miles didn't need anyone either, but he chose to work on teams. He was a survivor, like her, but he didn't shut himself off from those around him.

For the first time in a long time, Charlotte knew she needed someone in her life she could count on.

She needed Miles. Not just to help her rescue Madeena or take down Norris. She needed him to love her. "Thank you," she whispered to him.

He gave her a nod.

Blood was seeping through the gauze. Jax handed Miles more layers, dug out more for him as well.

"I couldn't help it," the girl said. "It hurt so bad."

"It's okay," Charlotte crooned. "We're going to find the man who did this to you and stop him."

"He wants…to kill my father."

"Did you tell him where your father is?" Charlotte said.

The girl sobbed, then moaned something that sounded like an affirmative.

"You need to tell us where he is, too." She hated asking the girl, but the only way to catch up to Norris was to know where he was headed. "We can stop him."

The girl shook her head.

"Control?" Moe's voice was low but strained. "Are you seeing this?"

"Roger," Zeb responded, then paused. "Shit. Is that what I think it is?"

The three of them exchanged a look, waiting for Moe to clarify.

"Looks like it to me," came his reply. Static filled the silence. The tunnels were difficult to receive transmissions in, but so far had been doing all right. "It's located on the inner wall perimeter, right above the target."

"Someone want to fill us in?" Trace, still outside with Parker, said after a tense pause filled the connection.

"Initiate evacuation," Zeb barked. "Now."

Jax's face pinched. "I have to stop this bleeding. We can't move the target yet."

Zeb's voice roughened with anxiety. "There's no time. Grab the target and move your ass."

What was going on?

Miles straightened, touching his earbud with his fingers. "We need five minutes. Can you give us that much?"

"I can disarm it,"—static danced with Moe's voice—"…hasn't been activated yet. We have time."

"Disarm it?" Charlotte parroted. "Are we talking…a bomb?"

A sickeningly long silence followed.

"That's exactly what we're talking about," Parker said.

Charlotte could mentally see the woman with her sniper rifle up on one of the towers. "But there's not just one. I'm looking at a minimum of four, spaced out and attached around that perimeter wall."

The place was loaded to blow.

"Get out." Zeb's voice was that of a father who expected his kids to obey. "Whoever set those bombs could activate them at any moment."

Charlotte gave Miles a pleading look. He cupped her shoulder with a hand and squeezed. "We're not leaving until we secure the girl," Miles said to Zeb.

"Four bombs, Jett?" Moe's voice was tight. "Well, in that case, chaps, I'm gonna need some help with the disarming."

Nico or Norris? Who had wired the place to blow? Had to be Norris, Charlotte thought. He needed to destroy evidence that proved he'd been here, especially in the torture room with Madeena.

"Go help Moe," she said to Miles. "We can't let this place blow up even if we make it out."

"What? And leave you?" Troubled lines appeared in his forehead and he shook his head. "No way."

"I'll be fine. Norris is long gone and Maddy can't move yet. There may be DNA or other evidence here that will help us nail Norris for his crimes."

Miles' jaw muscle jumped as he gritted his teeth, but he didn't argue.

"You, too," she said, poking Jax in the arm. "The two of you help Henley. I'll handle the bandaging and let you know when Maddy is ready to move."

The two men exchanged a worried glance. "If we move Madeena before we get her arms bandaged," Jax told Miles, "she could bleed out."

Charlotte took a roll of gauze from Jax's hands. There was still so much blood. It was all over their hands, their coats, but at least it had stopped dripping to the floor. "Four bombs, four of you. Parker stays on the tower as lookout while you guys disarm the bombs. Now go. I'll get the wounds wrapped up and get some fluid in Maddy. She's going to need a coat and shoes, too, or she'll have instant frostbite when we drag her out of here. I know where to find her some clothes, but I need time."

Jax stood. "Come on, man. She's right. Let's disarm those bombs."

Miles spoke into his comm. "Are you sure there are only four, Jett?"

"Confirmed," the woman replied. "Four."

Moe sounded more confident now. "I can walk you guys through disarming them. They're not complicated. Piece of cake, especially since they aren't activated."

Miles closed his eyes and woofed out a sigh. "God, I hate bombs."

Jax slapped him on the back as he headed for the door. "Don't we all."

Miles grabbed Charlotte by her upper arms and dragged her into a fierce hug. "I'll be back for you. Stay here. Once we're done with the bombs, I'll go with you to find clothes for Madeena."

Charlotte hugged him back, burying her face in his neck and inhaling his warm Miles smell. She shut off her comm. "Don't worry about me. Take care of yourself. I need you."

He muted his comm as well, leaning back and staring down at her. "I love you, Charlotte. I want us to have a life together after this."

She didn't know what kind of life she was going to have, but she wanted Miles in it. More than anything she'd ever wanted in her life. "Are you sure? I have a lot of ugly baggage."

He kissed her forehead and smiled. "I love your baggage too."

"Right-o, then." Her lips curved in a silly smile. She couldn't help it. Giddiness made her lightheaded. "I'm going to start making all kinds of plans."

His lips brushed hers and he stroked her hair before turning away and heading out.

Madeena moaned and Zeb barked in Charlotte's ear about losing her over the comm. Charlotte turned her comm back on, assured Zeb it was still activated, and went to work on the girl's wounds.

There were two rolls of gauze, bottled water, and some miscellaneous first aid items in Jax's backpack. Charlotte added one more layer of padding on Madeena's right arm and started wrapping, snugging the gauze as tight as she dared. She softly hummed an old Gypsy lullaby under her breath, half listening in as Henley relayed instructions to the three men joining him.

More than once, Madeena nearly lost consciousness. Charlotte had to keep coaxing her awake, repositioning her in the chair. She finally got her left arm wrapped too. With the amount of blood Madeena had lost, she might need a transfusion. How were they going to do that?

A bottle of painkillers was at the bottom of Jax's bag. The same kind that he'd given Charlotte. Hers were already wearing off, but she was hesitant to give any to Madeena, fearing they might increase her drowsiness. Charlotte downed a couple more herself, dry, and then encouraged Madeena to drink some water.

Charlotte knelt in front of the girl and took her hands. "We're going to get you out of here. Get you proper medical treatment. Just hang in there, okay?"

Madeena's eyes fluttered shut, then open again. "My father...that man will kill him."

"Not if we get there first. We can stop him, but I need your help. You have to tell me where your father is hiding out. Where you sent the bald man to find him."

"The bald man?" A familiar voice sounded behind her.

No. It couldn't be.

But she knew it was. Knew it in the way her hair stood up on the back of her neck. Knew it from the sound of Maddy's fearful cry.

Charlotte popped up and whirled around to find CB Norris in the exit. He held a gun in one hand and what looked like a detonator in the other. "Come on, Carstons. Show me a little respect. The girl should know the name of the man who's about to make history."

Charlotte's pulse stampeded. She reached for her gun but he had his cocked and trained on her before she could grab it. "Easy, there, kid," he said. "You don't want to shoot me."

The hell she didn't. She raised her hands, slid half a step over to shield Madeena from him. "What are you still doing here? Why aren't you gone?"

"You interrupted my party." He wiggled the detonator. "I wasn't done putting my explosives around the compound."

Suddenly, Zeb's voice was in her ear, low and controlled. "Keep him talking, girlie. I'm getting it all recorded."

Yes. Charlotte almost smiled. Her comm. As long as she stayed close enough for it to pick up CB's voice, they might get a confession.

He was never getting out of there alive. She had him. All she had to do was keep him from activating those bombs, and he wouldn't do that while he was still inside the compound.

Was Miles listening? If so, he was probably already barreling down the tunnel back to her.

But he hadn't said anything. Had Zeb turned off his comm?

Of course he had.

Didn't matter. She had this. Turning slightly, she made sure her hidden camera caught Norris' face, the gun he was holding on her. "Tying up loose ends, Agent Norris?"

"I knew you'd come back looking for the girl. I thought about taking her with me, trying to draw out Blackwater with her, but he couldn't give a crap about her." Norris' eyes sought out what he could see of Madeena, then came back to Charlotte. "Not much to care about, I guess."

Bastard. "So you tortured her about her father's hiding place and left her to bleed out. Honorable of you, hurting and killing a fifteen year old, innocent girl who's never known kindness or love in her entire life."

He half smiled. "I knew you'd have a weakness for her. Hits too close to home, doesn't it?"

Play dumb. Get him to admit what he did to your family. "I don't know what you're talking about."

"Your mother being killed, your father throwing you in with the crazies. No one cared about you, either, did they?"

There was nothing in her comm. No voices. No Henley still giving out instructions. She was sure Zeb had switched her comm to a different channel.

Behind her, Madeena cried softly. Charlotte wanted to tell her it would be okay, but maybe it wouldn't.

A strange calmness came over her. Norris was dangerous, but so was she. *Get the confession.* "You used my mother. You had her killed."

"I told you, it was an unfortunate turn of events. Orlo wasn't supposed to kill her, only rough her up a little. Scare her so she'd keep her mouth shut and not tell your father. You know why he threw you in that mental institute, don't you? He thought he could keep you safe. From me." He chuckled, smug in his confidence. "If I'd wanted to get rid of you, I could just have easily had Orlo take you out there as anywhere else."

Her dad had been trying to protect her? "I saw Orlo leaving the scene of the fire. I knew who he was."

"And you told your father, who knew he had to shut you up. If everyone thought you were crazy, you weren't a threat to Orlo or, ultimately, to me."

All these years, she'd hated her dad for putting her in there, telling people she'd lost her marbles because of her mom's death.

He'd been trying to keep her safe in the only way he knew how.

Charlotte glanced at the ugly, black gun pointed at her chest. "You should have left when you had the chance. I have a whole team here. You have no one. You won't escape."

Another chuckle. "You forget. Who told you about these tunnels and had you pass on that information to Nicolae so he'd think you were useful?"

Norris had. Back in the day when she'd been trying to get into Nico's syndicate, Norris had shown her a map of the secret passageways above and the tunnels below the castle in case she needed a quick escape. She'd used that information to make Nico believe she was a local, someone who knew more about the history of the area, and this castle, than he or any of his men. When he'd wanted to know how she knew, she'd told him her Gypsy ancestors had built the tunnels. He'd bought it.

"I never told you all of the escape routes," CB said. "Trust me, I didn't come this far to let myself be captured."

"But you're still here. Why? You've already set me up to take the fall for all of this, you don't need Madeena any longer, and you're outnumbered by a group of highly trained individuals. Why didn't you cut and run as soon as we showed up?"

The smugness left his face. "The exit I need is in here." He used the gun to motion her to step aside.

Charlotte stood her ground. There was only one way in, one way out.

Or was there?

CB's gaze dropped to the floor.

The floor. Charlotte tapped the board under her foot. Heard the hollow sound.

There was an escape hatch under her. Another tunnel. They'd interrupted him putting the bombs on all the walls and he hadn't been able to get back to the torture chamber and the one exit he needed before Charlotte had arrived with Miles and Jax.

CB's only way out.

"You're in a pickle then," she said, a bit of smugness entering her own voice. She'd have to make sure Madeena didn't get hurt, but Charlotte couldn't help it. She gave the man who'd ruined her life a big smile. "Because I'm not moving."

"You will once I move your lifeless body out of the way. I planned to shoot you all along anyway. If nothing else, just to pay you back for flipping my damn Jeep. I loved that Jeep."

God, he was so full of himself. She didn't doubt for a moment he was about to fire that gun at her chest.

So she did the only thing she could do. She pulled Zeb's ridiculously too-heavy H&K out of her waistband and pointed it at Norris' head.

"Ah, shit," she heard Zeb say in her ear. "Miles, we have a problem."

But there really wasn't one. Tired of the small talk, Charlotte slapped her other hand up to steady the gun and pulled the trigger.

CHAPTER TWENTY-TWO

Boom!

The sound was muffled, echoing up from the tunnel as Miles took the stairs to the ground level three at a time. A return popping noise, like fireworks followed. "Shit, are those gunshots?"

Zeb had told them to get back to Charlotte, that Norris was with her in the chamber. How had that happened? He hadn't heard anything over his comm.

Never should have left her.

His wet boots slipped on the stones. Hunter, right behind him, grabbed him by the coat and kept him from ending up on his ass.

"Situation update," he yelled into his comm as he squeezed into the tunnel he'd come out of earlier, drawing his gun. "Control, do you read?"

Static came back in his ear over the shuffle and stomping of boots behind him. He, Trace, and Jax moved through the tunnel as quickly as possible, Henley still topside to continue working on dismantling the bombs.

His shoulders bumped into the narrower parts of the tunnel and sent him bouncing off the sides. Hunter grunted, experiencing the same thing.

More gunshots echoed through the tunnel, this time louder. Booming and fireworks.

Charlotte and Norris.

There was nowhere in the chamber to take cover. Charlotte was already injured and would be protecting Madeena.

Get to her, now!

He couldn't lose another person in his life. Couldn't lose *her*.

Zeb's voice broke through the static. "...proceed with caution...shots fired..."

No shit.

They hit the bottom floor. Miles held up a hand to stop his SEAL train and listened. The shooting had stopped. No voices, no nothing. The door to the chamber was open.

Was Charlotte dead? Had Norris shot her and escaped?

A clamp squeezed down on his chest. His mind blanked for a second due to a surge of rage, a flash of past memories that threatened to immobilize him.

His training took over, thank God, and he signaled Hunter to move to the other side of the door. Jax slipped in behind Miles to cover him.

Miles edged forward enough to see part of the room. The chair Madeena had been siting in was tipped over, blood smeared across the floor where her body had been dragged. The table was on its side, the gleaming instruments that had once sat on it scattered on the floor. Bullet holes pitted the metal, the tip of a single dirty, naked foot peeked out from one end.

Madeena.

"Did your boyfriend tell you why he was in those mountains not far from your cabin that day?"

The voice startled him. A man.

Close.

Behind the door?

He hadn't ever heard Norris' voice, but it had to be him.

Miles met Hunter's eyes. Hunter motioned at the door's hinges.

Yep, Norris had taken cover behind the door. He had to be talking to Charlotte.

She's alive.

Relief ricocheted inside him, *ping, ping, ping*. She had to be behind the table with Madeena.

Norris' voice came again from the other side of the door. "He was looking for you. That team of his was working with SIS on a so-called training mission, but I'd already given you up to Vauxhall. Told them all about the fact you'd passed on tons of info to Nicolae. They were gunning for you, Carstons. Your SEAL knew from the first time he saw you who you were. That you were a traitor. When I'm done here with you, I'll make sure he's branded a traitor, too, for helping you. Of course, I'm going to kill him first."

The sound of Charlotte laughing rang out, echoing in the chamber. Not a carefree, happy laugh, but one of a woman who'd survived the worst life could throw at her and didn't give a fuck about threats from a piece of shit like Norris.

"You go ahead and try that," she said. "But let's get one thing straight. The only way you're leaving here, you wanker, is in a body bag or handcuffs. If I have my way about it, I'm voting for the body bag."

Miles smiled at her sheer tenacity. He'd always been a tough SOB, but Charlotte's bulldog attitude and determination put him to shame.

With three fingers raised, he started the countdown for his men. One...

"And just so you know..." she added.

Two...

"...you're about to meet my boyfriend face to face."

Three—Miles swung through the opening, firing at the thick wooden door, Hunter and Jax on his heels.

The shots were deafening in the chamber on top of the sound of splintering wood and shouting. Ears already hissing from the previous hail of bullets between her and Norris, Charlotte clamped her hands over them as Miles and the other men invaded the underground room.

Madeena was a limp biscuit, a dead weight, draped across Charlotte's ankles and feet. Sweat trickled down Charlotte's skull, into the wrapping Jax had secured there. Her heart jackhammered in her chest as she tried to stay lucid. The hand with Zeb's gun flopped to the floor, her arm too weak to hold it up any longer.

Stand up, she commanded, but her body wouldn't obey. Warm, sticky fluid ran from her leg, covering the floor where Madeena's blood had already stained it. Her eyelids fluttered closed and she forced them open. She had to stay awake.

The echoes of the gunshots faded off, commotion on the other side of the room suggesting Miles and the others were hauling Norris out from behind the door. Gritting her teeth against the searing pain in her leg that put the ache in her ribs to shame, Charlotte propped herself up on one elbow and peered through a small hole in the table she'd used as a shield.

Between two pairs of men's legs, she saw Norris lying on the floor, still half behind the door. His eyes were closed, his black knit cap askew on his head.

"Get your girl," Trace said. He grabbed Norris under the armpits and pulled him out from behind the door.

The hissing was mostly gone from her ears and Moe's voice startled her when he spoke. "Uh, guys? Hate to interrupt your little tete-a-tete down there, but if anyone can lend a hand, we have a situation."

Miles hustled to Charlotte's side. "Norris is down," he said as he knelt next to her. He brushed hair from her face and kissed her forehead. "You're going to be okay," he whispered to her, then said to Moe, "What do you need?"

"Yeah, sorta figured Norris was out of commission, but when he went down, he left us a little gift."

Jax had come around the other end of the table and was shifting Madeena off of Charlotte's lower legs. His fingers felt for a pulse at her neck and Charlotte held her breath, waiting to see if the young girl had made it. He glanced up at her and nodded.

Sweet Jesus. Madeena was alive.

"What kind of a gift?" Zeb barked in their comms.

Miles shed his coat. He stripped off his shirt, wrapping it around Charlotte's upper thigh and cinching it down. She cried out in pain but knew it was probably her only hope.

"The bombs," Moe answered. "They've been activated."

Miles and Jax exchanged a look. "Can you walk?" Miles asked, helping Charlotte sit up.

Her heart did a rapid-fire *thudthudthud* and her head felt like a balloon, so light it would float away. "Of course," she lied.

"The good thing is," Moe went on, "There are only two left since we disarmed the others. But even if these two blow, it could cause a ripple effect in the castle's foundation. Everything could cave in."

Miles handed his coat to Hunter, his voice sounding far away, even though he was right next to her. "Wrap the girl in my coat and carry her out. Jax, get up there and help Henley. I've got Charlotte."

"You sure?" Jax said, frowning at Charlotte's leg. "I don't think she's going to stay conscious long."

Charlotte laughed. She no longer felt her leg, her hip, her ribs. Nothing. The rest of her body was floating like her head. "I'm fine," she insisted. Her words sounded muffled to her ears. "Let's go."

Trace appeared above her, looking over the edge of the table. "Ah, shit," he said, when his keen eyes sized her up. He had Norris' gun. He slid it into the back of his waistband. "Megadeth, you take the girl. I'll help Poison with our MI6 agent."

Megadeth, Poison…such silly names. Charlotte grinned at Miles, realized his hands were holding her up in the sitting position. Zeb's gun, on the ground next to her, was fuzzy around the edges. At one point, it morphed into three guns instead of one.

Definite concussion.

She remembered this feeling from her childhood. This lightheaded, room-spinning, I-can't-feel-anything sensation she hated with a passion. All those days, all those nights at the hospital, strapped to a bed and going out of her mind with hallucinations, only to have the nurses replace those with the god-awful feeling that she might float so high, she'd float away. No one would ever find her. No one would even miss her.

Had Miles drugged her? A spurt of panic erupted in her chest. She grabbed his arm to steady herself, blinked hard.

Not drugs. No one had given her any drugs.

Charlotte looked from Miles' naked chest down to her lap, to the tourniquet he'd tied around her leg. Jax lifted Madeena carefully, laid her over his shoulder, gave Charlotte a thumbs-up, and left her view. Trace took his place at her feet.

There was still so much blood. Rivers of it, snaking out from her body, coating Miles' hands, the treads on Trace's boots. More blood than they'd found Madeena sitting in.

No, it wasn't drugs giving her this high.

I'm dying.

The past few minutes played out in her head in a tornado. She'd fired on Norris, knocked Madeena to the floor. Felt the ripping sting of the bullet eating through her flesh. "Norris…shot…me," she managed to gasp. Indignation flooded her chest. Her voice came out stronger. "That bastard shot me!"

Miles and Trace helped her to her feet. With a last burst of strength, she grabbed Zeb's gun, using both hands to bring it up.

The men didn't see him, but she did. As all three of them stood up from behind the table, CB was conscious and holding a gun on them. A small pistol.

She'd thought he was dead, but there he was, lying half on his right side, his breathing labored as he raised that tiny pistol and aimed it.

Not at her.

At Miles.

Miles saw it then. "Look out!"

His arm went around her belly to take her back to the floor, but Charlotte aimed and fired. Once, twice, three times.

Her body slammed down to the floor.

Miles was heavy on top of her. She heard shuffling, then Trace said, "He's dead."

She stretched out her neck, peeking her eyes past the edge of the table.

CB Norris lay staring blankly at her, a hole in the center of his forehead.

Kill shot.

More in his chest.

Charlotte sighed, Miles' yells faint and far away as he lifted her from the ground. She closed her eyes and curled into him, letting the darkness—the relief—take her away.

CHAPTER TWENTY-THREE

An explosion erupted behind them, the van rocking as its wheels skidded in the snow. Miles grabbed onto Charlotte, lying on the floor, and held on tight.

The blizzard had let up but the roads were shit. Zeb had put Hunter in charge of getting them out of the compound and away from the grounds. With Hunter's enhanced skills and reaction times, he was the best man for the job. They'd barely made it out when the one bomb they couldn't disarm went off.

A fireball rose behind them. The van righted and everyone took a deep breath. The vehicle was equipped for surveillance, not triage, but tackling Charlotte and Madeena's injuries by degree of severity had to be done.

Miles felt like his world was being torn in two. The woman he loved was near death. She'd killed Norris to protect him, to protect Madeena, and here he was helpless to save her.

"She needs blood," Jax yelled, checking Charlotte's pulse. "Where's that report from Beatrice?"

Parker had Charlotte's head in her lap. Moe sat in the corner, laptop in hand. "Coming in right now," he said. "Looks like Charlie's AB neg."

"Anyone AB neg?" Zeb said, handing Miles his coat as he checked on Madeena's wrists. The girl was half awake, her head rolling as the van skidded back and forth again. "We'll be at the clinic in minutes. Dr. Lascar will be waiting for us, but I doubt he's got any AB neg on hand."

AB-. Of course, Charlotte would carry one of the rarest blood types in the world.

"Doesn't have to be AB negative," Parker said. Closest to Zeb, she took Miles' coat and pillowed it under Charlotte's head. Charlotte's skin was white as the fur on the coat's hood. Her lips were blue. "A neg or B neg will also work."

Miles looked up. "Seriously? I'm B negative."

"That'll do," Jax said. He pulled tubing and a field-issued blood transfusion pack from his backpack. Ripping the top off a package of alcohol wipes, he handed one to Miles. "Find a vein."

As Jax rigged his system to collect Miles' blood, Zeb grabbed Charlotte's hand. "Hang in there, Agent Carstons. No one's clocking out today."

The backwoods clinic had seen better days, but the nurse and doctor that met them at the door seemed battlefield tested when they arrived a few minutes later. There was no time to get to a major hospital in Bucharest, not with the roads as bad as they were. Beatrice had sent directions to this clinic, told them they could trust Lascar.

They had no choice. If they didn't, Charlotte would die.

She might die anyway.

Before Miles knew it, Charlotte was on a gurney heading for a backroom draped in plastic. Miles, holding a bandage over the vein Jax had abused to draw blood, started to follow.

The doctor, a short man with gray hair and bushy gray eyebrows stopped him. His voice was heavily accented, but not with Romanian. "We have to find the bullet and stop the blood loss. That's our job, son." If Miles had to guess, he'd say the good doctor was from Louisiana. New Orleans, possibly. "Your job is to stay here and pray."

Zeb grabbed Miles' arm. Hunter took his other. "Come on, man." Hunter urged him back to the front room. "Let the doctor work."

"I can assist," Jax told Lascar, handing him the bag of blood he'd taken from Miles. "Never finished my residency, but handled plenty in the field."

Lascar motioned with his head for Jax to follow him.

Over his shoulder, Miles watched the nurse prepping Charlotte for the surgery. The woman's dark eyes came up to meet his over the edge of her face mask. She nodded at him, offering the only reassurance she could. Jax donned a gown and face mask and closed the door to the surgical room.

Miles paced the small waiting room. Parker found a kitchen down a long hallway and brought back juice for Madeena. A lost and found box near the entrance provided snow pants, a sweatshirt with Madonna's face plastered on the front, and a hat. Parker removed her boots and socks, pulling the woolen socks over Madeena's feet. Soon the girl was looking warmer and had perked up enough to ask for food. Parker and Moe walked her back to the kitchen and emerged a few minutes later with candy bars for all of them.

Miles shook his head when Madeena offered him one. He tossed the bandage from his inner elbow into the garbage and rubbed his forehead. Norris had died instantly from Charlotte's shot, and was probably buried under a ton of ancient stones and rocks. But a part of him wanted to go dig the bastard up and kill him all over again.

Minutes dragged into an hour, then another. He wandered the clinic, making laps through each of the sad, little rooms. The place looked like an ordinary backwoods family clinic. But as Miles started randomly looking through drawers and cabinets, he came across high tech equipment. An extensive drug supply cabinet hidden behind a wall in the doctor's office. Weapons beneath a loose floorboard in a storage closet.

The doctor wasn't just a doctor. Who he worked for was up for grabs. CIA? NSA? DIA? The Queen?

Beatrice had a lot of contacts from her time in the NSA. Lascar had to be one of them. Taped under the doctor's pencil drawer, Miles found a loaded Sig Sauer. Behind the office door sat a loaded rifle with a military-issue night scope.

Hopefully Lascar knew his way around surgery the way he knew his guns.

No longer able to contain his anxiety, Miles left the clinic and walked out into the night. Sunrise was only minutes away, he realized, seeing the horizon had gone from deepest black to a muddy blue. Would Charlotte live to see another day?

Cold seeped into his bones. Bone-chilling cold. Exhaustion made him woozy, white spots specked his vision. He leaned back against the clinic's bricks and watched his breath fog the air. Every cell in his body demanded he go back in there and save her, but there was nothing else he could do. His blood was all he could give her.

Fuck this.

He was helpless once more.

All his time in the SEALs and he'd never met anyone like Charlotte or had the adventures he'd had with her. Riding out a winter storm in the mountains, dancing with Gypsies, hustling pool tricks. She'd given him more in the past year—the past few *days*—than he'd experienced in his entire lifetime.

He wanted more. Much, much more.

The back door of the clinic squeaked open sometime later. Dr. Lascar stuck his head out. His surgical cap was still on his head, the mask hanging around his neck. His gown was covered with blood. "God Almighty, what the hell are you doing out here?"

Miles jacked himself off the bricks. "Is she all right?"

"She could use another round of blood. That first bag only held half a pint." He looked Miles over. "You look like a healthy young man. Think you could give us a bit more?"

"She's alive?"

Lascar looked at him like he was stupid. "No sense in giving blood to a corpse that I know of."

"No, sir." Miles smiled and held out his other arm. "Take all the blood you need."

CHAPTER TWENTY-FOUR

WASHINGTON, D.C.

Beep…beep…beep. The noise woke Charlotte, cutting through a foggy dream about Miles and Maddy. She was happy. They were happy too.

Beep…beep…beep.

Annoying, that beep. Why wouldn't it stop and let her go back to sleep?

She couldn't feel most of her body, like it weighed nothing more than a feather. Like she wasn't anchored to anything.

I'm floating.

She tried to block the beeping noise and recall her dream. She wanted to stay inside that dream forever. Miles smiling at her. Madeena running in a field and laughing.

And then, there was the little boy. He was playing with hand carved wooden animals.

No matter how hard she tried, the dream edged away, dissolving, refusing to offer her comfort. In its place, horrible memories whizzed by. Snow and cold and blood. The sounds of bullets. Norris raising a gun…

Beep, beep, beep.

Charlotte sucked in a deep breath and blinked open her eyes. The noise was coming from a heart monitor next to her bed. The lights over the bed were off, but sunlight filtered through a large window off to her left. She blinked and shaded her eyes.

Bouquets of flowers and balloons lined the shelf under the window, and a TV hovered in one corner with the BBC news running on it.

Hospital. London. Her heart rate ratcheted up another notch.

"Hello, Agent Carstons," a woman's voice said off to her right. "We finally meet in person."

Charlotte craned her neck and saw a lovely blonde with a tablet propped on her large, pregnant belly. The woman wore her hair up in a bun, purple framed reading glasses sitting low on her nose.

The floating feeling finished disappearing as Charlotte shifted in the bed. An explosion of pain went off in her leg, claws tearing into her muscles. She bit the inside of her bottom lip to keep from crying out. But she was alive.

The thought shocked her.

Where is Miles?

No doubt he'd brought her home and dropped her off to face the music. She'd lost the USB and killed Norris. Dead might be better than facing life in prison.

"You have me...at...a disadvantage." Charlotte forced herself to breathe steadily around the pain, but her voice came out croaky. Her dry throat didn't want to cooperate. "I assume Vauxhall sent you?"

The woman tilted her head slightly. "Vauxhall has tried recruiting me on several occasions, but I declined their offers. The Queen and I don't get along."

A grin tugged at Charlotte's mouth as she realized who she was speaking to. "You're Beatrice, aren't you? From Shadow Force International. I recognize your voice."

"I am, indeed." Beatrice wrestled her awkward body out of the chair. "I'm relieved you made it back to the States in one piece. We haven't lost a client yet, and I certainly don't plan to start."

"States? Aren't we in London?"

The woman sauntered over to the bed. Waddled was more like it. "Washington, D.C. Vauxhall wishes to speak to you, but you're under my jurisdiction as a client for now. When you're up for it, I'll notify them of your whereabouts and that you're available for deposing."

Charlotte liked this woman. A lot. "Thank you. I can't say I'm in a hurry to go to prison."

"The treason charges have been dropped. Henley set up the comms and cameras to stream live to me at SFI headquarters during the rescue of the girl. Agent Norris' conversation with you was enough to show MI6 you were being used as a tool for his own purposes. They have questions, and I can't protect you from all the red tape you'll to go through while they investigate, but until then, your mission is to recover."

The pain meds were definitely wearing off. The clawing sensation in her leg matched the beating of her heart. "How long will that take?"

"Norris' bullet lodged in the femur and had to be removed surgically. It did some damage, hence the temporary cast. Once the doctor releases you, and you receive a couple weeks of physical therapy, you should be able to walk normally again."

"Is Miles okay?"

Beatrice touched the screen of her tablet. "Yes, although he refused treatment for his injuries. You wouldn't be alive without him, Agent Carstons. You might have bled out if not for the fact his blood type was compatible with yours."

Miles had donated blood to save her. She would at least have something of him to take with her after her recovery, even though he was obviously not interested in continuing their relationship.

Not that she could blame him. "Norris said Miles and his SEAL team were hunting me. Back when this all started with Blackwater."

He'd known all along who she was while she cared for his wounds and seduced him at the cabin. Or maybe he'd skillfully seduced *her*, planning to arrest her once the snow melted and he could put out an SOS to his senior chief. She hated to ask, but she needed to know. "Is that true?"

"From all accounts of the mission I've been privy to, their primary target was extracting Dr. Alexander from Romania. There were MI6 agents at the joint training session. Their mission I can't attest to, but most likely it involved finding you. It is possible Miles knew who you were."

Possible. She'd have to pin him down some day and find out for sure.

Her skin itched where an IV needle was taped to it. "How long have I been out?"

Beatrice checked her watch. "Going on thirty-one hours. You suffered a head concussion, and with all the blood loss and the stress of the surgery, your body simply needed a lot of sleep."

"Madeena? Is she okay?"

"The girl is doing well. She's been begging to see you. Because of her parentage and the fact she has no legal guardian available to care for her, I've taken steps to ensure her temporary safety and well-being, but it *is* temporary. She is in this country illegally. If I turn her over to the authorities, they will deport her. Or she may chose to return on her own. I can't hold her here either."

"Did she give up the location of her father's hideout?"

"Wasn't necessary. Your Romanian relatives, the Gypsies? One of them contacted Miles a few hours ago to let him know they had tracked down Blackwater's camp. Apparently, you shared with them your search for the terrorist and after you left, they started their own search in order to assist your efforts. Miles was already on the plane back to the States, but I was able to alert the proper authorities. There's a SEAL team on their way to the camp as we speak."

Renalda had come through for her. Madeena had not had to give up her father. Two plusses out of so many negatives. "You said Miles was headed back. From where? You sent him on a mission that soon after he nearly died in Romania?"

"There was an issue with Nicolae Bourean. Miles insisted on taking care of it himself."

"Issue?" Charlotte struggled to sit upright, felt a fresh dagger of pain rip through her thigh. "What issue?"

Beatrice pushed a button on the remote lying next to Charlotte's arm and lifted the head of the bed. "SIS didn't make it out of Romania with him. I suspect Norris had a hand in notifying the Romanian government about what was going down at the compound and they stopped the extraction at the border. Your government and the Romanians butted heads over jurisdiction and SIS was forced to turn Bourean over to the Romanian authorities. Within hours, he escaped, most likely because of a bribe or threat of some kind towards his captors."

Nico was on the loose again. Blackwater was still free—hopefully not for long, but the man hadn't stayed under the radar all of these years by being careless. "So all of that, everything we went through, was for nothing."

"You saved the girl."

True. Maybe that was enough. "Madeena is in danger if her father and Nico are still running loose."

"Nicolae Bourean will never hurt anyone again, I assure you." Beatrice's blue eyes were sharp, calculating. "Miles and one of my other men, one you met who happens to be the best assassin the United States military ever had, found Bourean with no trouble. They extracted swift but necessary justice for you and Madeena. Miles told me he couldn't rest until he knew Bourean had paid for his crimes against you. You need not worry about the Romanian crime lord ever again."

Swift but necessary justice. Charlotte shivered under the blankets, the scent of laundry detergent and bleach reaching her nose. "I wouldn't blame Miles if he never wanted to see me again. I've caused him so much trouble."

Beatrice waddled over to the table under the TV in the corner. A large, black bag sat on the tabletop. She rifled through it and returned with a book. "He said to give you this. You would know what it meant."

Charlotte's heart did a funny cartwheel. She rubbed a hand over the dust jacket and brought the book to her chest, hugging it.

Harry Potter and the Chamber of Secrets. He'd remembered her favorite book.

"He said there's a message inside," Beatrice said, lifting the bag and slinging the straps over her shoulder. "I'll leave you to read it."

"Thank you," Charlotte said. "For everything."

"Some day I'll ask for a favor in return. An operative of your caliber could be useful to me and my team." Beatrice pointed to a cell phone lying on the side table next to the bed. "If you need anything, my number is the first speed dial button. You can reach Miles with the second. I'll alert the nurses you're awake."

"Beatrice?"

She stopped at the door.

"If I want to adopt Madeena, do you think that's possible?"

The woman's hand went to her belly. "I have friends involved in a similar situation in San Diego with a drug lord's sister they wish to adopt. A weird dynamic, but I think Sophie and Nelson are going to pull it off. I'll give them your contact info, Agent Carstons. They may be of assistance."

"Please, call me Charlie. All my friends do."

"Good bye, Charlie."

"*Kushti bok*, Beatrice." At the woman's curious look, she explained. "It means good luck. Gypsies never say goodbye."

Beatrice smiled. The door closed quietly behind her.

Charlotte let out a breath, hopes and plans colliding in her brain.

Then she opened the book to find the message Miles had left inside.

CHAPTER TWENTY-FIVE

He'd waited for Charlotte to call but she hadn't. Beatrice insisted she'd left Charlotte a cell phone, his number on speed dial.

No calls. No texts. No nothing.

Service was spotty in the Carpathians, he'd told himself. Even on board the Shadow Force International jet back home, he'd hoped it was simply lack of service that kept Charlotte from getting through to him.

Of course, Beatrice hadn't found it difficult. She'd kept him updated on Charlotte's condition, on the status of the MI6 investigation, and warned him he would be called on to answer a bevy of questions regarding his assistance in taking down one of MI6's most decorated operatives, regardless that the man was an asshat who'd broken as many laws as he had commendations in his folder.

Beatrice suspected MI6 and the Queen would sweep most of Norris' deeds under the carpet in order not to expose the holes in their spy service.

Miles suspected Beatrice had told the Queen to leave him alone or she would personally make sure the BBC aired all their dirt.

Maybe the book had been a stupid idea. Charlotte had almost died, for God's sake. Maybe the message—the way he'd left it— brought back memories best left forgotten.

But Miles knew in his gut why Charlotte hadn't called him.

He'd betrayed her.

CB Norris had spilled the information about Miles and his

SEAL team's mission. How they'd been part of the group hunting for Charlotte. He knew he should have told her a hundred times over, but he hadn't. His time in the cabin with her had been a surreal experience. He'd known she was the MI6 operative the SIS boys had been looking for, the one Andy had warned him about. But he'd had no proof, and he hadn't wanted to believe it anyway. When Charlotte had shown up on his door step a week ago, Miles had thought it no longer mattered.

Sunrise painted the horizon in pale peaches. Miles shaded his eyes as he disembarked from the plane, Trace Hunter on his heels.

They were both jet lagged and worn out. At least Miles was. Hunter looked like he was ready to take on another crime lord-terrorist pairing as he jogged toward a black SUV waiting for them on the tarmac. "Sure you don't want to swing by SFI and clean up?" Hunter called over his shoulder. "You smell like a goat, man."

Miles sniffed at his shirt. Hunter was right. "I'll wash what I can here in the lavatory. I need to get to the hospital."

Hunter stopped and waved a hand at the terminal. "Go. Wash up. I'll wait for you. I can drop you there on the way."

The hospital was not on the way, but Miles appreciated the taxi service. He jogged inside and did a quick wash off with paper towels and liquid soap.

At the hospital twenty minutes later, Hunter pulled into the west lot and parked.

"You don't have to go in with me," Miles said. "I know you have someone waiting for you."

He also knew Hunter hated hospitals. The last time he'd been here, his fiancee had been fighting for her life. Luckily, she'd made it. They were planning a big wedding next summer.

"Are you kidding?" Hunter grinned. Not something that happened all that much. It was sort of menacing, like the rest of the guy. "And pass up the chance to hit their infamous Vendo-land?"

Hunter knew Charlotte hadn't called Miles. He feared Miles was about to get his heart stomped on.

That made two of them.

Miles appreciated the backup. "If you're going to be my wingman, I need M&Ms."

"I'm on it."

They bailed from the truck and Miles noticed the snow was

melting. Spring was weeks away, but the preview was nice. He itched to get back to San Diego and some sunshine.

But sunshine and warm temps would mean nothing if Charlotte wasn't by his side.

Hunter turned off for the first floor vending machines. Miles headed to the elevator. Charlotte had been moved to the third floor after an overnight stay in intensive care. Beatrice had told him Charlotte's doctor was pleased with her progress after such a severe injury.

Miles was pleased, too, but not surprised. Charlotte was one of the toughest women he knew. She put some of the men he'd been in the field with to shame with her willpower and steadfast courage.

Upstairs, he passed the nurse's station and found her room. Taking a deep breath and running a hand through his hair, he hesitated a moment at the closed door. Why hadn't she called him? Why hadn't she responded to his message?

Nerves twisted his stomach in knots. Slowly, he eased open the heavy door and peeked inside. "Charlotte?"

No answer. Balloons floated in the sunlight streaming through the window. The TV was off; the room silent.

Miles stepped in. The bed was made, the copy of the book he'd given her lying on the pillow. A sticky note was stuck to the top with his name in bold, black letters scrawled across it.

His heart sunk.

With leaden feet, he crossed the tiled floor and ran his fingers over the edges of the book.

Charlotte had bulldozed into his life twice, knocking him sideways. Now, here he was, holding nothing once more, because even with her injuries, she'd managed to run off.

He punched the pillow, the book flying off to hit the floor.

The front cover popped open on impact. A beam of sunlight cut across the title page.

Gutted, Miles leaned over to pick up the book when he saw pencil marks on the page.

It took him a second to follow the circled letters. Understanding nearly made him drop to his knees.

Snatching up the book, he ran out the door to the nurse's station. A plump redhead was sorting files and startled when he slapped the countertop with his palm. "Charlotte Carstons, room 338. She's not in her room. Do you know where she is? Is she having tests or something?"

The nurse's eyes did a once over, and even though he looked like hell and still smelled like he'd slept with goats, she smiled. "Let me have a look, sugar, and we'll see."

A door at the end of the hall swung open and Hunter popped his head in. "Hey, man, she's in physical therapy. I just saw her."

Miles banged on the counter. "Thanks, anyway," he said and took off down the corridor at a run.

Hunter led him down the stairs to the first floor, past the entrance and to a separate wing of the hospital.

"What's she doing in PT already?" Miles asked, not expecting Hunter to know. "She had major surgery two days ago."

"I don't know." He pushed through a double door that had Physical Therapy spelled out over it. "But that's where I saw her when I was wandering."

Sure enough, as Miles came to a standstill looking out over the open PT area, he spotted Charlotte sitting on a table talking to a therapist.

Arguing might be more like it. Charlotte was talking, but the gal in white listening had her arms crossed and was shaking her head.

Charlotte's left leg was in a partial cast, her right ankle wrapped. A padded and bandaged arm stuck out from under her hospital gown sleeve. Her hair was up and he could see the stitches at the base of her skull. She looked like she'd gone three rounds with a bear.

To him, she'd never looked better.

Miles skirted through some elderly patients lifting small hand weights and others pedaling bikes.

"But I have to," Charlotte was saying to the therapist. "It's the most important day of my life."

The woman's ponytail bobbed from side to side as she shook her head. "I'm all for starting as soon as you can, but this is ridiculous. The doctor hasn't okayed it. You can barely sit upright. You still have a cast on."

Miles chuckled to himself. Nothing and no one could stop Charlotte once she put her mind to something. "I wouldn't waste your breath arguing with her," Miles said, approaching the table. "Besides, she's a glutton for punishment."

Charlotte's eyes swung to Miles, widening in surprise. "You're back!"

She hoisted herself off the table, nearly toppling into the

therapist as her casted leg refused to bend while the good leg did. For half a second, she was suspended in mid-fall before Miles caught her.

The book crashed to the floor once more.

Several patients nearby stopped what they were doing to watch. Charlotte threw her arms around his neck and hugged him. "I got your message."

He'd painstakingly gone through the first chapter and circled the letters to spell out *I-l-o-v-e-y-o-u-w-i-l-l-y-o-u-m-a-r-r-y-m-e?* "I got yours too."

Three little letters. She'd found all three on the title page, not even bothering to string them out so he had to actually look for them.

Y.

E.

S.

"You're not mad?" he asked.

"About what?"

"The fact I never told you my team was helping MI6 look for you?"

"Hmm." She played with his collar for a moment. "You can make it up to me on our honeymoon."

Miles laughed. "I think that's fair."

"So...when?" She was practically bopping up and down in his arms.

"When what?"

"When are we getting married?"

The therapist covered her smile with a grin. Miles glanced around. Hunter had a bunch of old ladies gathered around him and they were all watching the show. "When do you want to?"

"Today?" Charlotte laughed, the sound vibrating through his chest where she leaned into him. "Seriously, as soon as I can get this damn cast off. The doctor said it's temporary. The bone wasn't broken, just nicked. Three or four days and I should be good."

Three or four days. "I like the sound of today better."

"I'm not coming down the aisle in a wheelchair."

Miles heart expanded as he looked down into her chocolate brown eyes. Eyes he loved, just like the rest of her. "You're right. We should wait a little while, make some plans. I'm sure your dad and brother would like to be there when we tie the knot. If you want a Gypsy wedding, that's fine too. Maybe even in Romania so Renalda can be there."

Her eyes suddenly shone with tears. "You would do that? Go back there for me?"

"I would do anything for you, Charlotte. Don't you know that?"

She rose up on her good foot and brushed her lips across his. "Magic does exist."

"What?"

"Magic, like in Harry Potter. It does exist because we make it happen. The mind is a powerful thing. All Gypsies know that."

"I have no idea what you're talking about" he said, sweeping her up into his arms, "but I like you anyway."

She laughed. Carefree. Happy.

The best sound he'd ever heard.

"I have a better idea than holding the wedding in Romania," she said. "I need to get Renalda here for treatments. I'll bribe her."

"That's the spirit."

"Madeena can be our flower girl. I'd like to adopt her if we can get through all the red tape."

A wife and a child all in one shot. Miles' mind reeled. "Think she'll like California?"

"What's not to like?"

"So you're not going back to MI6?"

"Gosh, no. I may check in with the CIA, though. See what they can offer me."

"That a girl." He hefted her a little higher and kissed the end of her nose. "I know a couple of old Gypsy remedies to heel that leg. A certain MI6 agent taught them to me. Let's get you back upstairs so I can get to work on making you feel better."

Charlotte giggled and waved goodbye to the therapist, who handed her the book. Charlotte laid her head on his shoulder as he carried her past the other patients. Clapping and hooting followed them out.

Hunter grinned and slapped Miles on the back. "I'll get the car," he said, shrugging off the hands of his fan club and heading for the door.

"I'll be a minute."

"You don't have to take me upstairs," Charlotte said after they'd passed through the double doors and were in the hallway. It was quieter here. A long line of glass windows looked out into a garden. Several patients were strolling amongst the benches, daffodils pushing their yellow-green heads up through the last of the snow. "The doctor actually released me an hour ago. I'd say, 'take me home,' but neither one of us has one. At least not here in D.C."

Miles stopped. He'd never settled in one place long enough to call it home anyway. "Home for me is wherever you are, Charlotte. Lucky for you, I happen to be in good with the woman who owns the keys to a safe house that will blow your socks off."

"Beatrice?"

He nodded. "We can crash there for now. What do you say?"

"I say, I love you and I want to be with you forever. Let's go home, Miles. I'm so ready for this."

Hugging her close, he headed for the door. "Me, too, darlin'. Me, too."

Stepping out into the bright morning sunlight, Miles stopped on the curb to wait for Hunter. As Charlotte kissed him again, longer and deeper this time, he prepared himself for another exciting adventure.

The End

Thank you for reading FATAL HONOR.

Turn the page to read about the next installment in the
Shadow Force International Series.

FATAL COURAGE

SHADOW FORCE INTERNATIONAL, BOOK 3

He ruined her career…

In twenty-one missions, CIA golden girl Ruby McKellen has failed only once. Thanks to Navy SEAL Jaxon Sloan, the man who stole her heart and forced her to choose between him and her partner Elliot, she's on probation and Elliot is in prison for national security crimes. To prove Elliot's innocence and save her damaged career, Ruby is running an unsanctioned mission—but the only way to do get the proof she needs is to go to Jax with her tail between her legs, and begging isn't out of the question.

She wrecked his heart…

Jaxon left the Navy after the mission with Ruby in Morocco went south, but that one hot, unbelievable night with her will haunt him forever. Working for Shadow Force International now, his new assignment has brought him full circle—the CIA operative Jax's testimony sent to prison has escaped and Jax has been ordered to hunt him down. Just like in Morocco, the one thing standing in his way is Ruby.

A second chance at love could prove fatal…

When Ruby's life is threatened and Jax stumbles on information that might prove Elliot *is* innocent, guilt over putting the man in prison compels him to join her unsanctioned mission. What really happened that night six months ago? Is Elliot an honorable spy or a mastermind at manipulation? Ruby is the only one who can help Jax navigate the world of undercover lies and betrayal to find the truth.

In a battle of wills—and of hearts—Jax and Ruby must have the courage to face the truth about themselves, their past, and what it really means to betray someone you love.

About the Author

USA TODAY Bestselling Author Misty Evans has published over thirty novels and writes romantic suspense, urban fantasy, and paranormal romance. She got her start writing in 4th grade when she won second place in a school writing contest with an essay about her dad.

Misty likes her coffee black, her conspiracy stories juicy, and her wicked characters dressed in couture. When not reading or writing, she enjoys music, movies, and hanging out with her husband, twin sons, and two spoiled puppies. Get your **free Super Agent story** and sign up for her newsletter at www.readmistyevans.com. Like her author page on Facebook or follow her on Twitter. Bloggers and reviewers, if you'd like to join Misty's Rockin' Readers review group, send her a message at misty@readmistyevans.com and she'll hook you up!